A NOVEL

Books by Robert Kroetsch

FICTION

But We Are Exiles
The Words of My Roaring
Gone Indian
The Studhorse Man
Badlands
What the Crow Said

POETRY

The Ledger
Stone Hammer Poems
Seed Catalogue
The Sad Phoenician
Field Notes

CRITICISM

Essays
(*Open Letter:* Frank Davey, ed.)

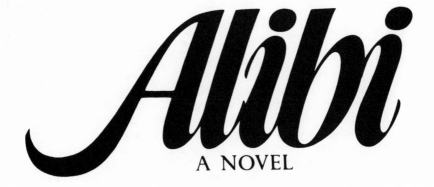

A NOVEL

ROBERT KROETSCH

Beaufort Books
New York • Toronto

Library of Congress Cataloguing in Publication Data

Kroetsch, Robert, 1927–
Alibi.
I. Title.
PR9199.3.K7A8   1983   813'.54   83-7122
ISBN 0-8253-0154-8

Published simultaneously in Canada by
General Publishing Co. Limited, Toronto

DESIGN: Brant Cowie/Artplus Ltd.
COVER PHOTO: Rosen/Miller Services Ltd.

Printed in the United States   First Edition

again, for Smaro

DORF'S PRESENTIMENT (A CHAPTER IN WHICH MUCH IS FORETOLD, BUT—)

*M*ost men, I suppose, are secretly pleased to learn their wives have taken lovers; I am able now to confess I was.

My discovery came as a great relief. At the time, of course, I put up quite a show of rage and indignation. I went out and fired a shot or two at the poor fool who had been so generous as to come to my aid and, as a consequence, I spent a few years under something of a cloud. It was work, finally, that cleared the air; when I returned abruptly from the States, I lucked into a job with a millionaire Calgary oilman whose pastime it was to collect anything that was loose. He needed an agent who was a completely free man. I was left alone to pursue assignments, to travel, to dicker, to bribe if necessary; I need deal with no one except in financial terms. How much? was the question. In sum, I was a happy man. And I might have remained such, had Deemer not sent me that unfortunate message.

I might explain that I have never once met Jack Deemer, at least not face to face; he's a great one for sending messages. His minions live in a kind of dread of memos or post cards or, for that matter, scraps of toilet paper scrawled with instructions for which there is no explanation, no place to seek clarification. My calamity differed only in arriving as a yellow, pasted-up CNCP telegram, waiting like a bomb in my mailbox when I flew in from Sicily with a collection of twenty-eight sets of dominoes.

Find me a spa, Dorf. That was the message. Nothing more, nothing less. Out of nowhere. For no reason. The dominoes, I might say, were a perfect find. Absurdly, I turned the piece of paper upside down and tried to read it that way. In a panic, I remembered Karen Strike. I wasn't quite sure what the hell a spa was. I remembered vaguely Karen Strike saying she had done or was doing or hoped to do a documentary on spas that were or would be forgotten. My mind likes asides.

We had talked at the opening of the Max Ernst show, at the Glenbow the previous November. Karen and I have a continuing, tentative relationship; we meet in galleries, at concerts, in waiting lines in restaurants, and somehow end up talking for twenty minutes or so. Just a little too long to call the chat a casual one, not long enough for it to lead anywhere.

I telephoned her.

"Dorf," I said, "Bill Dorfen. We had a glass of champagne at the Max Ernst opening."

"The man with the tall, sad face," she said. "We had six glasses of champagne. I was totally bonkered and you deserted me to go fly to some place in Africa for a rendezvous with a stuffed green rhinoceros."

"A white rhinoceros," I said. "When I got there it had already been sold to an Italian shoemaker. And besides, you deserted me to climb a palm tree, there in the Glenbow Gardens."

We talked for twenty minutes, Karen and I.

Let me confess that last Wednesday, the day of my call, was also my birthday. I had arrived home to a twinge of loneliness. A man is not forty-six very often and, after our talking for a while about spas and where I might begin to find one, I ignored my being fifteen years her senior. I had learned her age from a piece in the *Herald* on the local film co-op. I suggested that I owed her a drink. It was Karen herself who said we could kill two birds with one stone by having the drink in Banff. "There's an old spa up there in the Rockies," she said, "still frequented by hundreds of bathers who don't know the history of the place."

Like my boss, she's a lunatic on the subject of history. Dark was falling, and snow with it, by the time we swung off Shaganappi and took Number One toward the mountains. "Water cures were big in the nineteenth century," she explained, her left hand once, briefly, touching my right thigh. "The mineral hot springs were developed so the well-to-do might suffer their ills in comfort."

Karen affects a kind of disbelief in the better things of this world, money and love among them. That somehow goes with her interest in history. But she does have a considerable interest in staying alive, I discovered; I nearly managed to kill us, just outside the gates of the park, when I hit a patch of concealed ice. It happened when she opened her big Greek-island bag and hauled out a wrapped parcel that looked like a book. "It's not a book," she said, "it's a journal. For your birthday." Apparently I had let it slip, while we were talking on the phone, that the day was my birthday; I was flabbergasted by her concern. She put down the parcel between us and then leaned across it and gave me a peck on the cheek.

The car turned around but, fortunately, stayed on the road. We managed to get it pointed in the right direction just as a snowplow, lost in its own wild rainbow of powdery snow, bore down on us. A bit later, after we'd driven through Banff and were climbing up Sulphur Mountain toward the parking lot, Karen remarked that we *needed* a visit to a spa. I ignored her little sarcasm; she has something of a nasty tongue at times.

We parked my old green Dodge in a long line of fancy cars. Walking up the icy and snow-concealed road to the Upper Hot Springs, we were, not once, but twice forced to hold hands. Karen was wearing pretentious hand-knitted mittens. We went in through the glassed-over doorway of the stone building, bought tickets, she paying for hers, I for mine, and went down the stairs to separate change-rooms.

I put on my rented blue bathing suit and picked up my locker key. The place was crowded with men who insisted on standing around naked and pink and steaming, their shrivelled pricks like so many mushrooms blinded by the abrupt light of the white-tiled room. I walked around, not through, the showers, then down the cement steps and into the hot mineral water. Slowly letting myself sink, I pushed my way through the two steam-covered glass doors, out of the old stone blockhouse and into the winter night and the falling snow and the open-air pool.

I expected to see Karen.

(OR, IN WHICH DORF CLAIMS
TO HAVE GOT LAID)

I didn't know what she'd look like in the bikini she'd claimed at
the ticket window to have in her bag, except sexy; I didn't know
what the pool would look like either, on a winter night, even
though I've lived eighty miles from Banff National Park these
past few years. I had to go around the world three times to get
here. That's the way it is.

I let the two doors close behind me and everything was
fog. Thick, swirling fog because the steam froze as it lifted off
the surface of the pool. The sky was simply black above the fog,
the water lit from beneath, as if heaven and earth had got
themselves upset. I caught the cold air into my lungs; I ducked
down until even my lower lip was in the hot mineral water. A
foot or two of space separated the water from the fog. And that
space was full of floating heads.

Just heads, just floating. Like that. Motionless. Heads and
more heads, planted there, and growing. They weren't the least
bit troubled at not having bodies, there in that yellowish light,
under the lid of fog. Nobody seemed worried. Shit, I thought,
this is okay. I wanted to tell Karen, wanted to say, you've got to
use this in your documentary, get a camera in here, and only
then did I realize I couldn't see her anywhere. And I'd loafed on
purpose in the change-room, waiting for her to get to the pool
ahead of me; I panicked a little.

I don't mean I panicked, I just felt strange. Because I knew,
looking at all those heads, floating there, on the water, under
the fog, that I'd never quite be the same again. One has those
occasions, those recognitions. Just as I knew I had changed,
slightly, forever, when I levelled a gun at my wife's frightened,
absurd, scrawny lover and realized I could pull the trigger.

Snow was still falling. Snow had fallen all day, the

announcers had insisted, while Karen changed stations and I drove through the falling snow. Snow was general on the eastern slope of the Rockies; it was falling when we hit the concealed ice on the snow-buried road.

But the flakes, falling now, never quite managed to touch the surface of the pool. And the heads that weren't talking, in fact, were. They seemed to be talking to themselves; each face talking to itself. The light, blurred as it was in the fog, was brightest around a whole circle of heads, each head facing outward, a group of people on an invisible bench, it seemed, around the invisible inlet where the water from the mountain came mysteriously hot and gushing into the pool. They were Japanese, those faces — tourists, or skiers; their voices were all a conundrum. And yet the other bathers were more numerous than the Japanese. I was there to see why people were there; I had to find out.

The deck around the pool was covered in a good eight inches of trackless snow. And the floating head that spoke, that addressed me, had fine white crystals of ice on the fine hairs of the upper lip. Her upswept arched eyebrows, dark eyebrows I am certain, were thickened with ice. "I've been waiting for you," she said.

Absurdly, I answered with my name. "Dorf," I answered. "People call me Dorf." I raised my right hand, offering to shake hands, there in the small space between our heads, above the water, under the fog.

It was then I noticed I was carrying still the key to my locker. The key was on a cord that was supposed to go around my wrist, apparently. But the circle of string was too small.

One of my secrets is just this, that I'm sort of funny looking. A face that is almost too long. A body that is too long, also, without really being big. Almost big. Not genuinely unattractive; just funny looking. Just on the edge of it. And, as a result, beautiful women like me.

"Julie," she said. The floating head said that name. Then she said, "Jack." I thought that might be her second name or something. But then she added, "Jack said I might find you here."

Karen, just then, came through the water, her nose barely

above the surface, like a swimming animal, like some amphibious creature; she dove when she saw me and, exactly at that moment, I reached inside my too large bathing suit and slipped the loop of string around my slightly aroused member. I tried, in the diffused light, in the swirling fog and in the random scattering of bathers, to see where Karen surfaced. She is, if nothing else, the most cruelly efficient woman I've ever known, and maybe that's what attracts me to her. God knows, I am nothing if not inefficient myself. It was a stroke of luck that got me a job tracking down odds and ends in the corners of the world, and for that, if I do say so myself, I have a kind of genius. Yes, I can say quite truthfully, I never fail when Jack Deemer sends me on a search, galloping asshole that he is, and millionaire Calgary oilman to boot. Find me a collection of dominoes, Dorf. He'd remembered, unexpectedly, playing dominoes as a child. And I found them. Complete sets, twenty-eight of them in the corner of a shop in a Sicilian village where I stood a damned good chance of having my throat cut for the gold ring I wear on my right hand. Find me some shrunken heads, some Japanese armor, some aphrodisiacs.

But this time he wants a *spa*.

Karen waved. She seemed far distant, standing now, raising herself up into the fog; she was about to go through the two glass doors, back to her jeans and her T-shirt. "I'll meet you in the waiting room," she called. "If you stay too long you'll be wiped out." And she pointed up at a sign that gave some ridiculous warning.

She went through the two glass doors and I was alone with Julie. And that I, impulsively, kissed her, kissed Julie, was only natural. Why she turned and motioned herself through the water, toward the deeper end of the pool where no one lingered, was only natural too; I followed. Or, rather, I dallied, but dallied in her direction. We were, for all my feigned delay, already conspired together in a little ambition of our own. I could not see her body, except in so far as I could see into the water itself, with all the attendant distortions, as dictated by the laws of physics.

She repeated my name to me, almost as a question,

"Dorf?"; and I answered, explaining, whispering, there under the fog, our mouths almost in the warm water, my lips close to her floating head; yes, I'd had two grandfathers by the first name of William, both with the same first name, and my parents, farming people northeast of Calgary in the Battle River country, in a futile hope that I might receive at least one inheritance, named me after both of them. Billy Billy Dorfen. And all I got from my ancestors, it turned out, was the conviction that I needed two of everything: two cars, two university degrees, two bank accounts, two addresses, two mailboxes. For sure, two kicks at the cat. Two lives, possibly.

Julie touched her lips to mine as if she would silence me. Almost as if she, already, knew the details and did not have the patience for a recital. But I must tell her everything, and I went on, her hands touching mine now, touching my chest, my abdomen, finding my own lost body, there under the water's surface. I guess the whole thing with my wife, the divorce and all that, turned me off sex in a way; I'd spent a few years being a bachelor as if it was a new religion. Julie, her hair coated in ice, her ears too maybe, I don't know ... But her hands touched mine again, inviting them to respond even if I couldn't; I explained that I got the inheritance, in a way, after all. I really did. And a fabulous one it was.

Jack Deemer simply collects. It is not a matter of what to collect. He has that kind of money. And, as a result, everything came up roses for Billy Billy Dorfen. I'd disappear again, but now I'd return from around the world with stuffed tigers. I mean, with *real* stuffed tigers. Or with ceremonial masks. Or with walking sticks.

"I know," Julie said. Softly, though. Or patiently, I guess it was. And our hands, then, worked together, undoing the awkward knot I'd tied in the drawstring of my too large bathing suit. She was wearing a wedding ring, or at least she was wearing rings on her left hand; I felt that.

He's a recluse now, Jack Deemer — or at least so rumor has it — hidden away in his mansion on Prospect Avenue, there in Mount Royal, in the real center of Calgary. He's simply a name. And a legend, of course; the richest of the many rich men

spawned in the Alberta oil patch, like so many hatched sala-
manders, a man who, in the making of his fortune, killed two
other men. Or at least that's how the legend has it.

I felt her thighs rise along the outside of my own. No one
could guess what was happening, there in the pool. Her hair
was dark, almost pitch black, for all the ice encrusted on her
head. Perhaps we could see down into the water, to where our
hands, swimming, independent of our bodies, eased aside the
crotch of her swimsuit. Only the key, on its cord, was between
us, and I could only be reminded of the collection of locks and
keys I tracked down for Deemer, found in a village in Connecticut and purchased at a ransom price from a dear old lady. We
spent hours, she and I, fascinated by the levers and bolts and
barrels and springs that combine to make a lock. She told me of
Barron's tumbler lock and of Chubb's adding a detector; she was
inordinately proud of Linus Yale, and yet had to confess that
skilful tickling would open even the best of his contrivances.
She told me of keys so huge they were carried over the
shoulder; she knew of Chinese locks that were, seemingly,
without age.

Julie and I had to be careful not to attract the attention of
any of the other bathers. The lifeguard, in her glass box by the
pool's side, was lost in the fog, surely. We hardly dared move, and
yet, somehow, her hands guiding, mine lifting her toward me, I
entered her. We couldn't kiss there in the pool; we didn't dare.
She kept her head hardly an inch from my own, her features as
calm, as bemused as those of any other bather. She closed her
eyes, briefly, and I noticed that her eyelashes, too, were
perfectly filmed in ice. We were as if, ourselves, frozen in that
exquisite discovery of each other, two floating heads, motionless,
in the dark and the snow and the ice.

But what a hot joining underneath the surface. She came
before I did. I was having difficulty with the soothing effect of
the water, with the bathers around us. I simply couldn't move. I
was vaguely aware of the key between us, between Julie and me,
and I thought again of that old woman, that delicious old lady,
there in her Connecticut house, her locks, some of them,
mounted in doors that were mounted in the middle of a large

room, doors that led from nowhere to nowhere, the exquisite complexity of their locks available to any who would look, the secret connivance of figure and letter and sign, available, teasing the eye that would know, confounding the mind with the very unwillingness to hide.

"I'll have to kill you," Julie said. She might have stifled a groan, concealed it, by speaking. Her lips were hardly a tongue's reach from my own; I could feel the cold on my forehead. I could feel it on my ears; the ice on my wet hair touched my ears, tickled them.

Her simple, confusing remark tipped me over the edge into a slow, long, delicate flooding. I was aware of everything, and nothing too.

"Find that spa, Dorf. Find that spa for Jack Deemer, and I'll kill you. Remember."

And then she was gone. I was left standing there, comic, ridiculous even, alone in the pool, my bathing suit around my ankles, the string of my locker key around my sturdy member.

I raised my bathing suit and tied it again using a simple bow knot. I made a perfunctory search through the growing crowd in the pool. Skiers were coming in, young people, people ferociously young, some of them obviously drunk. They were splashing each other, shouting. The lifeguard came out of her glass box to issue warnings and threats.

My knees were weak. I had no idea how long I'd been in the pool. I swam and then touched my toes to the pool's bottom. I fished inside my bathing suit for my locker key and went toward the two fog-smeared glass doors. I was impossibly sleepy. And I guess I was crying a little.

IN WHICH DORF IMAGINES
THAT HE SHOULD HAVE WRITTEN A NOVEL
INSTEAD

If I were a writer of fiction I'd no doubt have begun my entries
with the telegram itself, that moment when I arrived back home
from Sicily and opened my mailbox and found, among the usual
ads for houses and firewood and pizza joints, the CNCP envelope
and its week-old telegram. I'd have begun with my sudden
excitement and fear, my not knowing, quite, what a spa was, let
alone what Deemer would want one for; I'd have dramatized my
panicky dialing of Karen's number, suggesting I did it partly to
get information, partly because at last I had an excuse to call
her, and I was horny. I'd have concealed the fact that in three
years I hadn't made love to anything — man, dog, beast, or
woman — not to anything but my right fist, and that, infrequently.

Karen was waiting in the brightly lit sitting room just
beyond the ticket window. Or, actually, she was not so much
waiting as studying a diagram on the wall that explained how
ice-cold water around Sundance Creek percolated down through
the rocks to a depth of 15,000 feet below sea level, was heated,
and returned to this mountain outlet at a temperature of 110
degrees Fahrenheit. There must be a lesson there somewhere.
She put her pad and pencil into her sagging Greek-island bag.

And then I couldn't speak. I had rushed to get dried and
dressed, not even stopping to shower; I wanted to tell her
everything, tell her of the threat to my life, ask her advice. And
there she was, making notes on the goddamned world. She'd
left the pool early to get on with her research, while I
floundered my way into the usual deep water.

I needed nothing so much as to sit down and think, but all
the chairs were taken: by strapping big women with gaudy

towels coiled on their heads, by bulky men, awkwardly trying to recover a sense of clothing, lifting cigarettes in their water-wrinkled fingers. I looked about me like a man newly arrived on earth; I was, I can only confess, totally exhausted.

Karen led the way through the glassed-in entrance, past the row of people waiting to be admitted. She stopped outside the door to find the hood of my parka, pulled it up over my wet head, then raised her own hood. We stood side by side in our parkas.

"What do you think?" she said.

She is the two a.m. terror of the soul: Karen, researching her documentary. She has a dream of one day making a perfect film, the perfect replica of a dismissed life. I was thinking about a woman who said her name is Julie. Her lovely thighs, holding me.

"I don't know," I said. "Life is a losing bargain in any case."

"I think I'll use it," she said.

She is asking Alberta Culture for funding so she can do her documentary on the forgotten history of forgotten spas. Not the famous ones; rather, the forgotten, the neglected ones. As if we must not be allowed to forget past follies.

"Go ahead," I said, after a moment's hesitation. "Use it."

"What's bugging you?" she said. "Good God, you can be a humorless prick."

Instead of waiting for my response she stepped away from the shelter of the door, turned left, turned me in the same direction, and pointed toward the tower of steam that stood over the pool.

"Look," she said. "What an opening shot."

I groaned in my embarrassment at her gift for the cliche. That made her laugh, thank heavens. The freezing steam, garishly yellow, bizarre almost, real and unreal, columned its way into the dark sky.

And yet I had to go onto the parapet and look down into the pool; and, yes it was possible, just possible, at times, to see through the fog into the pool, into the water itself, for the pool was lit by submerged lights. It would have been possible, I realized, for an onlooker to see Julie and me in the intimacies of our passion. Was Karen, in her devious way, telling me she had seen us? I was recklessly on the edge of telling her what I suspected she had seen; I wanted to point at the blank water, describe a man and a woman, their mutual fingers intertwined, gently tugging aside the crotch of the woman's green bathing suit, the thick, dark hairs like seaweed; perfect, ingenious tentacles, imprisoning the man's desire —

Karen caught my gloved hand. She made me turn to our right now, away from the cavernous pool below us. She took me across the road to the higher, smaller, rock-rimmed pool where water fell darkly out of the mountain, splashing into its own heat, the close stink of sulphur rising with the ghostly steam.

"And this is the end, I suppose," I said.

We walked down the driveway toward the parking lot, neither of us speaking a word. It was dark, blue dark, under the falling snow; spruce dark, mountain dark. We found my car and brushed at the windshield. We drove past the Rimrock Inn. And then Sulphur Mountain was dark. The road went through a kind of scary darkness along the falling mountainside. The trees beside the road were blurred by snow; the road itself was blurred to a track. Maybe it was a coyote that dashed in front of the car.

"Why did you hit it?" Karen said.

"Good Christ, I didn't *try* to hit it."

"You didn't try to miss it."

"I didn't say I tried to miss it. Look at that road."

"Aren't you going to stop?"

She'd heard the thumping, under the car, as well as I. "It's too goddamned late now," I said. And then, lifting a hand at the snow racing toward the windshield, I ventured, "We'll get killed ourselves in this."

"I have appointments tomorrow," she said.

And I was thinking, against her ignorance: Find that spa, Dorf. I'll have to ... That woman, there in the pool, her thighs caressing my own, her pubic hair like a wave of the sea itself, wrapping over the shore; and over the two of us together, above the pool, through the fog, eyes watching. Karen Strike's pale, luminous, documenting eyes.

"We can't," I said, abruptly. "We can't drive back to the city tonight. Eighty miles of this would be suicide."

I was surprised when Karen agreed. All she said was, "Can't you learn metric, Dorf?" Then she pointed at a signpost; I made the sharp right turn, skidding a little. "Whoopee," I said.

I began the drive toward the Banff Springs Hotel. Neither of us spoke a word. I found, on the road, under the night-blurred outline of the hotel, a parking place; I backed into the space, snow on my rear window, easing the car into the long row of snow-covered cars. We were walking in under the snow-laden, dark-creviced spruce when Karen asked, "Have you ever seen Godard's *Weekend?*"

"Never heard of it," I said. "It's a movie, isn't it?"

"You'd enjoy it," she said.

The west door wasn't yet locked for the night. We entered into the subdued light, the shadowed doors of closed shops, lit windows. Siwash sweaters for Japanese tourists. Moccasins. Tartans. An antique shop. The row of paintings of famous Indian chiefs: Crowfoot, Big Plume, Medicine Calf, Old Sun, Big Bear, Red Crow. We went up the stairs to the main hallway, with all its baronial pretensions. We went to the desk, Karen waiting for me to speak.

And we were fortunate. The snow had forced cancellations. We took the elevator to our room: the girl in the tartan skirt, she had dark, radiant, insane eyes, I saw that; she didn't ask what floor we wanted, simply stopped the old cage on the eighth floor and we stepped out into the hallway, Karen and I, stripping off our parkas as we walked, I carrying the key to our room in my teeth.

I was at once wildly horny and filled with a kind of gentle tenderness. The infernal key was worn, and Karen helped me get the door unlocked. If it hadn't been an April evening, if snow hadn't been falling, heavily now, again, we might have seen from the window of room 865 the valley of the Bow River, the white wall of mountain peaks that seem to cut off all hope of escape. I'd paid the extra five bucks for the mountain view; I'd decided, registering, to put everything on my expense account.

But the window was black with darkness, the room insufferably hot. I struggled and, finally, slid the window up in its old frame. Then we could see snow, streaks of snow in the immediate yawn of dark; I watched it while Karen went through her bag and, with hardly a murmur, came up with a toothbrush.

The room was bright under the slant of ceiling that comes down too close over the bed nearest the window. The walls are richly bright with a wallpaper that is striped in gold and brown and an off-white. There is no desk in the room, and that bothered me; I'd decided, riding up in the elevator, to go back to the car and get the journal I'd received as a birthday gift.

We sat, each on a bed, facing each other; all our years of vague acquaintance come to that moment. When you're out of the city half of each year, when you never know when a message will send you off to Singapore for a dusty boxful of miniature Buddhas, you end up having few friends. I guess *none* would be a more accurate term. It's pretty terrible, really. Except that I don't mind being alone, it gives me time to think. Karen and I are acquaintances, people who meet more by accident than by design — as we'd met at the Max Ernst show, she talking about spas and films and Ernst the outrageous artist, while I observed that he was, even before his being an artist, a collector of sorts: witness his collection of primitive art. I'd insisted, under the influence of six glasses of champagne, that Jack Deemer himself, my notorious employer, was an artist in his own right, a kind of looney sculptor intent on tacking together, or assembling in warehouses at least, all the loose pieces, all the high-class garbage of the riddling earth. "Jack Deemer," Karen had said in response, just before she climbed the palm tree, "is a two-bit, low-down, chiselling thief."

"I'm going to take a quick shower," I said. Karen was prattling on about the spa and taking off her snow boots. Hiking boots, I guess you'd call them. Those fancy, padded things. My body smelled of sulphur; the room, quickly, even with the window open, began to smell of sulphur.

It was Karen who'd suggested, over the phone, let's drive out to Banff. She knew it was snowing. It was her idea. I'd only suggested a drink and a preliminary conversation. There used to be a real spa in Banff, she'd explained, those hot springs there, with a hospital, spa doctors, the works. And now she was at me again about it: "Buy this place for old Deemer," she said. She laughed that easy, mocking laugh of hers. "A spring, a forest, a mountain — if that'll keep him from seeing that he's got to die."

She had it all figured out, she was certain. Jack Deemer, there in his mansion behind its guardian row of spruce, its tall and northward facing windows staring down onto the clustered skyscrapers in the bowel of the city; Deemer, his house and his trees and his privacy looking down from the rich seclusion of Mount Royal, had seen one day, maybe late one evening, instead of his own Midas wealth, his own death.

Karen lifted up one of her boots and sniffed the warmth inside. "Of course, you'll be a hero for saving him," she said. "You'll be rewarded endlessly. You'll have it made."

I was taking off my clothes as she spoke. I quite simply undressed. Said nothing. Karen was holding a boot in her hands. I undressed right down to my skin.

The words HOT and COLD, it turned out, were on the wrong taps over the deep white tub. I gave a cry, leapt from behind the curtain, slipped on the floor, caught myself.

Karen burst in at the bathroom door, I, already, trying to touch myself with both large hands, and I do have large, awkward hands, trying to touch my burn.

"Kiss it better," I said, almost shouting.

BURNING, BURNING

*A*nd then Karen began to laugh. Karen finding me a towel and at the same time beginning to laugh. "You're useless to me now," she managed to squeak out through her laughter. I, my private parts scalded, unable to touch myself, unable to let Karen so much as come near me with a bath towel.

"Well, shit," I said. "Shit."

Karen, laughing. A release, a freedom, maybe even an escape from her own anxieties. There is often a train moving along a flat horizon, in my reveries. I saw it just then. I wait for the train to end and another crosses behind it. Karen was undressing while she tried to contain her laughing; at least she had the decency to be embarrassed at her callous indifference.

I lay down on the bed under the slanting roof, naked, belly up. I lay there like that near the open window, letting nothing but air touch me, and Karen went into the bathroom and came out; she came out wearing only panties and her T-shirt with its message: MAKE DO. She lay down on the second bed. "Do you want me to turn out the lights?" she asked.

"Yes." I paused. "No, wait. In a little while. Shit." I tried, again, to touch myself. "You don't think it's fatal?"

"Yes. It'll fall off by morning."

"Wouldn't a kiss help?"

"No. And I'd be tempted to bite. Dummy."

"I was horny," I said.

"I still am," she said. "Dummy dummy dummy."

We talked that night. We told each other stories. Perhaps that is what changed our relationship. After all those years of merely acknowledging each other, Karen always on the edge of climbing a tree to escape our intimacies. I mean that. After a while she turned out the lights. And then we discovered there was some light in the darkness, after all. Perhaps from the lit and snow-buried skating rink, eight stories below our window. Karen, once in a while, got up and went to the window and, bending forward, looked out, looked down, and I could just faintly catch the outlines of her lovely buttocks; I wanted to slip her panties down and pillow my head.

She explained, went on at great length in fact, explaining that she'd applied for funding for her documentary. Educational TV. She was waiting for the opportunity to make a feature film. And meanwhile, she worked with a film co-op in the basement of a Unitarian church on 16th Avenue, taught two courses at Mount Royal College, and did some PR work, during the height of the theater season, for Rick McNair. Patch together a life. Make do.

"Now you need one yourself," Karen told me. "A spa, that is." She laughed, softly, in the darkness; she laughed out through the window, at the invisible wall of mountains, at the snow falling on the deserted skating rink. "Water is good for a burn." And she left the window then; she found me in the darkness. And she did kiss my burn. But even that hurt, and I touched her head, her lips, away from the burn and the darkness. She ran her impatient tongue up the ridge of one hip, across, and down the other.

"A spa," Karen said. She was lying on her bed now. "A mineral spring. A hot spring. Tubs and swirls and massage tables. Rubbing rooms. Cooling rooms. It's a story that goes way back — the Romans did it up brown. They threw in pleasure with the cleansing."

"One time I went to Baden-Baden," I said, "to pick up a collection of wood carvings. I dropped six hundred bucks in the casino."

Karen didn't laugh. Then she said, "They have a treatment there for senility. You ought to tell Deemer about it."

Karen is city-born and bred, has her own house just below the Mount Royal compound, in the valley beneath. But her family is a ranching family, in the foothills country south and west of the city, and they hate the oil crowd with a fine passion.

And that's why I told her the secret, I guess. Still another version of desire and guilt and the old hunger to connect, somewhere in the darkness. I had dozed off a little. I knew she

was just as lonely as I, that confident Ms. Karen Strike. I told the
story quickly, not naming Julie at all. I was trying to tell the
story: the woman approaching me, our finding the key in my
hand. The woman's long fingers; I remembered, her long,
perfect fingers, molding the water's heat to my swelling need. I
wanted to tell the story. Then I heard myself add, "Her name
was Julie." I said it tentatively, there in the darkness, as if she
might be Karen's best friend, as if Karen might leap up and leave
the room, leave the hotel, the night, the mountains. "Our bodies
were weightless," I said. As if that might be an adequate excuse,
an alibi, a reason that would exempt me from any human rules
of which Karen was the keeper. "Sliding together. Without
weight. We had to make an effort, to press ourselves together."

"You rat," Karen said. "Tell me more. I like it."

"The water was the temperature of the inside of her body.
Thus my whole body — "

"Jesus, Dorf," Karen said. "Don't say *thus*."

"It was as if all of me," I said, "right up to my neck, had
entered her body, which in turn — "

"That's better," Karen said.

"I was weightless, but so was she; I could lift her whole body
in my hands. She could move all of me. She pulled me in between her legs and let me float again and pulled me close again."

And I went on talking, listening to Karen begin to caress
herself, there in the darkness. Yes, I did not know who the
woman was, had never seen her before, but she knew me,
somehow, and she had approached me in the pool, had
seduced me. Julie was her name; she had told me that as if I must
never forget, at least I thought that was the name she had given.
She had dark eyes, eyebrows that were dark too, except they
were coated in ice and maybe weren't as dark as I imagined
them to be, and she knew the collector. She knew Jack Deemer.

And that's a funny thing. I didn't mention, at least not then,
Julie's threat, her saying that to find the spa for Deemer would
cost me my life. Because I didn't want to spoil Karen's response.
Her pleasure. But while I talked I began to realize I could not
find the spa until I knew for whom I was finding it, and why. And
the best way to find out about Deemer was by finding out from
Julie.

"Tell me about the woman," Karen said. "You're talking about Deemer again. I've decided I hate him."

And right then, at that moment, I realized I would have to tell a lie. I had to make up part of the story. After my resolve that I would, finally, on my birthday, begin to tell the whole truth and nothing but. Because at forty-six you aren't really forty-six; you're into your forty-seventh year. The number, that too, isn't and is a lie.

"Tell me some more," Karen said. "I mean, about the pool."

"Why?"

"I'm touching myself."

"What does it feel like to have a cunt?"

"For God's sake, Dorf, get on with the story."

And I said I would. But I talked about the collector. Everyone knew about him, the man who had so much money, the man who made such a fortune in Alberta oil he was collecting collections. Collecting the world, people said. That's the way they liked to put it; the statement made them part of the conspiracy.

But no one had actually seen much of Deemer in the ten years since he made it big. Whoever he was, he was, at least that much was known, a nobody. People guessed he was from a farm somewhere because he understood the farm boys who first worked on the first rigs, knew their scorn for unions and exploited it, knew their loneliness and flew in booze to isolated camps when they didn't have fresh eggs or milk, knew the macho backgrounds that made them willing to lose a thumb or a hand or a leg or a life to find oil while working for a cheapo driller who might or might not pay them in the end. Deemer came from such obscurity that no one knew him and went to such a state of success that no one knew him. It was that kind of transformation. It seemed to leave out the merely human. Except that he had to kill two men in order to accomplish the change. He had left that much evidence behind. Two corpses.

"A bath of desire," I said. I liked that, had used it twice before Karen protested. "She came through the water, like a swimming animal, through the overhang of fog and the whipping edges of the snow."

I was telling myself the story. I had to hear it before I could understand, and I had to understand before I could proceed. I was in one hell of a corner. I thought of the telegram, there on the floor in the left hind pocket of my green corduroys: Find me a spa, Dorf.

"My documentary," Karen said, "can be about the places you find and can't use and don't want. About all the places that don't save anyone." And she added, bizarrely, "Can I kiss you now?"

And my answer, then, was what bound us together. Looking at my journal now, looking at what I wrote then, trying to make sense of it all, I realize we were sealed at that moment into a bargain. We are all lonely. Don't kid yourself. I could hear the quickened, wet motion of her hand, the softly slapping motion of her hand as if, against some deep affection, she punished herself for being naughty. My ears were witness. It was an intimacy beyond touch.

"Places in the mountains," she said. "Some of the hot springs that have never been developed. Those that are known just to the local people. And some of those spas that once flourished, that are neglected now." She caught her breath. "We'll find them. Won't we, Dorf?"

She would make a film. She would make a film about lost and healing places. She would follow me as I went from place to place, would follow me to my death if she had to she said, unwittingly, filming the search. It would make her reputation for her. She'd be away, after that, away and running and winning.

"You," she said. "You knew when we drove up here tonight that we wouldn't be able to drive back."

"Maybe."

"That was sort of deceptive."

"You knew it too. Better than I did."

She laughed a small laugh. "Then why didn't we tell each other?"

I remembered: when I was a kid, there was a little spa not far from where I lived. Maybe thirty-five miles. Sixty kilometers. I never went there myself. Meeting Creek. It was a place where the Indians used to gather, the Cree and the Blackfoot, for centuries I suppose, curing wounds or heartaches or flat feet. A place where the homesteaders went for a couple of decades. They'd take the cold mineral water and turn it into steam. Steam baths. I'd heard the old men, the old women, talking about the good old days when they went there and got cured. And they'd laugh, secretly, together. I was just a kid. I hardly listened.

"People never tell," I said. "That's the way it is. They can't."

"They should," Karen said.

"They should, they should," I answered.

"Then say something," Karen said.

"I want to be loved," I said.

Karen came. She came hard and long, there in the darkness; I could barely see her. I was happy. I wanted to tell her that. I was happy, there in the crazy dark, with the lost peaks, high and broken all around us, and the wounded slope of Sulphur Mountain pouring its blood into visitors' dreams. I couldn't find anything to say. I heard Karen's voice. The motion of her hand stopped, and once I thought she said my name.

"What?" I said.

"Go to sleep," she said. "Dummy."

NEGATIVE #1:
AND BREAKFAST, AFTER

*P*erhaps we all, by some sleight of hand, live two lives. We have each two lovers. And each time, making love, we dream the other. That's fair enough.

I got up with the jaded sun and went into the bathroom and washed my face. Dressing was the difficult part. I had no blisters, but I could barely endure the touch of cloth to my tender pink skin. I went down the hall toward the elevator, hobbling as if I'd been kicked in the knackers. The insufferable young woman on duty in the iron cage could hardly suppress a laugh. I went down to the huge Alberta Room and ordered coffee.

A dozen people, at any given time, were standing in line at the bowls and platters and the steaming hot metal trays; hands reaching, pale hands and dark, taking fresh fruit and glasses of juice, toast and croissants, butter, jam, honey, kippers and eggs and bacon. The taking hands; the taking mouths too. Maybe fifty people, Christ knows, I didn't count, here and there at the bright orange tablecloths, quietly or noisily eating breakfast. I watched and listened. A few late skiers. A few Japanese tourists. A number of middle-aged men who had put on their ties before breakfast and gathered over slices of ham to talk about heavy oil. A group of people, men and women, younger, who were social workers; they'd come here to have a convention and to get away from it all.

Deemer could buy the place, I knew, and ask everyone to bugger off. For a moment I was on his side, hating all those people and their hearty appetites and their laughter and their confidence and their intimacies. Young couples, honeymooners no doubt, sitting there sore between the legs and staring mistily into each other's eyes and managing to bump their croissants and their fingers together. While I was thinking: blood, semen, sweat, shit, hair, fingernails, toenails, piss, pus. The infinite dribble of excrement that is life. Why go on? For the mixed pleasure of an orgasm? For the brief decency of a mind-scorching drunk? For the blustering of a few words that have chanced to become a business deal, a legal document, a medical report, a speech, a sermon, a newspaper column, a journal entry, a telephone call, a riddle, a library, an obituary?

Karen found me in a pretty foul mood. I stood up before she could sit down, led the way to the food; I heaped grapefruit sections into a bowl and took a croissant and a plateful of scrambled eggs. The eggs were watery. I liked the way they looked awful on my plate; I took more than I could possibly eat, looking forward to the time when they would be cold and gooey as well as too pale.

The waiter had poured Karen's coffee while we were getting our first course; he'd filled my cup for the third time. I passed her the saucer with its white plastic containers of cream; I tested the weight of the CPR silver knife and fork. But I didn't start to eat.

"Would you mind?" I said. I poked at my sections of grapefruit. "You mentioned that water is good for a burn." I felt unshaven, a boggy ditch. "I think I should spend some time at the spa."

"I have students to meet," Karen said. "You promised." She gestured toward the bright light streaming in through the tall windows. "The road will be plowed by now."

"Exactly," I said. I filled my mouth with grapefruit sections. I talked with my mouth full. "You'll have no trouble driving," I said. And I added, "He blurbled."

"There's no such word," she said. She looked at me with a mixture of pity and disgust.

"You take my car," I said. And then I was surprised myself, at my own confidence. "It's what today — Thursday? You can come back Friday night, after work, and pick me up here. I should be fine then." I pointed discreetly with my silver CPR fork down at my scalded member. I was sitting with my legs spread.

Karen licked the melting butter off her slice of brown toast. Then she indicated my full plate. "Oh, the Great Wound," she said. And then she added, "Diet is part of the cure, Dorf. Along with abstinence. Eat your eggs."

"Damnit," I said. I was impatient. "Friday night. You'll be here for dinner … Look, I'll give you the key to my apartment. Could you pick up some clothes for me?"

"No," Karen said. "What the hell is this?" And then she went on, foolishly, "You're strung out on that middle-aged, dark-eyed, abandoned woman of abandon."

"That's hardly a fair assessment," I said. "I never said she was dark-eyed. I said she had perfect, dark eyebrows."

Karen got up from the table and went for more toast. Now, also, she wanted some of the strawberries and the cantaloupe she'd passed up on her first run through the line, and a croissant, a warm croissant, with a patty of butter. She can eat like a horse.

"Where's the good-looking kid in the plaid vest with the coffee?" she said. "I could use some service."

"Let me get him for you," I said, sarcastically. I turned around on my chair to signal for more coffee and without thinking bumped my own tenderness. I damned near went through the ceiling.

"Do you really suppose you'll find her?" Karen said.

"I didn't say I was looking for *her*. I said I'm worried *stiff* about my scalded *prick*." And then I added, "I forgot to gas up yesterday. We'll have to gas up before you leave."

"Maybe Julie has a car," Karen said. "You won't need yours anyhow."

"I think you're jealous," I said.

"Jealous, my ass. I'm worried about your total incompetence. Your mother might sue me for letting you hurt yourself. I don't think unaccompanied children are allowed in the pool."

She kept that up while I poked at my scrambled eggs. She was obviously enjoying her own rather dismal sense of humor. "Don't use any of that exhilarating wit in your film," I cautioned at one point. Then I began to detail the clothing I'd like brought back from my apartment; I listed a tweed jacket, clean corduroys, two of my western shirts — and to my surprise she not only agreed but suggested I wear the rather expensive grey shirt I was wearing the last time she saw me. She said the grey shirt looked good with my curly, greying hair.

"It absorbs champagne well," I said, "as I discovered that night."

"You were abominably well mannered," she said. "I thought you were going to ignore me when I spoke."

"I spoke first," I said. "I'd been eyeing you all night."

"That's a lie, you were raving on without even noticing who was listening."

"And you weren't listening, you were flirting with that Enright fellow, that man who was there for CBC, talking to him about the film you might make. In fact, that's where I first heard you mention spa; you didn't even intend me to hear it."

We were arguing about something, I don't quite know what. Lovers have discord with their own memories, their own desires. Karen claims to like older men. No doubt she has heard the goat-man god, making his rude and lusting noises under the window, long before this; Deemer announces his claims, even on the unknown. She finished up a second helping of scrambled eggs. I was appalled.

"I'll run to the lobby," I said. "You stay here and finish eating, I'll go reserve my room for three more nights."

"You're being presumptuous," Karen said, through her eggs and her cynicism. "You'll be catching the bus this afternoon."

"Want to make a bet?" I said.

DORF FINDS A LAUNDROMAT INSTEAD OF
A SPA AND IS NEVERTHELESS PLEASED WITH
HIS PROGRESS AND CLAIMS TO MAKE REMARKABLE
DISCOVERIES ABOUT HIS EMPLOYER AND FINDS
HIMSELF ALSO VITALLY ATTRACTED TO THE WOMAN
WHO HAS PROMISED HIM AN EARLY DEATH

I went up to my room, found Karen as usual brushing her teeth; we both put on our parkas. We both made loud silences. We followed each other, side by side, to the elevator. And then the small rituals of a snowy morning: brushing the snow off the passenger's side of the car, passing the long-handled brush over the car to Karen. Kicking one boot against the other. Karen behind the wheel, easing her way onto the snow-white road. "Hey, this is fun," she said. "Mind if I wreck it?"

We went down Banff Avenue, made a left turn and then a quick right into the Texaco station across from the King Eddie. I paid the man for the gas. Then Karen spun her way through the snow and was gone.

And the first woman I found was not Julie. I was to find Julie later, much to my sorrow. But the woman I found at first, there in Pinkie's Cleaning Centre on Caribou Street, was only tall and beautiful and dark-haired and dark-eyed; she was doing her laundry.

I thought at first she might be Julie. I had nothing to launder so I took off my parka and took off my plaid shirt and put the shirt into a washer and put my parka back on and bought soap from a machine and plugged in the required quarters and sat down.

The woman was folding panties. She was wearing a fur coat, mink, and she was folding panties; and the panties, against all the splendor of that coat, were splendid too, one pair golden, another lime green, one pair as blue as a noon sky, one pair the color of fire, suggesting beaten brass, filigreed; panties embroidered, emblazoned, crocuses for her belly, a pierced red heart on a background of black. And maybe it was that, the collection itself, that kept me from seeing anything else.

She turned toward the window, held up a tiny ball of orange cloth to the blurred light that came through the frosted glass. I watched the gauzy, crumpled panties stretch smooth. Too small, still, for her, unless she too was small inside that coat; she paused to check something, the stitching perhaps, or the elastic. And it was then I noticed her left hand.

She folded the panties, the left side over the middle, the right side over, the crotch up. Then she put that pair onto the lowest of the three stacks of panties on the low table between two rows of washing machines, the machines set in alternation, one white, one green, one white, one green.

Her left hand was like the claw of a bird. I guess she saw that I had noticed. "It's all right," she said.

Her dark eyes had the pain and the fright and the indifference of a bird's. One time, when I was a boy in Edenwolf, that lost little town up there near the Battle River, I pointed a shotgun up at the bottom of a crow's nest and, to my horror, my transfixed horror, the sudden explosion brought a crow fluttering, wounded, down at my feet, a crow, unable to fly, that only looked at me and waited.

She wasn't Julie, but I couldn't turn and leave. I talked, made conversation. She was there in Banff to take the waters. Three times a day to the pool. Her face was beautiful. "It helps the joints," she said. She pointed with her right hand to the invisible left hand in the sleeve of her mink coat.

Her name was Estuary. Of all the names to hang on a woman, that one just about takes the cake. "Is it Romanian?" I asked, surprising myself. "No," she said.

I dried my shirt, after washing it, and put it back on. Estuary laughed at me, and I liked that.

We went for a bus ride, took a tour on a Brewster bus. We caught the bus, just across the street, where I might have caught a bus into the city. I took it, that trip to nowhere, farther into the mountains, because I had nothing else to do until the pool opened. Estuary went because she too had nothing else to do, nothing in the wide world. It was like that. But the driver winked, knowingly, when Estuary handed him our tickets. He took the tickets with a kind of affection from her left hand.

He was a fool at the wheel, that driver; he was a smallish man with big, surprised grey eyes under the brim of his tour driver's cap. He told his captive audience that he'd been a geologist in his younger days. He'd come to the mountains years ago, he explained, for his health. And he laughed a wild, carefree laugh. The audience, perhaps thirty people, all of them middle-aged or past, laughed with him. He occasioned a kind of conspiracy. The passengers were on his side immediately; they trusted everything he told them, everything he promised about Castle Mountain, about the Sundance Range and Johnston Canyon and Redearth Creek.

"There are some great spas in Romania," I whispered to Estuary for no apparent reason. "A friend told me about them."

The driver's name was Fish. He was an absolute fool on ice, on snow, on cliff edges, on hairpin curves, on downhill slopes. Every gesture had to be a risk. When there was nothing to worry about he drove without looking, glancing back at us instead. And yet, by the end of our three-hour ride, everyone loved him. Don't ask me why. Maybe we were glad just to be alive. He'd showed us two hundred post card scenes, snow-buried forests and towering peaks and the cold green edges of glaciers, up there in the sky.

I tried to identify Julie. I spent too much of that day studying faces. It got to me. All I could see, after a while, instead of the mountains, was pain and loss and fear and loneliness. I didn't like it. The corner of a mouth that betrayed a loud woman. The twitch in a man's eye muscles. I began to admire Fish. He was well preserved and well over sixty. I began to wonder if he looked anything like Jack Deemer.

Fish didn't want a tip when we got off the bus at the bus depot. He asked me instead if he could buy me a beer. I should have been on guard, I suppose; gossip and a scheme can sound somewhat alike. Assuming there's a difference.

I haven't mentioned Estuary. I guess I should explain that,

after an hour or so on that bus, we ran out of things to say to each other. So we held hands. We just sat there, and then I took one of her hands in mine. The funny thing is, I'm not so sure I remember which hand of hers I was holding. I was looking around a lot.

Estuary didn't come to the King Eddie with us. She said she had to go directly to the Upper Hot Springs. Fish led the way and I soon discovered that I wasn't the only person with a thirst. There must have been ten of us, a dozen, in the group.

I was glad that Karen wasn't there with her goddamned notebook, recording the way in which I wasn't getting on with my task. Forty-six years old and goofing off as usual. But I did watch for Julie. Sitting still on the bus had been good for my burn, I felt that. I watched for Julie and all I saw was something like two hundred people, wranglers and ski bums and staff from a dozen hotels and motels, beautiful young women and handsome young men, all of them the picture of health, all of them trying, if nothing else, to get soused; the King Eddie is a beautiful place to do it in, with the heads of wild animals stuffed and watching from the dimly lit walls.

I suppose I got soused myself. I bought one hell of a lot more beer than I drank. And I drank more than I needed. What I'm trying to say is I was pretty well corked, smashed, by the time I tried to describe Julie to Fish. I had only begun when he broke in.

"You're a worrier, Dorf. I can tell that."

Actually, I was thinking about Estuary's panties. That rainbow world she had collected for herself. What else is there but the dream? I connected the panties with Estuary and Estuary with the woman I was looking for and the woman I was looking for with a dream of being healed. I was hurting, I knew that much. We cannot have what we want, and we hurt. But the trouble was I was working for a man who could buy anything he wanted. That's what people said about Jack Deemer.

I drank a lot of beer. I ate a bag of potato chips, and I got thirsty again and I drank more beer. How and when Fish came to mention Big Julie I don't remember, because I no longer cared. I was free of care when he said the name.

"You know her then, I assume," I said. Sometimes I get

scared and that was one of those occasions. "Estuary," I added, for no apparent reason. "I'm sorry she left us. I like her panties."

"Big Julie Magnuson," Fish said.

"Not the same woman," I said to Fish. "This woman was sort of biggish. But you'd never call her big."

"She lives with Jack Deemer. The oilman. You ever hear of him?"

"I've heard of him," I said, richly enjoying the irony.

"Funny bird, ain't he?"

"I don't know," I said.

"Thought you said you knew him," Fish said. It was so loud in that beer hall you couldn't hear yourself think. Fish leaned close. He was obviously enjoying the company of three or four of the women in our group; he begrudged me what little time I was asking. "Remember," he said. "Remember the cougars."

I pretended that I remembered. But then Fish did the remembering for me: Deemer killed a couple of men in the oil patch. I tried to look surprised. But he was talking to impress the ladies, Fish was. The first one was killed by Deemer when he was so poor he could get away with it, the second one when he was so rich he could get away with it. The first one, at least, had something to do with Big Julie. Fish didn't quite remember the details. But he did know Julie, or rather, had known her; not the present Julie, of course, but the Julie she was before she became this one. The Julie they called Big Julie, in the camps. The Julie who worked in the camps, who could fuck and fight with the toughest of the men. Deemer was something of a coward, Fish explained. Or maybe he was just smart.

Fish himself was an oil geologist. Had been one. Deemer was just a guy with a sharp eye and cool way of calculating a gamble, but Fish was the real thing, knew his rocks inside out and worked with drill cores and seismic explosions and ate camp food until one day he was sent to look at a mountain. And he missed the truck that would have taken him back to the city. He threw away his pencils and he hadn't left since; he hadn't been out of the mountains in something like twenty years, he no longer remembered for sure. He got laughs from the three old ladies by asking what year it was.

I looked around at the animals' heads on the walls. And that's a funny thing; that's when I remembered. I'd known another collector when I was a kid. He was a farmer, four miles out of the village of Edenwolf. But every fall he was transformed into the perfect hunter. Every fall he went to the Rockies west of Pincher Creek, and he hunted for the perfect mountain sheep. He wanted a set of those curled horns that make a perfect circle. He died one fall in the mountains. People in Edenwolf claimed he found the perfect ram one fall, and stalked it, and shot it. And got his curled horns. And died on the way down the mountain.

But Deemer wasn't like that. Maybe he was just a coward. Or maybe he was trying, I decided, over a fresh glass of beer, maybe he was trying to put the world back together again. After killing someone. Maybe, instead of just trying to buy the world, he was hoping to buy it and reassemble it too. According to his own design, of course.

And maybe Fish had been away from the world for so long he no longer knew what it was like.

"Where the hell are we, Fish?" I demanded.

"You're pissed, Dorf."

"What the hell is this?"

"These ladies got to go take their treatment."

"What the hell treatment is that, Fish?"

"Their rheumatism cure. Up at the pool."

Up at the pool. Up on the mountainside, up in the pool. I was acting drunker than I really was, so I could get back to the subject: "Remember what cougars?" I said.

And this time Fish had his audience. Those ladies were ready to leave and to go to the pool, but they would listen to Fish. "Those cougar kittens," he said. "When Deemer's partner died. When he died, in the bunkhouse, all by himself with the cougars."

We had to know more and said so.

"She saved these three kittens," Fish said. "After one of the men shot the mother."

We ordered more beer.

"It was breakup and the drilling crew went out to Fort McMurray, only Deemer and his partner stayed with the rig, and the cook stayed with Deemer and his partner. And the cook's name was Julie."

"We guessed that," one of the ladies said, though I couldn't figure out how.

"So Julie and Deemer come out of the bush one day and they tell the mounties the other guy is back in there, dead as a doornail. Woke up dead one morning. Food poisoning they thought. Deemer and Julie were four days getting out of that camp through hell and high water, packing a canoe from one stretch of open water to the next. Wet all day and all night. Nothing to eat but a goose that Deemer managed to kill with his 30-30."

I wasn't as thirsty as I'd been.

"It took two mounties a week to get into that camp. Two greenhorns, pretending they knew how to travel in the bush."

I was watching the head of a bobcat, mounted on the wall across the room, over a skier who had his right foot in a cast, the cast on a chair.

"They licked that skeleton clean. Polished it with their loving tongues. Slick and clean." Fish was getting into it now; his ladies kept a cat or two themselves, you could see that much. "Three cougar kittens in that bunkhouse. Maybe four. And the most perfect skeleton that any young mountie ever laid eyes on."

I asked for details. I had to know more. What was the *real* relationship between Deemer and Julie? I mean, I had to know, and I said so; I was willing to start a fight to find out.

"That says it," Fish said.

"Says *what?*" I shouted.

"Says it all," Fish said.

"Licked the skeleton clean," one old lady said to another. They were a bunch of bitches, getting off on that disaster.

But they were also just slightly offended that anyone would tell such a story at the expense of the good reputation of cats, even if the cats were actually cougars.

"How do you know it was murder?" I said.

Fish gave me a look as if I had to be the stupidest man he'd ever known. "That well was Deemer's first million." Then he shrugged. "These ladies are dying to take their baths."

I forgot the razor and tooth paste I'd bought. I had to go back into the bar, into the stink and the heat, and I almost didn't catch the group before the taxi whisked us away on our ride up the mountain.

It's a funny thing, but I led the way into the building. Into the Upper Hot Springs. And yet, Fish seemed to know everyone there. It was dark now, overhead, up there around the tree tops, up there around the stars. Dark, shit, yes. And yet he could see.

And the floating heads were there too. I went pushing my way around, nosing my way around. I was there and the heads were there and the fog was there. I think all of us missed her.

Julie wasn't there. Big Julie Magnuson.

I talked with the three old ladies. They might have been three of my aunts from Edenwolf, but in fact they were somebody else's aunts, one of them from Montana, one from Swift Current, Saskatchewan, one from Toronto. They had in common the aches in their bones. I talked to their pink and frosted faces. And they looked at me, because they saw that my muscles had only a few years of illusion left. Maybe they even desired me. I hope they did. But they looked at my face, which I guess I'd have to call handsome; they looked at the ice that coated my hair, and they let me into their circle.

I began to realize I could pick them out. Among the tourists come to look, the skiers come to relax strained muscles — I could recognize the bathers who had come to be cured. The old women, suffering from the fever of their rocking chairs or their television sets. The old men, persuaded that the spa water would untie the closing knots. For some reason I began to imagine entries in my journal, the entries I was now two days behind on: Life is only to be endured. Yesterday was my birthday, I was forty-six; I decided, yes, I'm going to keep a journal, I'm going to love two women, I'm going to tell the truth. Life is unendurable. The trouble is, I enjoy it. Yesterday made sense, I can see it all now, but today doesn't. Maybe that's what journals are about. Or Karen Strike's documentary.

I was missing Karen again. I missed her more than I missed the woman I was looking for. And I'd more or less tricked Karen into going away so I could look for the woman I, right then at least, didn't want to find. But that was a lie too. I did want to find her. I started, once more, to go around the pool; I was hardly able to take my eyes off the two glass doors.

Fish introduced me to a man who had a terrible migraine headache. Fish seemed to know half the people in the pool, more, maybe everybody.

"This isn't going to cure him," I whispered to Fish about the man with the migraine headache, the big, round head that was being polite, smiling while I whispered to Fish.

"Sometimes it does. Briefly."

"For five minutes?" I said.

"Not for that long," Fish said.

I couldn't stand it. "Why does he come here, then?"

Fish didn't give me a decent answer. Instead he said, "He's been coming here for eight years."

"The same problem?"

"The same headache."

I should have swum away from the two men. Instead, I shouted. I shouted at both of them. The heads around me, the floating heads, looked startled. More than that, they looked offended. As if I'd awakened them out of a deep and wonderful sleep. "This is all a fraud," I shouted. That's one of the things I said. But then I went on and asked about Julie. Maybe I was upset. Or I'd had too much beer at the King Eddie, and the sudden heat, the hot mineral waters and the heat and the fog and the frost, combined with Fish and the man with the migraine and the three old ladies from everywhere, curing their aching bones; it was all too much and I shouted something about cats. "Feed the fucking cougars," I shouted. "Cougar food," I shouted. I'm embarrassed now, even as I write down what I said. I can't remember.

The lifeguard came out of her glass box. It was so fogged up I was surprised she could see; I hadn't noticed her. I didn't notice her until she leaned down from the edge of the pool as if

I was a misbehaving child, as if I'd dived in an area where people weren't supposed to dive.

I tried to reason with her. She gave me one minute to get out of the pool.

WOMEN, BEWARE THE IDEA OF LUCK,
AND MEN BEWARE GOOD FORTUNE

*K*aren Strike came back one day early. She was waiting in the lobby of the Banff Springs Hotel and, in my trust that human beings care for each other, I assumed she had rushed back from the city in order to be with me. When I walked in through the front entrance I found her sitting in an easy chair, an armful of clothes on the chair beside her. My clothes. Three shirts, a jacket, two pairs of trousers. Perhaps it was the sight of my clothes, without me in them, that upset me slightly, my clothing flung down as if I'd left in something of a hurry.

"Well, hi," I said.

"Hi yourself." She looked up at the stuffed buffalo over the door.

"Jesus, you're a day early." And then I added, "I've just come back from the pool."

"I was there three hours ago. You weren't."

"I wasn't, three hours ago." And then I added, defiantly, "I was getting snockered."

"Dorf," she said, "how could you disappear in *Banff?*"

I could see she was relenting.

"I didn't find her," I said.

That was both saying I know what's on your mind and, you're wrong, idiot. She looked absolute, there in that chair, slightly angry at having been kept waiting, almost sorry that she'd come at all. She is tall, a shade thin, her hair a kind of dirty blonde that both excites and repels me. She has a perfect pair of legs and knows it and takes every opportunity to expose them right up to her crotch. In that she bears some resemblance to my former wife. She was wearing a skirt and blouse that were vaguely Oriental, something from a Tibetan shop, I assume, on the 8th Avenue Mall in the city. Something just close enough to skid row to ease her conscience.

"Two things," she said.

"Fine," I said. "Great. Shoot."

"The first one we can throw away," she said. "I'm horny."

"Great," I said. "Just fucking great."

"And second," she said, "I got the grant. The contract. I've hired a cameraman to come up here tomorrow and look around."

That was why she'd been so damned anxious to get back to the city. To check her mail. And now she had rushed back to me with the news. "I won't be here," I said.

"Of course you'll be here."

"I've got work to do."

"You'll be here. You're a prisoner, Dorf. Go look at yourself in a mirror." She smiled a little smile of mild amusement and mild disgust. "You look like something the cat dragged in."

"I can leave whenever I like," I said. "I wouldn't look for that woman if I was dying of thirst and she was the sole possessor of a case of Perrier water."

"Let's take these things to *your* room," Karen said. "I'm sick of being your servant." She picked up my clothes. "And by the way," she said, with her gift for mere repetition, "how's the Great Wound?"

"I perish for want of love," I said. "Let's go."

We went to the elevators. I found the key in the front left pocket of my corduroys. On the way up I checked the time on Karen's wristwatch, since I refuse to wear anything that keeps the hour: it was just a little after eleven. I reminded Karen that we'd agreed to have our postponed drink together, celebrating my birthday. We threw our things on the beds, returned to the elevators, and rode down to the mezzanine. At the door to the bar I suggested we take a walk first, to clear my head, before we settled in to serious drinking.

We walked hand in hand past the china shop, into the huge lounge — the Riverview, I believe it's called, though we couldn't at that hour see the Bow River or the mountains. Karen went to a window beside a writing desk, looked down and pronounced the skating rink deserted, saying so in a pompous tone that I assumed was meant to mock my sincerity. But I noticed that she clung, still, to my hand.

I insisted that we proceed down the long marble floor, arm in arm; we marched between the two rows of huge brass pots, I insisting that we pause now and then before a potted plant, examine it, guess at its name, look around.

Karen became quite irritable. She released my arm and marched over to have a look at a rather conspicuous print: "Robert Burns … Reading His Poem of the 'Winter Night'" — I went back later to study it. Curiously, the Duchess of Gordon, at the center of the assembled audience, for all the winter night of the poem, is resting her slippered feet on a footstool and looking warm and fragile … "Take a peek at this," Karen called down the long, hollow room in a voice that was nothing if not too loud. "Your sharp-clawed falcon should like this — "

It was that uncouth remark that brought Julie's head into view. She was sitting on a high-backed sofa in front of the monstrous fireplace at the face end of the lounge. Not until too late did I, approaching, see that she was with a young man.

In the confusion of introductions that followed I shook hands twice with a Mr. Marty Grieg who was described as a climber, part of a rescue team.

Instead of looking at this Mr. Grieg — I had seen his name, recently, in the papers, some famous rescue or other — I stared at the two heads of bighorn sheep carved in stone and seeming to support the stone slab over the large and galloping fire. Julie said nothing to me and I as much to her; she was wearing an indecent amount of gold, gold bracelets, a golden necklace, a gold brooch in the shape of a peacock, its tail decorated with infinite small gems that caught and turned and broke the light.

This Mr. Grieg was full of his accomplishments and his contempt — for those who, as he so wonderfully put it, make mistakes, get lost, or overreach their capabilities — and, I began to perceive, he was dearly in love with death. He had that kind of pale, thin intense face of young men who climb mountains and look for death. Poor Julie did a marvelous job of appearing to be interested, listening while he explained how he'd climbed some impossible slope to bring down a skier who'd broken his back while helicopter skiing —

"Have you ever heard a peacock's cry?" I said, abruptly.

Karen chose that moment to turn and flee.

Julie looked surprised.

"One morning," I said, "I was in southern France looking for a rare book on the Albigensians. I was awakened by a cry that chilled my blood for the rest of the week."

I turned on my heel and was gone.

A DARK, STONE
STAIRWAY

*J*ust like that, I turned and was going and was gone. I meant to
overtake Karen. Something, I could see, was upsetting her. I
intended to apologize, even though I wasn't quite aware of what
I could possibly have done to upset her. But she was upset. I
had promised her a drink. Or Julie had ignored her. Or Grieg
was a truly offensive prick, with his bragging.

Someone bent on ransacking the hotel could not have
done a more thorough job than I. Karen had simply and in an
instant managed to vanish. I went directly from the Riverview
Lounge, through the Oval Room with its peach walls and its
glassy chandeliers, into the library. I startled an elderly couple,
locked in embrace in that Tudor room, a couple as ancient in
appearance as the table against which the lady rested her
buttocks. In my embarrassment at their indifference to interrup-
tion I turned and quite by mistake went into the Ladies' Rest
Room. Karen was not there. I had time to admire the delicate
tiling before I fled, turning to the right, stopping for a sip of
water at the fountain, hurrying into the Cascade Ballroom where
once, years ago, I myself embraced a woman in dance; the
doors to the Conservatory were locked; I stared in at the myriad
plants, that odd collection of plants from the scattered corners
of the mere earth.

It was then I began to recognize the hotel itself, the Banff
Springs Hotel, as another kind of collection. It offended me, the
sheer deliberation that had gone into the collecting; Deemer, at
least, had the grace of his exuberance, tempered by a perfect
ignorance. He believed he could collect everything, and set
about doing so.

I turned about and marched through the hallway to the

Oval Room, past Julie and Grieg where they sat in front of the fireplace and talked as if nothing had happened; I marched past them as if I'd not noticed them or was preoccupied, but that marble floor stretched a full mile in front of me. I was dizzy when I got to the far end, walked past the elevators, resisted the temptation to retreat to my room and a good book; and, yes, I was tempted to return to the library for a book, selecting something that promised a quiet read, the small titillations of sex; instead I went to the gallery overlooking the late Gothic pretensions of Mount Stephen Hall.

I was looking down from my shadowed obscurity into that vast hall when Karen came out of the shadows below me and crossed the limestone floor toward the grand piano at the far end of the room.

I said nothing. I might have called down to her; I took my time, my good and sweet time, deciding; I admired the trees and animals in the dark blue tapestry-like drapes, suspended against the night, far across the room from me. The curious light in the room, muted, ominous, lit up not the glass of the window but the lead that squared each small, leaded pane. There were coats of arms and more coats of arms, like cryptic messages from Julie, placed in the air about me; there were flowers carved on the doors and the drawer-fronts of heavy oak sideboards, carved as if with a two-headed axe; yes, I was walking, I was going somewhere, nowhere, walking; I was walking through a cloistered walk; on my tiptoes I paused, Medici prints on the walls about me, more of those exquisite flowers, those exquisite faces that reminded me not of the Gothic dark of Julie's indifference but of her exact need, her precise and radiant horror at her own desire; I passed through an archway, the hotel was archways, more archways, with the beamed ceilings in violent, male contrast; Karen touched a key of the piano. She touched a single key and was surprised at the echoing sound. She turned away.

I found a dark, stone stairway. I went down, carefully I went down, the heavy stone steps. Into a darkness that was watery thick.

I saw Karen go into the Oak Room.

That I hesitated was no reflection of indecision. I had already made up my mind. Rather, I was deciding on my stance. Would I be forgiving? Would I be demanding, arrogant, hurt?

She did not hear me enter.

The room has a floor of stone and on it a rug that seems a Twenties imitation of something infinitely old; I rather liked it. Three recessed windows imitated the squares in the rug; the panelled walls, dark, almost invisible, were a maze, too, of squares; the ceiling, I noticed at a glance, was made up of a pattern of joined circles and squares. There were heads in bas relief in the row of wall panels that joined with the ceiling. I was losing my sense of direction, even my sense of up and down. What light came in at the window might have come from a star or from a furnace.

I closed the door behind me. I turned to make certain it was shut and saw that the panelled back of the door had disappeared into the panelled wall.

I had found, after all, the perfect lock. I remembered the old lady in Connecticut with her elaborate keys, with her elaborate locks and their bolts and stumps and gliders, her collection of doors mounted in the middle of the floor in the middle of a room, as if by that bizarre conundrum she might confuse all thieves into their own insanity.

But now the door itself vanished, the room only remaining. The world was transformed in that instant. A world without door is not a world that any one of us recognizes. We are conditioned by doors, shaped by doors; the very notions of entrance and exit give direction to our lives. Time itself was erased; I saw that time is an artificial construct, something we've invented, a kind of airy equivalent of doors.

Karen took hold of me. I use the expression deliberately. She did not seize or capture or fondle. She took hold of me. Those other possibilities had been erased by the erasure of the door. Human gestures lost their humanity; we engaged, instead, in the merely animal.

And then we understood the freedom that is an animal freedom, a freedom from the illusion of time. Now was everywhere. The hawk's high cry or the first night of frost, the egg in the nest, the seed that finds bruised earth, the rain that falls at the breaking hour.

In that boxed world, Karen and I were natural. Her holding held away my slightest claustrophobia. We did not speak. Yes, we did not speak, we tried not a single word on each other, we uttered not a single lie, the two of us together; arms were enough. The silence confounded, rebuked, and then, finally, acknowledged nothing but our quickened breathing.

To my surprise, her cunt was wet. My fingers retreated to that warmth.

Inside the absolute closure of the doorless room, I listened. Whether it was the silence or the animal smell of Karen's body that made me erect, I don't know. We live by the body's five senses. They speak to each other only. They are the openings that give us the world. Those receiving senses, they ask no deceit, no withholding, no pretty and winking logic, no elaborate regret. They are not contrivances of disguise or design. They are inhumanly patient.

I know there were chairs in the room, spaced evenly about the four walls, empty chairs; and they, too, were only objects in nature. In nature, I insist; the artifice of the chair, that too was gone. Windows and drapes were as much and as little as a sprig of grass, a feather on a windowsill.

Karen, when I fell to the rug, straddled me. I lay down in the middle of the rug in the middle of the room. Karen eased her wet body onto my impatient wound.

The pain was hardly to be endured.

That I could not find relief from my pain was no fault of my own. I was past all coming, into a static suffering. I was misery itself. I was the suffering that all men have endured, to give pleasure. I was my own failure made good and heroic, the giving man, given to the whispered need of a woman. I endured and I endured. I moved against the strong, soft movement of her need, my arms held her holding arms.

I don't know who invented the door. We heard it creak open, Karen and I; we heard it creak shut again. Just that. A sound, like a spoke of light. As if the moon itself had tickled loose the lock that wintry night, in spring. I understood, and said we must go to our room; even as I am certain now, looking back, that it could only have been Julie who peeked in and then could look no further. Julie, seeking me, spying on me, even. Julie, seeking me, in the night, in the hotel. Finding me. Drawing back from the first perception of oblivion.

My Julie, saving me for her own ambitions.

A LONGISH CHAPTER (DORF, ALONE)
DESTINATION: THAT PLACE WHICH ELUDES US
THAT SADDEST DREAM OF ALL OUR HOPE
HIGH AS A MOUNTAIN
BEFORE, AND AFTER, TOO
THE MAN WHO COLLECTED NOTHING
AND FOUND IT EVERYWHERE

*T*he waitress brings my capuccino and a Danish. The couple at the next table, here in The Espresso Cafe at the bottom level of the hotel, below the Oak Room, below and beyond ... The young Japanese couple, the boy showing off his English for his girl, but confused now, saying slowly to the waitress, "What ... is ... Dan ... ish?"

I stir the steamed milk down into the coffee. I look away from the cup, away from my journal, out into the Bow Valley. To the right, overlooking both the hotel and the valley, is the slanting edge of Mt. Rundle.

Birthday today. Meaning, five days ago. I cross out *I am* and write in *He is* ... He ... I ... What does it matter? I am, he is, at last, this morning, trying to catch up. Birthday today; that was last Wednesday. Monday today.

Karen, I write, looking with curiosity at the name. Almost frightening, that word, Strike. STRIKE. I print it in capitals. Her TV documentary has, if nothing else, a title: "The Mechanics of Healing."

She has a killer instinct of her own, I understand that now. Her cameraman, when he arrived late on Saturday morning, instead of looking at the mountains or at the Upper Hot Springs, or for that matter, at me, spent most of his time looking at Karen's ass.

She, of course, was delighted; she had two men following her around while she talked about takes and camera angles and the question of whether or not they should simply record or set up situations.

"Fake the real," I suggested. We were standing on the parapet, overlooking the pool; even as we stood there together, the three of us, a charming little triangle based on Karen, I could not help but visualize a couple in the fog-distorted pool below us: the man, tall, too lean perhaps, suggesting a kind of terrible hunger; the woman dark, voluptuous; I could hardly resist giving the details to Randy.

The cameraman was named Randy. He waved his faggy little right hand and said the real would suffice. Condescending prick that he was. The real would suffice. He liked the brooding emptiness, he said, the column of grey fog reaching out of the white landscape into an empty sky. "Healing," he said, "as a kind of absence, a reduction to nothing," and he tried to get his cold little fists into the hind pockets of his new jeans. Bless you, I thought to myself, aren't you too sweet for words.

Karen led her entourage up the side of Sulphur Mountain, hoping to get a look at the source itself, the place where the water comes spring-like from the rocks and the clay. Randy, I could see, was afraid he'd get his new jeans dirty. I saved him by saying to Karen, "There's a little-teeney house now, built over the source. We could use a photograph from the archives." I'd been doing my homework and then some in the Peter Whyte Archives on Lynx Street; Karen had somehow conceived the notion that I did nothing but loaf. Once, in a fit of exasperation, she'd told me I was ripping Deemer off. "I thought you hate the rich," I said. "I hate theft in any form," she replied, pretending to her usual moral superiority.

I suppose I had to rub it in; my research was making hers look bad. "Or a photograph of the Brett Sanatorium," I suggested. "With patients lined up on the verandah. Begin there."

She said nothing.

"A great opening shot," I said. "They came to Dr. Brett from as far away as Japan to be treated for arthritis. His victims bathed in the mineral waters and drank whisky and went away feeling better. He made a fortune."

Before I could go on Randy interjected with the novel observation, "I could stand a drink myself." He was sulking; he added that it was Saturday afternoon, insinuating by his tone of voice that he had better things to do than take pictures of hot water.

I said I'd drive him downtown if he was in a hurry; he claimed to have a dinner date. So I whipped my car into a line of traffic going down the mountain, and distracted poor Randy by talking about R. G. Brett, the spa doctor who went on to become lieutenant-governor of Alberta; yes, I explained, there you have a man who went from this very place as if obliged to heal the whole damned country of its misery; I sort of got wound up on the subject of spas. In Roman times, I explained. Before that, in Greece. The use of water to cure disease: "Look at your Hippocrates. Look at Celsus. Look at Galen. Water to cure fevers. Water to cure infirmities of the brain." I gave Karen a little poke in the ribs. We were all of us sitting in the front seat. "Sir John Floyer," I said, "the English physician, believed and demonstrated that a cold bath will cure damned near everything that's wrong with you."

I saw that Karen was irked by my telling her about her subject, so I suggested, when I pulled up behind a parked car, that we all slip into the King Eddie for a quick beer. Before Randy met his date, I added; I was turning my head to wink at Karen, and accidentally bumped the car ahead of me. To my horror, both Randy and Karen accepted the invitation.

Fish, of course, was in the King Eddie. He had to shout my name across the room as if we were old buddies. And, of course, he was surrounded by the usual ragtag mob of the dying and the dead.

Six people leapt up and went in search and found three chairs, and I lifted them one by one over the patrons' heads. Somehow we new arrivals squeezed the three chairs into the circle around the two tables, then squeezed ourselves into the chairs. Someone pushed two glasses of beer in front of me.

Karen took to the place like a pig to mud; she was, in an instant, deep into conversation with an old man who wore a scar down the middle of his face, as if he'd been split open with an axe and put together by a blind seamstress. Randy was seated where he could play footsies with her.

"Big Julie," Fish said. Shouted.

"I heard you," I said.

"She's renting my bus next Tuesday," he said.

"Too bad," I said. "I'm thinking of heading back to the city."

Fish shrugged. "I just thought you might like to know. She's going out to Yoho. From there they plan to do some climbing. Some guy teaching survival."

A shiver ran down my spine. I helped myself to a glass of beer, added a dash of tomato juice, took another sip.

Fish was in his glory. He was surrounded by his passengers. They might have been on shipboard, sailing a darkling sea. They were children of a strange joy, all of them. I recognized the three old ladies and they recognized me and asked where I'd been. I was embarrassed at my tardiness and promised to join them soon, one night. And the lady was there with the bird-like hand; she dared to use it, now, to raise a glass of beer. Estuary. She raised a glass of beer in my direction and said, to my astonishment, "Thank you."

I felt a secret pleasure. Why, I don't know; I was thrilled and humbled. I smiled in return. I tried to give her a kind of it-was-nothing shrug, but I felt the affection that denied my casual response. I glanced at her a moment later and thought of her collection of panties, the panties lime-green and lovely as that small and delicate fruit, that green-tinted fruit with its special smell; I thought of her red panties, violent and needing to be torn, barely containing a thicket of pubic hairs; I thought of the silken blue of her sky-blue panties, slick now and smooth with a soft wetness; no, not that pair, I told myself, she's wearing a wild and purple lace tonight, not thick enough to stop a tongue —

Karen caught my attention by throwing a balled up napkin in my direction. We were supposed to drive up to Lake Louise; we had reservations to have dinner at the Post Hotel. She looked me a question: was it time to leave? I understood her wishes, her needs, even her affection for Randy. Do you think we should stay here? I mouthed, not making a sound. Her face lit up; she made a circle around the table with her right forefinger, indicating she liked the circle, the friends, the antics; the beer slinger, seeing her, nodded. She had inadvertently ordered still another round of beer. I laughed with her in what seemed a secret conspiracy.

I knew I must ask Fish more about Julie and her proposed trip into high country. It was certainly time I got back to the city. I had work to do. But to do that work, I must know more about Deemer. To know more about Deemer ... My mind went in that kind of circle. I distracted myself by telling whomsoever would listen about hydrotherapy, the wonderful tradition of treating disease with that most cleansing of all the elements, water itself; I was full to the top of my head with Chinese ice-water treatments and the mineral contents of the waters of Saratoga and the medical theories of Vincent Priessnitz of Graefenberg.

As it turned out we got quite drunk, all of us. Not Randy, though; he insisted on leaving our party to go across the street to his dinner date at Joshua's; I begged him with all my might to stay. He would have nothing of it, saying he had to get back to the city that very night; he could ride back with his dinner date, it turned out.

"Stay," Karen said, "and ride back with Dorf in the morning. He's going into the city in the morning, aren't you, Dorf?"

I found myself somewhat rattled by the question. I had no idea up until that instant that I might not be going back to the city in the morning. Indeed, I'd already planned to visit my travel agent, bright and early on Monday; it was time, once again, to take to the air. Working in the Peter Whyte Archives, as I had so assiduously, I'd settled on a half dozen likely spots where I might find a neglected or forgotten spa that would suit Deemer's need for a hermit-like solitude, places where he might live forever and go unnoticed.

I'd conceived a kind of fascination with the idea, imagining

I might try them out myself, free of the everlastingly nagging sexual needs of one's body. I'd conceived a religious concept, I suppose, of my potential escape. Only after I'd exhausted its every turn would I yield my cell-like existence to Deemer's impulse to collect.

Karen thought I hadn't heard her question. She asked it again.

"I was thinking I might get my car looked at," I said. "Monday morning, bright and early." I tried to look positive. "We could be in the city by three in the afternoon at the latest."

Randy went prancing off to his dinner date. I was sorry to see him go, his droopy little moustache and his open shirt, not to mention his exposed belly button, added something different to our gathering.

Karen tried to give me a dirty look. I ignored her and signalled for more beer.

I suppose it would be fair to say we got corked. Polluted. Smashed. When it came time to go to the Upper Hot Springs, we didn't. I asked a few discreet questions about Julie. I shouted them discreetly in Fish's ear. She'd appeared out of nowhere to make her arrangements with Fish. I asked if she was possibly staying at the Banff Park Lodge. Not likely, Fish explained; she probably has a luxurious cabin of her own; Deemer would do that much for her.

"How so?" I said.

"She's got him by the balls," Fish said.

"How so?" I insisted.

"She's a good deal younger," he said. He looked across the table to Karen instead of at me, as if he meant to indicate that Karen is younger than I am; hardly a profound observation. "Julie," he said. "When she and Deemer teamed up in the oilfields, she was in her twenties. He already felt he'd hit it too late. He made it big all right, but too late. He'd missed something. He was so rich he'd die before he got all his money counted."

You couldn't hear yourself think in there.

"He was too old." Fish said. "Deemer was too old by the time it all began. He knew that. Told me that, once, over a couple of beers in a hotel in Donalda. He was trying to buy up some farms. He wasn't satisfied to have the rights to the oil, way down below the surface; he wanted the surface too. Strip-mining country. Up there where you come from."

I didn't remember telling Fish where I came from; I still don't think I ever told him. It was a little bit scary talking to that guy.

"Maybe the air above it too," Fish said. "Above the surface. Maybe he wants that too."

"I don't know," I said. I don't know why I said that.

"The only solution for Deemer," Fish said, "is to go on living forever."

For some reason, I thought of Julie again, her telling me that if I found the spa she'd have to put the spike in me.

We went to his apartment, to Fish's apartment, if you could call it that. When the bar closed, about a dozen of us climbed into a couple of cars and drove through a lot of snow-slick streets to his basement apartment.

Fish doesn't believe in owning anything. He lives in what has got to be the rattiest place I've ever laid eyes on. A two-burner hot plate. A window for a fridge: he opens the inside window and sets his quart of milk against the pane of the storm window. Two stools and a small table; I began to feel the second stool was an extravagance. A slab of foam rubber and a grimy sleeping bag on the floor in the second room.

There were a few books on the shelf in the closet inside the door. His change of underwear was on the same shelf; a change of clothes hung under it.

We had a good time. I guess I provided most of the beer; I don't quite remember. I knew that if I got drunk enough I wouldn't be tempted to go back to the city in the morning. Sunday mornings can get pretty heavy. But a good, bad hangover would keep me in bed. So we sat on the floor and drank beer and argued about house plants. One of the three old ladies began to insist that Fish should fill up his rooms with house plants.

"I collect *nothing*," Fish shouted. I'd never seen him lose his cool before. The lady, obviously, was upsetting him.

"Nothing," he repeated. And he seemed to be persuaded that he was telling the truth.

There was nothing in the world that Fish would bother to purchase and protect and own. Nothing. We sat around him on his carpeted basement, cement floor; we listened and argued and shouted and drank more beer and disagreed.

Only Karen defended him. She was on her make-do kick, with half the buttons of her Tibetan blouse unbuttoned. But even she had trouble defending his will not to own so much as a few house plants. The bathroom was just off his kitchen and we were in a sense standing in line while we sat on the floor and drank. It wasn't a bathroom; it was a toilet and a basin. Fish, obviously, took his baths in the Upper Hot Springs. He went to a public bath the way people used to, still do, I suppose, in lots of places. A public bath. The Roman baths with their swimming baths and their vapor baths and their baths of hot air. From the spoliatorium to the unctuarium to the calidarium ... That kind of undressing and reuniting; I began to see how taking a bath in private was a strange thing to do. Sitting in a tub by yourself. Standing under a shower, rubbing your private parts with a bar of soap. What the hell.

I kept thinking of Julie. Julie, on the coming Tuesday, climbing a mountain. Studying high-country survival. At the worst time of year. Well, not quite. Later still would be worse still, when the snow started to come down the mountainsides.

High up, and hesitating, all of us. We should have gone home. A dozen of us in that small apartment, soaking in our own sweat. It was stinking hot and the smoke would take out your eyes. I guess we were happy. We drank and we talked; Fish offered to take off his clothes, just to keep cool, and an old lady told him he'd have to wear a fig leaf, and then it turned out that Estuary was an expert on all the kinds of fig plants there are in the wide world, six hundred varieties or so, Christ, and I was more than a little drunk, and I said, "Don't tell Deemer, he'll want them all."

Deemer's collecting, and his collections, making no sense. So now, against all the randomness, he wants to collect, possess, some special and immovable part of the earth itself. Some place of entrance and exit, right there, wherever that is, where the mystery might or might not be. Pig in a poke. If I can find the poke, that is. "Dorf," I said aloud to everyone, and no one. "I want you to find me a poke with a pig in it. And a haystack with a needle in it. And get your ass in gear."

And there I sat, cross-legged, and I could feel the cold of the cement floor through the thin, worn, dirty carpet, there in that overheated room. There I sat, trying to open a bottle of beer with a pair of pliers, trying to get my ass in gear, trying to plot my course. "I'm chopping my course," I said to Fish. My tongue was thick.

"You're plodding your course," Fish said.

"Which of us is pocketing the truth?" I said. I meant that for Fish too.

"Deemer," Karen said. "You dummy."

"I didn't ask you," I said.

It was Karen who drove me home. Or back to our room I should say. The roads were slippery. I was too drunk to drive.

That was late Saturday night. Early Sunday morning.

AN OPEN BOOK: OR,

FOR OR AGAINST
FOR AND AGAINST

*M*onday night in our room in the old log hotel, there in Lake Louise, Karen read my journal. She read it while I was downstairs in the bar having a drink by myself, treating the climax of a two-day hangover and, when I went back up expecting to find her asleep, I found her instead propped up on our two pillows, reading the entries in the journal that she'd given me for my birthday.

"Do you assume," I asked her, "that because you gave me the journal you have the right to read my entries?"

"Spare me the 'do you' bit," she said. She has a small scar on her left wrist, just below the joint. She waved her scar at me. "You left it where I'd have to find it and read it, so I did."

Not only had she snooped and found and read my journal, she'd decided to tell me she'd read it, and she'd decided to have a fight with me about it, instead of apologizing.

"I left it where I can find it when I want to write in it," I said, "because I'm always a week behind in making my entries in the goddamned thing."

"You're twelve hours behind," she said. "Except that you don't mention you spent all day Sunday puking into the toilet bowl in Room 865, with its low ceiling that gave you claustrophobia."

"I beg your pardon," I said.

"You should have asked what listening to you barf by the hour gave me," she said.

"I damned near died," I said. "Maybe you didn't notice."

Instead of replying she flipped the journal open on a page that she'd obviously pondered and studied. "It says here that you 'didn't want to spoil Karen's response. Her pleasure.'"

"That's absolutely correct," I said.

"But you don't explain to either of us how a grown man happened to scald his prick, like a chicken about to be plucked, just at the moment when he might have done a little pleasuring."

"The goddamned taps were misnamed, that's why. You checked them. Twice. You agreed. Cold was hot. Hot was cold."

"You're sure you weren't feeling guilty about Julie and your hot-water quickie and looking for a little bit of punishment."

"Spare me the two-bit psychology, Karen," I pleaded. "You can put in all the fancy, sexually-repressed motivation when you make your great documentary, so-called. Meanwhile, back in the hotel, I was getting ready to screw you blind."

"It doesn't say that in your journal," she said.

"It says," I said, "if my memory serves me correctly, that you were getting off on my telling you about Julie."

"I was getting off on *you*, Dorf. Don't ask me why. Sometimes I almost like you, with your incredible need for women and your incredible ability to deny it. I'm attracted to your loneliness. You can even be gentle, when you forget yourself. And above all else you're a monster, and we all like monsters."

She closed her eyes, the bitch, and lay there, waiting.

I chose to speak very softly, very quietly. "You aren't troubled," I said, "by reading someone else's journal?"

"Not when it's yours," she said.

"Then I won't tell the truth," I said.

"You can't resist telling the truth," she said. "That's why I need you for my documentary."

"Then I won't say anything at all."

"But you'd rather talk to yourself than to anyone else. You're fascinated. You invent yourself, each time you sit down to make an entry, and I feel envy. Watching you."

"You said I tell the truth," I said.

"That's the truth," she said. "You do those real 'takes' on this Dorf guy that you're trying to put together."

"Wait a minute," I said. "You're the film exposer in this crowd."

"How do you know," she said, "that I didn't give you the journal intending to read it?" She laughed richly at her own humor. "I was interested in spas, Dorf, long before I told you what the word means." She laughed a very private laugh. "And I'd even heard of Jack Deemer."

"Congratulations," I said. "And if you'll excuse me now, I'll run to vomit again. Those brandy alexanders didn't do the trick."

"Or did they," Karen said.

LOOKING FOR THE LOOPHOLE
IN THE SKY

*W*hat could I do? I needed my rest. We'd driven up to have our dinner in the Post Hotel on Sunday night, instead of Saturday; I wanted to pretend we'd made a mistake about our reservations in the restaurant, but Karen had to go and tell the truth, explaining to the maitre d' why I looked like death warmed over. We took a room in the hotel. Monday I slept all day while Karen skied. She had no classes that Monday, teacher improvement day, or something.

We made love, Karen and I, but not on any cosmic scale. I insisted I had to sleep, I had to be fresh in the morning: we were to drive over the Great Divide and do some amateur climbing. "Jump up right now," Karen said, while I was trying to find some Kleenex, "and write in your journal that you just now came before I got decently started."

"I want you to ascend tomorrow," I said, "to still other dizzy heights. And put your watch there on the table where I can find it."

What happened in the morning is less clear; in a way I guess I have to say I did locate and meet Julie.

We drove into Yoho, Karen and I, to where Fish had dropped the climbing party. Karen and I had rented enough skiing equipment so that we might haul her four hundred pounds of camera equipment out onto the snow and allow her to take a snapshot. We didn't plan on doing any climbing ourselves; it was my suggestion, intention rather, that we might be there to welcome the climbing party on its descent. I had actually purchased and concealed in a pocket of my parka a flask of brandy intended for the occasion; I was to be Julie's own precious St. Bernard.

The light is a ferocious white, up there on the slopes. We were away from the ski lifts with all their pillars and cables and sky-riding chairs and their thousands of paying customers. At best we saw a raven. It hung the loop of its own disorderly flight across the valley. We were up quite high by that time, climbing still, working our way up toward some open slopes so Karen could take some mountain shots that would no doubt be old cliches in new color. Karen, at her worst, is terrible.

As a result of my being angry, I walked directly into Julie's trap.

Julie had no doubt recognized, or learned from Deemer himself, that I'm the determined sort of man who lets no obstacle stand in the way of accomplishment. I had been told to find a spa for Deemer; I would find a spa for Deemer. She saw that. And, gifted with that seeing, she decided the sooner I was polished off, the better. I guessed as much as she had guessed. But what I didn't see was just this: that my friend Fish might be part of the plot to excite me onto the killing grounds.

It was I who first spotted the climbing party. Karen didn't seem able to tell a tree from a caribou; she had on such elaborate sunglasses it was a marvel she could see at all. I spotted the party of four moving down toward the treeline.

They were on skis. I had somehow expected a party of persons all tied together and abseiling, equipped with pitons and chocks and hammers, along with the usual ropes and harnesses, a heroic string of climbers lashed to a white mountain and bare rock. I once picked up a small collection of books on climbing for Jack Deemer. He sent me to Austria, which seemed normal enough; unfortunately, most of the books were in German and I've picked only a smattering of that tongue. *Verdamnt!* But the books themselves were beautiful; the illustrations, especially, created a world where each human life hung suspended on a delicate cord over a desolate chasm.

As I say, I spotted Julie and her sycophants. They had simply been out to learn how to climb on skis instead of riding up a hillside in a gondola car. What I did not guess was that she had so arranged that I would indeed spot them. In my haste to overtake those same so-called climbers, I suggested to Karen that we take a shortcut across an open sweep of snow and join with them where they would enter a stand of scrubby evergreens.

"I think we should meet them down at the highway," Karen said. She was hung with cameras and equipment and looked as if she might fall down the mountain out of sheer imbalance.

"Let's go on," I suggested. "We can intersect with the others over there —" I pointed across the dazzling field of snow, indicating that we could simply angle across, slightly down, and let gravity take us to a rendezvous. "I've brought along a ration of brandy for everyone. You can take some pictures."

Karen, by virtue of growing up in the foothills, pretended to a superior knowledge of slopes and snow; god knows, I have spent most of my life in winter and don't need further education in that matter. "I'm heading back," Karen said, "and if I thought you had a brain in your head I'd ask you to come with me."

At that moment, Julie, on the far slope of the mountain, seemed to guess our indecision. She waved both arms, rather dramatically, over her head. It was, for me, a siren call. Karen, too, saw the signal and turned and left in a huff.

I might have shouted after her, Wait. Instead I said, into that last silence, too softly to be heard, apparently, "Listen. What was that?"

IT WAS THE FIRING OF GUNS
YOU HEARD, DORF; GUNFIRE
IN THE SNOW

INTO THE SNOW

It was the sound, not the sight, that first warned me that Julie, by a skilful combination of deception and outrageous flirtation, had lured me into the very path of a government-sponsored catastrophe. It seems a substantial detachment of the Canadian Army, somewhere below us, had been assigned to fire a 105-mm howitzer at the unoffending snowdrifts, high on the mountains along the Trans-Canada Highway; all this on the marvelous theory that by creating avalanches you prevent them. Something along the same line as committing suicide to avoid death.

I was in the middle of the avalanche path when the first shell struck the snow, up above me, and exploded. It was as if a vast symphony orchestra had been, unbeknownst to me, waiting; Julie herself had been the only visible person, she, the conductor, on a rocky perch; I had seen her before the sound got to me; the disproportion that so fascinates the human mind; the man chopping wood, the axe raised again, then the sound of the splitting.

I had time to turn. And then, my back turned, the sound was upon me, overwhelming me, borne on a gust of air, a blast of wind; a sound that was as soothing as it was frightening, it was so much an absolute, so much its own reality that when I was at last overtaken, pelted by flying snow, then picked up by the first tumble and woosh of the actual slide and avalanche, caught in the scream of downward, I swam in sound as much as in the snow itself.

OR ELSE
THE COURAGE NOT
TO BE AFRAID

I had the sense to kick myself free of the skis; I was somehow wading waist-deep in snow, somehow wading in a motion that had no bottom, no base that I could reach with my booted toes; I let myself go with the sound that had been a blur of blinding light, pure whiteness; I was tumbled head over boots and actually knew I was, at one point, laughing, giggling like a child. I felt it, though I could not of course hear my voice.

And then, as abruptly as there had been sound, there was the loud silence of my breathing. As if Julie, on her high podium, had sliced the very air away from under me with a gesture of her hand. And then I realized that, while I could not quite hear, I could not quite see either, in a light that was filtered almost to darkness by the snow. I had time to recognize all that while I lay buried.

While I lay dead I suppose I should say. For to be buried alive is surely to be dead. I had no expectation of being found. Granted, I was decently warm, there under the snow. I had some little sense of security; my abrupt cave wore the dimness of a cradle in the night-room of a child. I knew my right leg or foot was injured. I had the sense to get my right hand up in front of my face and somehow push a little space into being around my mouth and nose.

I am a man who suffers somewhat from a mild claustrophobia, a consequence no doubt of my childhood in the open parklands of the Battle River region. And yet, to my surprise, I felt no fear of that enclosing. Our folklore abounds in accounts of persons buried alive, or coffins opened to find that the corpse had not been a corpse at all. My own grandfather, on my mother's side, is reputed to have kicked his way out of his own coffin at his own wake when he heard his wife and a friend laughing obscenely in a corner of the bedroom where corpse and coffin lay in mutual rest on two kitchen chairs. I, on the contrary, struggled now; I had, finally, time to gather my wits about me, time to think and, thinking, I began to realize I'd been the victim of a quite different plot.

Julie had lured me into that area to have me killed off, though why remained a mystery. What a marvelous accident all would say; the dumb-ox walked out into an avalanche path while artillery shells went whistling overhead; he was obviously trying to kill himself.

I even toyed with the idea that she might well have been sent by Deemer himself. He would lay a trap to destroy all the secrets of acquisition, as the builders of a pyramid were killed after all the booty had been laid in: his collection had come to be worth millions, his attempts at spending money had, it turned out, succeeded only in making him richer, as each collection I acquired for him proved to be worth more than whatever Deemer had paid. I knew about the swindles, the legal cheating, the misleading evaluations, the carefully planted innuendos. Money makes money. And I knew, from Fish, that Deemer had ways of dealing with those who might deserve a share of his wealth. I thought of the poor man in that oil drillers' shack, out in the bush, facing a rifle. At least Deemer had moved up to cannons.

Strangely enough, dead as I was, and I believed for certain I was a dead duck, I found some small comfort in the recognition that I, the hunter, had become the hunted, the collector's agent made part of a collection. I was big enough to admit that in some small way I deserved my fate. We live and die by such distinctions, such abrupt and unexpected changes of role. I had been bundled up and carted off. In a fashion. I was into the old alabaster after all, and this a translucent white that allowed me to recognize my losses and my gains. I was gone from the mere world.

THAT LITTLE PLOT
OF MEASURED EARTH
EMBRACES ALL AND NONE

O death, where is thy stink. A rather unpleasant odor, I must say, seeped out around the neck of my jacket. And yet, it was not entirely without its nuance of reassurance. Actually, I was rather comfortable; I suppose my broken leg had not struck home wherever it is that pain strikes. I thought of the mice of winter burrowing under the snow, finding plants and making homes; I thought of the partridges of my boyhood nestling down deep until they were covered, vanished from the hunter's roving eye; and I had been something of a good hunter, and a deadly shot too, as a boy.

I managed, after a considerable while, to squirm around enough to get my right hand into a pocket of my parka. In the right-hand pocket of my parka was the flask of brandy; I twisted the silver cap free of the flask without taking off my glove. I managed, thrashing about a bit, to get the flask to my silent lips. And why I had not cried out, did not once, ever, cry out, I don't know.

I drank rather heartily. I had begun to think about my former wife and her frightened lover rejoicing at the news of my sudden death. I was filled with a certain resentment; I imagined, by way of compensation, a funeral the likes of which the citizens of my home town of Edenwolf had never seen. Jack Deemer himself would be there; he would come out of his reclusive hiding to offer his praise, then to insist on erecting a modest, at least by his terms, monument: To the Memory of William William —

No, it was too much. Not even on a monument of imported Italian marble could I tolerate that unlikely naming. I ran through the alternatives. William W. Dorfen. Or perhaps: William

"Dorf" Dorfen. Or, quite simply, with everyone knowing without having to be told, my initials: W. W. D. What memorial would be appropriate to a man condemned to live two lives; a man given two names, but both of them exactly the same?

I began to regret, dearly, that I hadn't brought along my journal. What a marvelous way to spite Julie. We, all of us, surely, aspire to a few heroic or profound last words. Deemer no doubt had a collection somewhere. I tried to think of something. Instead, I began to worry about my sphincter muscle's recent failure, my frozen ass being found in a lump of frozen shit.

Even as I thought those thoughts my right leg began to pain me. I drank from the flask of brandy with a kind of deliberation. I tried to move and the pain was intensified. It seems that while I thought I'd freed myself from my skis, I'd in fact failed to get the right ski off my boot. The left ski, it turned out, had gone down the slope ahead of me, and indeed served to confuse the search party into thinking I was farther down the slope than I actually was. I had neglected to snap the snaps that prevent a loose ski from running away.

I did not hear the small army of skiers that marched in a wavering row up the long hill toward me, each poking a stick or pole into the riddle and chaos of snow. I did not hear the shouted commands of their leader.

I was, however, awakened by the pressure of the end of a ski pole being rammed up my ass. It was the great and famous Marty Grieg himself who both organized the search and who jammed his longish pole damned nearly clean through me. He would be given, again, for his heroic effort, quite a write-up in the local newspaper, I could rest assured; my own clear-witted self-control would go unmentioned.

Thank heavens that Karen Strike had been present to recognize and to report the accident. Had I been there alone with Julie and her gang, I'd have been listed as missing until early summer when, the last snow melted, my mutilated body would have been found by a tourist no doubt up on the high, bare slope, my torn body ravaged by grizzly and wolf alike. Instead, as the fates would have it, I was bundled onto a sled, strapped and tied in a way that would have made a coffin a comfort; I was sent, thoroughly drugged, dismissed it would seem while the searchers opened wine to their success, down the slope to a waiting ambulance.

A WARNING
WHICH DORF WILL NOT HEED
IS, NEVERTHELESS,
ISSUED

*F*ish, when he came to see me, had a load of passengers waiting in his bus outside the hospital. He was in a disconcerting hurry. "A little detour," he said. He slapped my cast and damned near gave my leg a second fracture. "I wanted them to hear about a man who was covered by an avalanche and lived to tell about it." He picked up a ballpoint pen off my night table and bent as if to scratch the usual nonsense on my cement leg.

But then his face changed. He looked almost horrified, poised there, ready to write.

"I think she was trying to kill you," he whispered.

"Whatever gave you that impression?" I whispered in return, mocking his discovery. "My death?"

He shook his head. "I'm serious. I mean it. I'd stay out of her way if I were you."

I managed a laugh.

"Goddamnit," Fish said. "I'm telling you something."

"I'm laughing," I said. "Hand me a Kleenex."

"Dorf," Fish said. "It's not too late to give up. Stay here in the mountains."

"So why *are* you here?" I said.

Fish shrugged. He managed a foolish grin inside his grey beard. He was born with a shit-eating grin on his face, that man; he looked about one century old right then, for all his good health.

"I worked with Deemer once myself," he said.

I just about fell out of bed.

"But you said — " I said.

He wouldn't hear me after that. I tried to ask him questions. When did he work for Deemer? Or with Deemer? Was Julie there then? Why did he quit? ... But he might have gone deaf. He glanced around as if the bedpans themselves might be working for Deemer. He talked about our friends in the Upper Hot Springs, curing their lumbago and their hangovers. Only when he was ready to leave did he remember that he was supposed to write on my cast. He found the pen again and touched it to his tongue, as if that would help.

He was gone before I bothered to check what he'd written. And then, holding up a small mirror so I could read the message, even backwards, I saw it: "Until next time." In quotation marks.

Fish hadn't signed the message; maybe he didn't dare. Or maybe it wasn't his, maybe he was only the messenger. Maybe he only carried the messages. I lay there for a good two hours, slowly realizing the situation I was in. And I realized, also, there was no way in the world I could stop myself from looking for the spa.

To make a long story short, I rang for a nurse.

Signing myself out of the Mineral Springs Hospital was easy; it was full of skiers who were on their way somewhere else. Karen had galloped off in my car, so I hired an ambulance to take me to Calgary and to my apartment where I might pick up my passport and some clothes and call my travel agent. Waiting to hear from her, I stared about me and was horrified. My temporary address, taken years ago, was just that. And yet it was the only place I lived, my permanent home. Both and neither. A furnished two-bedroom apartment with one bedroom full of papers and junk that I intended one day to sort; my whole life with a rent sign on it. I was about two jumps ahead of Fish. And my leg was killing me. And the goddamned crutches nearly broke my arms.

The Wardair DC10-30 left Calgary on schedule. I like charter flights (and that one took some wangling, on such short notice); they force me to buy a return ticket. I ordered my first drink somewhere over the northern bush, relieved in the assumption that I'd be blessedly alone for a couple of weeks, an assumption that was to come to a stunning reversal before my second drink had turned into a third. I'm old-fashioned enough, even at my age, to insist on drinking my Cinzano straight up with just a small twist of lemon.

I was thinking about Calgary as I flew away at a welcome 535 miles per hour. Over the Atlantic. Against the sun's departure. All the lost travelers of the Arctic quest for a passage to the Orient. Silk and spice by the dreamload. But I was headed the other way. A day-long night. As if the chinook that was blowing in Calgary had picked me up, would blow me around the world's corner. Away from my avalanche into an avalanche that more than once covered half the continent that I was determined to flee.

And who the hell was on the airplane?

Europe is a dream too. But not of silk and spice. Maybe, I thought, maybe Deemer's mad collecting is just that, and that only, a calling up of ghosts from a million ancestral pasts. It is only that, a hailing and a hollering too, a head in the rain barrel listening to its own echo, a lost voice hearing a voice from the far cliff. The cry that comes banging back from the barn wall. The creaking sound from the attic.

Yes, I was not yet decently into my third drink when one of my sisters spoke to me. I mean — a real, genuine sister. Blood sister. Out of Wilfred Dorfen and Madeline Spetz, uniting two families that once conspired to make me rich. Wilf and Maddy, handing out one name two at a time. And there she was, my eldest sister, the eldest of three, tapping my left shoulder. I had an aisle seat because of my leg. Probably my sister had watched the demonstration I'd put on trying to board a crowded plane on two wooden sticks, and had been embarrassed to approach me until she'd consulted with the ancestral dead. I was, aside from being appalled, thunderstruck. Quite simply and completely thunderstruck.

My sister, Sylvia Thorn, and God knows at least her husband's name becomes her, loomed out of nowhere, leaned down and poked me in the side, so to speak, startling me out of my contemplation of a nearly empty plastic glass and its twist of lemon. I have taken, in my many travels, to carrying with me a small ivory container from the Ivory Coast in which I have prior to departure time deposited a few shavings of lemon peel. Airline service is not what it once was.

My dear sister Sylvia is one of those unfortunate persons referred to as the salt of the earth. She's the wife of a farmer who is indecently prosperous, there in Edenwolf, where we grew up. In fact she married in haste her horny young man by the marvelous name of Ed Thorn and by the time my mother retired the happy couple had put together enough cash to make a down payment on the home place, upon which they fostered a triumvirate of offspring.

"Are you still on the wanted list?" was Sylvia's way of beginning a conversation. She clings to her wonderful notion that I am in some primal way an outlaw, and that even to talk to me might constitute a breach of some regulation.

"What on earth," I said, "if you'll pardon the expression, are you doing on this flight?"

"Cut the bull, Billy," she said.

I was tempted to explain that I loathe being called Billy, but family connections do entail some sort of obligation.

"You are going to London?" I said.

"Gatwick," she said.

"You can't simply stay in Gatwick."

"I'll decide where to go after I get off the plane. Take a train into London. Or rent a car. Or, I suppose, I could simply catch another flight to somewhere else."

Don't ask me why I felt a twinge of panic. Perhaps I was worried about her. "Are you all right?"

"I'm perfectly happy. Never felt better in my life. Both girls have finished university. Young Billy is in grade twelve."

Young Billy, impulsively named after his uncle, much to the family's later regret, was described quite often as a surprise. As I had been too, I suspect, observing that I am fifteen years junior to my eldest sister.

"And Ed," I said. "How's he?"

"He won't leave," she said. "Hockey playoffs."

My sister has become, it turns out, something of a force in

the international egg trade. Indeed, she was on her way to a meeting about eggs and chickens and, I would suppose, something to do with egg cartels and the group dynamics of chickens' asses. She was going to the meeting early in order to have what she referred to, repeatedly, as her first real vacation in twenty years.

"I'm renting a car at the airport and driving around a bit," I said. "If you're stuck for something to do, come along."

"What about your crutches?" she said, pointing at my cast, not at the crutches themselves which had been concealed from me by a solicitous stewardess.

"I'll manage somehow," I said.

"You'll kill yourself," she said. And then, beginning to turn away, she added, "I'll think about it." She started to say something about not wanting to make any plans.

It was then I made the little fuss with the stewardess. It seemed silly, after all, for my sister and me to be seated miles apart in that loud monstrosity. I said as much to the stewardess. She explained that all seats were full. I explained that most people are movable. We had a ruckus of sorts in which she threatened to cut off my access to the bar; I explained that drinking had nothing to do with it and if push came to shove I had a bottle in my hand luggage.

The upshot of it all was the elderly gentleman seated in the window seat to my immediate left, the retired professor with all the hair in his ears, asked if he could possibly change seats with my sister.

Sylvia nearly talked my head off for the first three hours. She insisted on bringing up again the matter of my being "on the wanted list," which I take it had something to do with her sense of humor. I explained that, yes, after my divorce became final, I did spend a brief period of time voluntarily residing in a place where police surveillance was easily available.

"And the kids?" she said. "Your girls."

"I see them every summer, come rain or come shine."

I tried to change the subject. I was much interested, somewhat to my own surprise, in catching up with the family news.

After my father died on the mountain, carrying his perfect mountain sheep down from the ledge where he'd shot it through the heart, our mother proved to be, once again to quote my sister, a giant of the earth. She and my three sisters not only kept the farm operating, they turned it, as well, into a going concern, something my father had neglected to accomplish. They had even taken the trouble to have the sheep's horny head mounted; it completed my father's collection of the heads of the regional big game, and it looked splendid, up there high over the toilet bowl.

I had not much to do on that farm, run by Amazons, and yet great things were expected of me. I was supposed to grow up suddenly one day and just as suddenly take over the running of the empire — or at least, the farm; I was to continue to make it grow and prosper, the usual thing, more calves, more purebred Percherons, more wheat that would sell as registered seed. But then, by some little trick of fate, the chore fell to my eldest sister instead.

Sylvia was so much older than I that we never quite learned to play together. I liked the solitude of having busy elders on a farm that covered two square miles of pasture and wheat fields and sloughs and stands of poplar. Bluffs, my father called them. Poplar bluffs.

Sylvia did most of the family shopping. My mother was too busy to go into town and she would send Sylvia, trusting her with both the car and the money. I liked especially to be waiting when Sylvia returned. I would play while she was gone; I used sticks as horses; I rode my horses through the poplar bluffs, around the sloughs, out onto the prairie and back. But I liked best to come galloping up to the car when Sylvia returned from town, drove carefully, slowly, into the yard. I galloped so hard that I was sweating; the sweat shone on my skin, made my shirt wet even in those dry summers. Sylvia pretended to be a fairy godmother of some sort, come with treasures. She would bring me a licorice plug or wrapped candy kisses or peppermints or jellybeans, the red and the black ones that I liked best, or even a chocolate bar, Burnt Almond or O Henry. She would give me a treat and then she would bend and let me kiss her with my shining, sweating face. And sometimes she would stop pretending; she would let me give her a real kiss.

We talked for a long, long time on the wings of that high flight. She had a couple of drinks though, and they made her sleepy. I mentioned my little success. I was telling about a collection of birds' eggs I'd purchased in Central America from a one-legged collector; Deemer had been delighted with the find. It was, in ways, the find that endeared me to old Jack; after that he gave me a free hand. I was saying as much to Sylvia, promising to get her into the warehouse, there in Calgary, to have a look. I was telling her how, when I rode my stick horses through the poplar bluffs and around the slough, back of the barn, I learned to spot the nests of the springtime birds, the orioles in their swinging nests, the magpies and the crows in their great tumbles of organized sticks, the hidden eggs of the redwinged blackbirds, of a duck now and then, of the wild canaries, even.

"Remember?" I said. To my big sister.

DORF HIMSELF
SENDS A MESSAGE

*A*nd the sadness of a tragedy is just that: the miss is never by a mile, only by an ell, an inch.

When I noticed that Sylvia was snoring I began to write in my journal. Or I tried to write. But the couple across the aisle from me became a distraction; the man, I saw, was trying to get a finger inside the lady's panties without my noticing what went on under her casually folded jacket, and that made it difficult for me to write, but difficult, also, not to write, because I knew that when the man thought I was writing he thought also that I wasn't watching, and he worked again at his ferocious little task, his unseen fingers working, and I knew so painfully how he felt, remembering Julie, there in the pool, in Banff, not allowing me to move. I ordered another Cinzano, and another. We are so seldom perceivers of the apple falling, rather, of the apple that has fallen, did fall. I told myself that. Remember, I said. Remember everything. And I wrote down everything I could remember. I wrote and I wrote, there in the sky, over the Atlantic, over Ireland, over England. And I watched my neighbor with the affectionate fingers, his fingers moving, mine moving. I suspect the fortunate lady, pretending to sleep, her mouth turned close to the man's tweed shoulder, finally had her orgasm just before we landed. I saw her bury her mouth in the rough grey cloth.

We were hardly off the plane, Sylvia and I, all of us, there in England, when my hankering for Karen got the better of me. Mere lust, I realize now. But I was foolish enough then to send her a telegram. To tell the truth, I felt like Jack Deemer himself, old Jack the almighty, sending her a telegram in which I announced that she must join me in Bath the day she turned in her final grades. I'd let her know where I was staying.

NEGATIVE #2:
FOOTLOOSE, ON CRUTCHES

I tried to explain to Sylvia my need for Karen.

"In that case," Sylvia said, "why did you up and abandon her without so much as leaving a note?"

I found the question a stupid one.

"I'm not married to the woman, you know," I said.

"Marriage isn't your bag, is it?" Sylvia countered, exercising her usual facility for going gently to the heart of things.

"I was married for a number of years," I said. "I have two lovely daughters, as you've reminded me."

"I take it this Karen woman is younger than you are?" my sister said, venturing bravely from question to question.

"She's no spring chicken," I said, hoping to find a comparison appropriate to my sister's ears. "On the other hand, she's not a harridan either."

"You said she's making a movie."

"When did I tell you that?"

"You were talking about her when I fell asleep."

We were all this time watching for baggage. I had, actually, very little recollection of mentioning Karen; the woman was hardly ever on my mind. It was only when I was watching the fellow with the warm and loving hand that I'd thought of her at all. I began to fear my sister was privy to memories which my own mind hadn't acknowledged; one fears that of sisters.

"She sounds like a lovely person," Sylvia said.

"A bit given to running the world," I said.

"Well she *does* make movies."

My sister was obviously enormously impressed by that little detail.

"She's making a documentary," I said. "Some spendthrift

government agency is putting up the bucks. A grant. You know. Like subsidies to the egg cartel."

"I hope she has recorded your brilliant insights into economics," my sister ventured.

Fortunately, just then, one of her suitcases, reinforced by a lariat, came lumbering up from the bowels of the earth.

That the world is a connivance of forces beyond oneself has escaped Sylvia; trust is the glass she holds to her eyes. I went along with that trust, partly to delight in remembering it, partly to explore its application as an antidote to my own predicament. We rented a car at the Gatwick Airport and in the course of finding the M4 avoided London completely; indeed, we damned near struck out for France with Sylvia confusing not only left and right but east and west as well. Because of my game leg I had to trust the driving to Sylvia, who not only drove like the farmer she was, but insisted on making bad jokes about my useless leg on top of it.

We had no absolutely terrifying moments until, trying to take the exit that would allow us into Bath, Sylvia once again confused, briefly, left and right, and damned near met a lorry head on. In my excitement I reached to wrest the steering wheel from her control. Sylvia, in trying to change gears, hit the windshield wiper. The approaching driver managed a limp laugh and I thought again of Marty Grieg's face, the insufferable fool, staring down into my white grave there in the mountains, in the avalanche snow; Grieg staring down from above as if I'd been brought back from the dead and he was already composing his front-page heroism for the Banff *Crag and Canyon;* I had tried to struggle up and climb out of the hole by myself —

Sylvia had somehow expected horses and buggies. And yet it was I who cowered in the onrush of traffic.

"If you're so scared of getting killed," Sylvia said, deftly driving down the wrong side of the road, "why do you mess around with dangerous women?"

"And who, pray tell, is dangerous," I said, "besides yourself, of course?"

"This Karen Strike," Sylvia said.

"And what led you to that luminous insight?" I asked.

"She's got us racing like maniacs to Bath so we can send her another telegram and tell her where we are."

"Take your time," I said. "There's not a hurry in the world. It's just that I haven't slept for hours and days. I'm not like you, I don't sleep on airplanes, at least not while someone is talking to me. My leg hurts."

I went on a bit. I tried to explain that Karen Strike is so busy with her own career and her own ego that she doesn't have time to hurt a flea. Now this other woman, I was tempted to add, this Julie Magnuson would slit your throat just for the pleasure of watching the blood coagulate. She's not simply dangerous, she's a terror. But I thought all and said nothing as one should in the presence of a sister.

"Are you serious about this woman?" she said.

"How quaint," I said. "I haven't heard that expression in years." And then I added, for my own satisfaction, "Which woman?"

"Are you serious about her?" my sister repeated.

"Yes," I said.

"I'm glad to hear that," Sylvia said. She reached over, in the midst of all that onrushing traffic, and patted my cast. "You need a woman," she said. "I sense that about you. You've always been that way."

"Tell me about it," I said, pretending to joke. I held my sister's fingers for a moment or two.

Sylvia, by swerving brilliantly in front of an approaching bus, managed to avoid running over sixty-five cyclists. "Look," she added unperturbed, "that must be a pub." She pointed at a sign on which was pictured a keg of beer next to a foaming mug.

"No kidding," I said.

Sylvia had never been to Europe. She had taken it upon herself during the preceding winter to prepare for the trip by boning up on silver spoons and roadside pubs and ruined castles and The Royal Family.

We were, by some miracle, in Bath. We somehow found the Information Office, cheek by jowl with Bath Abbey. We stood in line and paid for a hotel room without seeing either the hotel or the room and before we returned to our chariot of destruction I managed to fire off a telegram to Karen. And I managed, also, to pencil in at the last moment: I'M HERE WAITING. HELP.

BROTHER

We stayed, Sylvia and I, in the Carfax Hotel on Great Pulteney Street. We were hardly dodging our way along the river, with Sylvia pointing out the boys fishing on the weir, as if I couldn't see—We were hardly onto the famous Pulteney Bridge, Sylvia there recognizing shops in which she must spend a fortune and where I, desperately, noted the name of a pub, The Boater, before she was explaining, whether I wanted to hear it or not, that the Allens had themselves taken lodgings on our street. And whereas I at first suspected the Allens must be neighbors of the Thorns in Edenwolf, it turned out they were eminent persons in the world of Jane Austen. Sylvia was thrilled to death.

I reminded her that just south of us a few miles Hardy's fictional characters, more robust, more genuinely honest about desire, had wrestled with their unaccountable fates. Not so many miles distant Tess of the D' Urbervilles did in with a pair of scissors the man who tried to offer her house and home.

"I think you've misread the story," Sylvia ventured.

"I think I read it," I reminded her, "while I was under something of a cloud myself. I should imagine I would, if anything, have been biased in favor of Tess."

The Carfax proved to be a perfect hotel, with a long stairway and high ceilings and white, cheerful interiors that reminded me continually of good health and Deemer's dark need.

Sylvia and I had a room together. It was a way to save a bit of money since prices were shocking to both of us; and, of course, with my injury, I could tolerate a little looking after. I explained to Sylvia that when Karen arrived we could make other arrangements. Perhaps we could find another room in the Carfax.

Sylvia insisted that we explore the city for an hour or two before getting some sleep. Bleary-eyed as I was, I consented to get into the car still one more time, crutches and all. There was no stopping Sylvia until we had obliterated ourselves. I was all for going to bed. I remember vaguely that we came to five huge plane trees, or at least Sylvia said they were plane trees, then we drove recklessly up Brock, headed, Sylvia assured me, for the great curve of houses that is Royal Crescent. I remember seeing an ice cream truck, Angelo's, parked on the street in front of No. 1 Royal Crescent. I wanted an ice cream cone. Sylvia stopped the car, bought vanilla for me, strawberry for herself. I asked her to kiss me and she laughed.

I turned away from her cheek and while I was taking the first lick at my cone I saw the splendor of those famous houses, the long, long curve of stone and pillar and window, the half-ellipse that encloses and shuts out a secret world, the 114 columns in the Ionic style, there on the hillside, with its porcelain view of the town below, of the countryside beyond.

I looked down at the blocks of stone under the wheels of the car. I had seen Royal Crescent, that architectural triumph of aristocratic lunacy based on the bleeding of an entire empire and I knew that even Jack Deemer, with all his money, would have to settle for something less. I knew that. I said nothing to Sylvia, but I had come so far and only to see that Deemer, with all his oilfields, couldn't quite have this. I felt sad.

I took a lick at my ice cream cone. "I'm dead-dog tired," I said to Sylvia. She wanted to drive on.

I had finished my ice cream by the time we got back to the hotel and found the parking lot. I was just able to get ready for bed, there in the corner where the sink was, brushing my teeth and washing at my red eyes and trying not to take my crutches to the four walls.

My bed folded out from a cupboard, next to the upright plastic coffin that turned out to be a shower. I damned near killed myself by having the bed fall on me. Sylvia leapt out of her own bed and got me undressed and tucked in safely and, burying herself in her own huge, heavily blanketed bed, ready to turn out the light, she surfaced for long enough to throw me a kiss across the room.

A LONGISH CHAPTER IN WHICH MUCH
IS REVEALED

*B*reakfast was served in a cosy, brightly lit, almost elegant space in the basement. Sylvia tried to sleep in each morning, but never quite succeeded. And, each morning, I managed to hop along behind and check at the desk without having her notice my concern. She liked to rush to our table and order a pot of coffee.

On the third morning the telegram was waiting for me. I didn't have a chance to read it before hobbling to my chair and my coffee and Sylvia's plans for the day. We had a tiff, over our toast, that morning, Sylvia and I.

"Eat your toast," Sylvia said.

"I don't like cold, dry, butterless toast," I said.

"Put some butter on it, she said, indicating the little butter pot.

"It will still be dried out and burnt and ice cold," I said.

"It isn't burnt," she said. "Why did you add that?"

It was like being back in our childhood home. Sylvia regarded herself as the guardian of truth and language, as if there was, somehow, a connection between the two.

"I don't like my toast served vertical on a wire rack and refrigerated," I said.

"Billy," she said, "you deliberately refuse to tell the truth."

"In my slight exaggerations," I said, "in my careful and deliberate tilting of the mirror, you might, if you chose to look, recognize truths that have forever been denied you."

That was a little more than Sylvia could take.

"A lie is a lie," she said, resorting to a tautology as moralists are wont to do.

Strangely, we were in the City of Bath for two more days before Sylvia one afternoon remarked that we'd not yet been into the old Roman spa.

"It's my crutches," I said. "How can we maneuver our way through that mob?"

"Try the healing power of the water," Sylvia said. She had always about her something of the practicality of a farmer's wife.

We did go in that afternoon, Sylvia and I. I had, of course, done my research beforehand, trying to determine if this might be the place that Deemer, through his mortal agent, sought. I must confirm the statistics: a city of 85,000 people; one of the most beautiful cities in the world, located 160 kilometres west of London; the flow of mineral water: half a million gallons daily at a temperature of 49 degrees Celsius; yes, the site of the Roman city, *Aquae Sulis*, established shortly after the Roman conquest of AD 43, right here on the River Avon; but even this preceded by people of the Iron Age and Sul, their god of healing.... I must make a list of the attractions, check them out; I must check out too the various means of communication, the weather, the possibilities of rabid privacy, the range of medical services. And I'd have to venture into the spa itself.

But I was sad. I knew I had come to some limit and I couldn't get over my sadness. We paid our money and we lined up and we went in and we read the signs. We tagged along with the multitude into the stony depths. The gilded bronze head of Minerva, looking a little the worse for wear. And the Gorgon's head too. Aesculapius, with his tame snake, a sure sign that healing was to be had somewhere in the vicinity. If you ignored the big stone coffins, the tombstones, showing an average age of thirty-eight. A great collection. I joked with Sylvia about her age; she was way ahead of the game. But I was sad beyond all reason.

There was no one in the pool. Something or other had poisoned the healing waters. We were allowed only to look at the greenish water itself. At the tourists, at each other, looking at the greenish water.

We had found and we had entered the sacred place of healing. And all I could see, anywhere and everywhere, was evidence of ruin. The Roman Empire itself turned into a collection of broken stones and a warming system, a hypocaust system that doesn't any longer work.

And Deemer wanted me to find a place that would save him from all that. I felt despair. Pure despair. I was up against it, I saw that. A great idea — ask him to come here, buy a piece of the action and spend his remaining years in contemplation of the inevitable end.

Sylvia hated the Roman stuff and took a great liking to the eighteenth-century overlay of loot and elegance. Beau Nash was her speed. The Pump Room was her bag, not the swamp that had once healed Roman soldiers. She wanted costumes and extravagant rooms and an orchestra near at hand. And she persuaded me to tag along on her search, maybe because I wanted to be persuaded; maybe because I wanted to find a goddamned spa for Deemer and get on with my own dying.

We had tea in the Pump Room. Or I had tea. Sylvia had carrot cake with lemon and almond icing and two cups of milk-drowned coffee. The silver needed polishing. The dishes were chipped. The carpets were worn and grimy and seedy. But, against all that, against the sound of cups hitting saucers and the hard heels of the waitresses hitting the hardwood floor, was the music of a trio; a woman on cello, a white-haired man on violin, a bearded boy on piano: they made Sylvia swoon.

What I needed most was a sedan chair. We walked past and then around and then into Bath Abbey, probably because it was free. Sylvia is not above pinching her pennies. I insisted on stopping beside the fountain. There outside the Abbey was the statue of a woman pouring water and the accompanying sign: WATER IS BEST. And I was careful to read to Sylvia the words that followed: "Erected by the Bath Temperance Association June 8, 1861."

"Erected," Sylvia said. And she laughed. "I'm ready for my pint," she added.

We went looking for a pub. And, yes, it was all downhill, you better believe it. Right there in Bath where Dr. William Oliver invented the biscuit as part of the cure.

"This takes the biscuit," I said.

"Your leg hurting you?" she said.

"Killing me."

She went to a pub like a horse going home in a storm. We found a lovely pub. I pointed to two chairs at a small table by a big window. But Sylvia wanted to stand. She liked to join the stand-up crowd at the bar; she was collecting the little pads the barmaids set drinks on to take home to Ed. She was irked, this time, when I insisted we sit.

I put my crutches on the big windowsill.

"I don't think it's broken at all," Sylvia said.

I pretended not to understand. I took a swig.

"Your leg," she said.

"That's right," I said. "I enjoy hopping around on crutches."

"Wait till Karen gets here," Sylvia said. "Then we'll see how well you stand up."

I was, I am now, I will forever be, offended by my sister's crude sense of humor.

"Everything goes bust and I'm advised to drink water," I said. I took a sip of the dark brown ale. "Carbuncular asshole of the deep-fried grief of the onion rings of existence."

"Come come," Sylvia said.

"This is the bottom of the bottom," I said. "If Deemer could purchase the whole universe, where would he put it?"

"Get hold of yourself," Sylvia said.

"This is the farcical finite," I said. I was feeling pretty low. Quitting would have seemed like a step up the ladder. "Old Jack Deemer," I said, "he drills a dry hole and loses a few million, so he sends me out to buy three more million-dollar collections."

"That reminds me," Sylvia said. Usually when she said that I was in for some Edenwolf wit and wisdom. Like the one about the one-legged man at the ass-kicking contest. "Dry hole. Reminds me of Mr. Deemer. And that woman of his."

My heart simply stood still. I must have survived two heart attacks before I spoke.

"What woman?" I said.

"That woman. I forget her name."

I could have strangled my sister right then.

"Remember," I begged her. Trying all the while to pretend I wasn't falling off my imitation antique chair.

"That was years ago," Sylvia said. "In the oil patch."

"Hmmm," I said. Except that it came out throaty.

"You were down there in the States," Sylvia said. "You were away. Where were you, anyways?"

I had no voice. My throat was a dry hole.

"It was his second big find," Sylvia said. "The second time Deemer struck it rich. I wish I could remember the name of that woman." She peeked into a flimsy paper bag containing a huge sweater. "His second field. Not the one up North. That was earlier."

"Was it Julie?" I dared ask.

My sister looked puzzled. "Was *who* Julie?"

"That woman. Deemer's friend."

"That's it," Sylvia said. "Or Judy."

"Just tell me what *happened*," I pleaded.

"I thought I told you."

"Told me *what?*"

"About the murder."

"You've done no such thing."

"What were we talking about?" Sylvia said.

"Nothing," I said. "Forget it. Please, forget, don't try to remember."

My sister has a talent for driving me mad. "This woman of Deemer's — they caught a scout spying on a tight hole. A new field had been discovered; that well was the clue and this scout had found out and Deemer didn't want anyone to know— "

She interrupted herself. "Julie. That was her name."

"That's what I said," I said.

"How did you know?" Sylvia asked.

"Forget it. Just tell me what happened."

"She killed him."

"I trust she was hanged for her offense."

"Are you kidding?"

She asked me to get her another half pint. When she became serious about something she ordered an extra half pint.

"Let's go for a boat ride," Sylvia said. "Where we saw that sign: Avon Cruises, Bath, Limited."

She somehow found that amusing.

"Bitter?" I said.

"Mild," she said. "This time. Or one of each. Two half pints, one of each, let's compare them."

"We've compared them every four hours since we arrived here," I said. "You were saying?"

"No," she said. "This scout, he was spying, on a pitch-black night. He was hiding in among some deserted ranch buildings by the drill tower; he was sneaking in close, trying to see and hear, trying to count." She craned her head toward me as if she would count my heartbeats. "Those old ranches are scary places. But they make good money, those scouts. He fell into an old dug well."

"Then Julie didn't murder him," I said almost triumphantly.

"Bone dry, the well," Sylvia said. "He broke a leg. And when the workers heard him, finally — Julie took him food and water."

"You mean," I said, "this Julie saved him."

Sylvia shook her head. "'You got yourself in there,' this Julie said. 'You get yourself out.'"

"But she didn't really murder him." I insisted on that.

"'Keep the canary singing.' That's what Mr. Deemer told his crew. 'Let him sit in his cage for a few days more.' Only I guess the man panicked one night and tried to crawl out. He knocked the sand loose and it started running, coming down like water. Only it was sand. We went to the funeral, Ed and I. It was the Hotchkiss boy; he grew up just across the river from us. You must remember his father."

I went to the bar to get a drink for Sylvia. Drinks for Sylvia. A scout, I reminded myself, is simply an innocent man who does the dirty work for someone else; he deserves consideration like the rest of us. My hands were shaking so badly I spilled coins into someone's gin and tonic and had to stand him another drink.

Sylvia, when I got back to the table with her two half pints, was looking at the sweater she'd bought for Ed. A huge, oily affair, turtle-necked, that would shed water as well as keep out blizzards and fog and hide a potbelly.

"We should go back to that shop," she said. "I want to get one like this for young Billy."

LOOKING,
IF ONLY FOR A WAY OUT

We left Bath one day before Karen was to arrive. I'd mentioned the telegram only vaguely to Sylvia. I didn't tell her that Karen was to fly from Calgary in a matter of hours; when Sylvia became curious I said we could leave instructions at the hotel desk. I'd heard of an old spa in Wales that sounded like the real McCoy.

I knew Sylvia wouldn't understand, but the truth is, I was having nightmares about avalanches. A huge wall of snow kept coming down toward me, down toward me, in my dreams. It loomed there above me, moving in slow motion, billowing and folding, kicking out its cloud of dust that wasn't dust but snow, falling down toward me, making no noise, only falling. And my skis went down the slope alone.

After crossing the great, arcing bridge over the Severn, after lifting ourselves up high over the river and setting ourselves down again, we apparently took a wrong turn.

We came to a castle. There it was, to the right of us, just off the crooked road, a castle that looked so much like a castle that I thought it must be something else. Sylvia suggested that we stop to have what she called a look-see.

Raglan Castle, it turned out — we were in Wales. We paid our pence and went onto the grounds. I was rather bored by the wreckage and the ruin, and the castle itself was a bit too late for my taste, fourteenth and fifteenth century. Something of a make-believe castle. Except that the well was a real one. A hole in the ground. Down to water. Say what you will, that's one of the mysteries. I was shook up again.

My sister, of course, loved every cold stone of the place; she insisted that for her it was a great moment in her life, a gateway of sorts; and to offer what support I could, I held her hand. We walked like two children from chapel to parapet. I assumed it was a recovery of childhood for her, a making real of what she had always imagined. We climbed a tower and were looking out through the slit-like windows. Imagine my surprise when my sister said abruptly, "I wish I'd had a crack at that Henry the Eighth."

"Good heavens," I said.

"For Christ sake," Sylvia said, "can't you say something besides 'Good heavens'?"

"I wonder if I know you, dear sister," I said.

"I wonder if you do," my sister said. "Good heavens."

We had only time, that night, to get as far as Abergavenny. I thought of our prairie towns by way of contrast. What horror, I asked, without getting an answer, drove our ancestors out of all the beautiful villages of Europe? I was struck into a feeling of diabolical unease. Sylvia, on the other hand, was positively into the castle business; we had to drive and limp and hobble through the quiet streets, passing up pub after pub; we found a trace of Abergavenny Castle, we dawdled around, trying to peek over the stone walls and through locked gates. "William de Breos once owned this castle," she explained, "the most treacherous and cruel man ever to inhabit the Welsh Marches. Right there in that castle," she insisted, pointing, "back in 1175, some of the finest chiefs of Wales were massacred; treachery," she insisted. Cruelty, betrayal; plotting and scheming and lying and deceiving and murdering; violence unto death.

I swear she had every high hope of being set upon right there. I said as much and she made a feint at kicking one of my crutches out from under me. But all we found was an old slingshot, lost in some weeds that made my skin prickle when I went to pick it up.

The insane landlord of our bed and breakfast place, a gallant-seeming fellow who pretended to have at heart only our pleasure, sent us on what he called a scenic drive through, or *over* I should say, the Black Mountains.

I suppose a man should have more sense than to ride through Welsh mist in a car driven by a woman who assumes that every road goes on indefinitely in a straight line and that trees, rocks, cliffs and chasms are only placed at strategic intervals by some optical trick to please the passing tourists.

I very nearly died of fright.

"What would you do," I said to my sister, "if you knew someone was trying to kill you?"

"I'd run for my life," she said.

"What if that person was terribly attractive, perhaps even needed you, perhaps even loved you?"

"I'd run for my life," my sister said.

"Jesus," I said. "You don't understand how serious this is."

"Give me an example," Sylvia said.

"Well," I said. I was stuck again. "Let's say, for instance, that this woman you mentioned, Deemer's woman, what's her name — Julie; let's say she, for instance, lets somebody know that he is, well, living on borrowed time so to speak."

"A well is a hole in the ground. The Hotchkiss boy didn't come back alive." She swung to avoid a sheep. "And they say there was a guy in the bush up in the north somewhere who didn't come back either. Except in a sack."

"You're not getting the point," I said.

"Ask Deemer," Sylvia said. "Ask Deemer what to do with a woman like Julie. Since you don't want to hear my opinion. I'd run for my life."

"He's unapproachable," I said. "He's a conundrum. A mystery. He's up there on his hill and the rest of us are down here. He's a prick with ears."

"Don't ask him, then," Sylvia said. "Ask yourself."

There were something like two thousand sheep in the middle of the road. Sylvia nearly put me through the windshield. She swerved around a black sheep, around a sheep that was, literally, black; she came within an inch and a half of driving straight over a cliff. Then, by God, would you believe it, she slams on the brakes and gets out of the car and starts to talk sheep with the shepherd who couldn't take his eyes off her; he insisted we share his thermos of tea. I lay down on the grass, face down with my eyes shut, listening to the sheep. I couldn't look. Those sheep, there on the hillside, looked like a friendly avalanche.

THE PERFECTION OF LLANDRINDOD WELLS DISCOVERED, AND OTHER DEVELOPMENTS

When, some hours later, and I have no idea how many hours it was, we burst onto the top of the world; when we emerged from still more valleys and crooked roads and hairpin turns and concealed roundabouts in concealed villages; when we, literally it seemed, burst through the top of the world and were at our destination, I could only ask Sylvia to let me out of the car in order that I might relieve myself against a wondrous green hedge.

Llandrindod Wells is a perfect spa town. It is made up of Victorian brick houses, huge houses — or perhaps they are Edwardian houses, not Victorian houses at all. Their perfect, large windows, so mathematically correct and proper, excite the inmates to blatant spying, excite the passerby at once to feelings of guilt and to voyeuristic pleasure. Here, too, and not so long ago, one could drink the waters from the saline, sulphur and chalybeate springs while listening to music that soothed and healed and caressed. I urinated freely.

Llandrindod Wells is noted, was noted at least, for its treatment of rheumatism and obesity. I gave myself a flick and stumbled back into the car and Sylvia drove to our hotel and I stumbled and bumbled out again. Or, at least, I was doing my damnedest to get out of the car, what with my crutches and all, and something like two hundred maps scattered around and everywhere.

The woman who came to my assistance was Karen Strike.

Karen Strike snatched the very earth from under me by reaching out to lend a hand. There she was, tall and skinny and blonde and healthy as a dray horse, putting a bellboy out of work at the door of the Metropole Hotel. She was waiting, had been, for me. Expecting me. Wondering where I'd been, what had detained me. She is the end of the world on two long legs.

And I cannot say I was unhappy to see those same legs. Karen had, I at first assumed, picked up my message at the hotel desk in Bath, had somehow, traveling by public conveyance no doubt, beat us to our destination. She had beat me and Sylvia.

I tried to make introductions. I introduced Sylvia as my sister, and then couldn't remember her name. My sister, I said again. I called Karen Miss Strike.

"I phoned Deemer," Karen said, not in the least perturbed by my confusion.

"You phoned his office," I said. "Good."

"No," Karen said. She nodded to my sister, understandingly. "I phoned Jack Deemer. He said you'd be here. I came here directly from Heathrow."

"You phoned his office," I corrected her. Again. "I phoned in myself before I left Bath. His secretary is some kind of a genius; she keeps track of everything."

"I talked to Jack," Karen said.

You could have knocked me over with a feather. I was lifting suitcases out of the back seat of the car, leaning on one crutch while I did so; while the two women watched. Sylvia was going through her purse as if she'd just then lost her passport and her ticket and her travelers' cheques.

"He sounded lonesome," Karen said.

"An imposter," I suggested. "Perhaps he employs a look-alike."

Karen ignored my suggestion. "He mentioned you," she said.

"How so?" I asked, setting a suitcase on the otherwise healthy toes of my game leg.

"I asked if you are reliable."

The insolence of the media people is endless. Karen pretends to be the suffering artist. It excuses everything, even the fact that she's a public snoop. She has her roles confused; she can't tell if her camera is a paintbrush or a spyglass. She had forgotten, even then, that it was Jackie Flanagan, a fellow teacher, who relieved her of academic duties back in Calgary so that she might fly off and do her research toward a film. Or drink double gins with foreigners.

"So he fired me right on the spot," I said.

"He said you've never failed him. You're remarkable. You work in circles, in tangents, in loops, in triangles. But you always get to the center."

Somehow I felt a great swelling of relief in my body; I was strong. I was in a hurry to get on with the job, eager to look at the town. I asked Sylvia to put the car away.

"I take it you came to like him," I said.

"I didn't say that. Cantankerous old bastard. I asked about that Julie of yours and he hung up on me."

Don't ask me why, but I was secretly in cahoots with old Deemer again. My game leg be damned, I had work to do. He was keeping tabs on me, old Deemer was, out of trust and affection; a lot depended on my success.

It's a plotted world we live in. Karen had her camera equipment stacked like cordwood in the lobby of the Metropole; she claimed she couldn't so much as hire a cab, let alone a cameraman; but her equipment made Deemer look poverty-stricken.

The place was deserted one minute; the next, two busloads of octogenarians arrived and began to swarm into the place. They were all women. Two busloads of old ladies with four pieces of baggage each. Their ambition was simple: they remembered back, those ancient ladies, to the days when Llandrindod Wells was a place of everlasting health, and they'd come for one more swig of the invigorating waters, one last breath of the bamboozling air.

I went into the bar to take the waters myself. Karen was unpacking with the speed of a goldminer who had just hit the Klondike. Sylvia was out driving our rented car around and over the local inhabitants. She sometimes suggested I had a hollow leg, not a bad one, and I was treating it accordingly when the two women came through the door looking like fellow conspirators and childhood friends.

"Deemer," I said. Tentatively. Signaling with a glance to Sylvia that she should stay out of this. "You actually talked to him?"

"He's old," she said. "His voice is so old. But strong too."

"Now which is it?" I said.

"Both," she said.

"That's no answer," I said. "I hate answers, but that's no answer."

"He was gruff when he spoke," Karen said.

"He likes his power," I said.

"A kind of husky gruffness." Karen was fidgeting with a light-meter. She was forever holding something up to the light. "Maybe he was trying to be gentle."

"About as gentle as a pet cougar," I said.

"You two are like two kids," Sylvia broke in.

"I like cougars," Karen said. "Love them."

"Lizzie Lansing," Sylvia said. She nodded toward Karen. "Your friend looks like Lizzie Lansing."

My sister, in Llandrindod Wells, in Bath, on a jet flight to hell, was certain to see someone who had to be the spitting image of a friend of hers in Edenwolf.

"The same cheek bones," Sylvia said. "Like a blonde Indian." As if she knew what an Indian looked like. "Remember? Lizzie Lansing. That time you bit the ears off her teddybear."

I guess that's when I threw a minor tantrum. I told both Karen and Sylvia that I was sick of having my life described and analyzed and remembered and predicted. I wanted to be left alone. "Leave me alone," I shouted, making the whole room fall silent.

And I nearly bit my tongue off. Not wanting to gossip. Not wanting to tattle.

I can be calm about it now. After all these years, yes. Lizzie Lansing was my kid sister's best friend and the main reason why I didn't have a kid sister. Jocelyn, my youngest sister who ran off to Edmonton and married a Greek, was only five years my senior. But she was always with the neighbor girl, with Lizzie Lansing, and the only time they let me play, the one time I can remember, was when I caught them, Jocelyn and Lizzie, admiring each other's young breasts. There in our hayloft, two young girls, astonished at their own young breasts, the budding nipples, the translucent skin; I was watching from inside the cupola where I'd climbed to steal pigeons' eggs, and when they shouted at me, when they saw me and shouted, I lost my precarious balance and fell; I fell and I fell; I was forever falling, and I landed in the heaped hay and was buried. And I might have been smothered; I might have died right there and then if the two girls had not scrambled, naked and together, into the newly dumped hay, the hay that had just been dumped from the overhead sling. I liked that too, the hay released and falling and tumbling down, an avalanche of fresh, green hay.

The two girls, naked, lay down beside me. They snuggled close, one on either side, holding me. They said I could pretend I was the husband. They let me play the game with them; but they wouldn't let me take off my clothes. I couldn't take my clothes off. I lay dead still, itching inside my hay-filled clothes, with the two girls, one on either side. And then they went on talking with each other, giggling with each other, playing their game as if, for all my presence, I might not ever have existed.

"Lizzie," Sylvia said. There was no changing the subject, once she'd located it. "I think she expected you to come back from the States. She was surprised when you got married."

Our drinks were lined up on the bar. Karen, like Sylvia, loved to stand up at a bar and knock back her booze. I suppose she pretended she was making a full-length feature.

"Deemer speaks to no one," I said. "I know that for a fact."

I stalked out of that handsome old bar, there in the Metropole Hotel. I left the two women to finish our three drinks, their company be damned. I'd die of thirst before I'd talk to two prevaricators.

A CURE OF SORTS IS EFFECTED,
OR, IT MIGHT EVEN BE SUGGESTED,
FEIGNED

I must let this entry stand as I originally wrote it, in the interest of making clear my own integrity; I have emended and sum-marized elsewhere only to establish a narrative account whose clarity matches my insight:

April 11. We lie in bed, these lonely nights, thinking of each other's bodies. And, yes, it was my idea that we stay in three separate rooms. I suppose I should have, in some madness of my own, suggested we all stay together. They are ready to do just that, Sylvia and Karen; they are, already, thicker than thieves; they act as if they've known each other for centuries. I am the moral prig.

But at least I was alone when the phone call came this morning. This sun-bright morning, here in Llandrindod Wells. I am on an expense account; I have the expensive room, complete with telephone. Neither Sylvia nor Karen needs know that Julie Magnuson woke me up at seven a.m.

And I remember, indeed: out of my dream of trains that meet and blur together and separate, came the voice of Julie Magnuson. She was in London, on her way to Portugal. Because she was going there, to a spa.

She invited me to join her.

My dream. Two trains, one east-bound, one west-bound; they are about to meet; I can't look away; they meet, they blur together. They separate again. They open a wide, blank space. A silent space on the horizon. Good God, the silence. The silence of horizons.

Julie Magnuson was speaking. "Dorf? Is that you? Dorfen?"
I was holding the receiver as if it might be a pillow.
"Dorfen? Billy Dorfen?"
"Uh-huh."
And then she was talking. Pouring out words. She had found me. She'd been phoning for two days. The goddamned Welsh phone system. She had tracked me down through no end of phone calls, back to Calgary, then to London, then from London, then to Bath.
"Did Karen catch up with you?" Julie asked. "A woman named Karen Strike. Making a film. Doing research on neglected spas."
"No," I said. I was lying; one necessary, little lie. But in a way I was telling the truth. "I'm here with my sister. My leg is getting better. Don't worry."
"I can't afford publicity," she said. "Scandal," she added.
"Don't worry," I said. Again.
"Portugal," Julie said. "That's where it is. Luso. Write it down. *Luso.*"
I picked up a pencil. She spelled the word, the name, over the phone. I would understand, she said, when I got there. And before I could say I wouldn't show up, I couldn't possibly make it, I didn't want to go, she had hung up. Death talks softly. Death has a low and seductive voice. A small voice, there on the Welsh phone system. Death hangs up the phone. I love two women.
And that day, for the first time since we'd come together, Sylvia and Karen and I, we went for a walk. I managed, one block out of two, to do without my crutches. We went to the stream that had been the place of healing. I was nothing but kindness all the day long. I was a man who had been invited to attend his own funeral. And I felt a new respect for the blooming trees, there in Rock Park, for the old bedspring in the waterfalls, for the running shoe in the water, under the wooden bridge. We walked ourselves ragged, following down past the old Pump Room toward the place called Lovers' Leap. I realized I'd been suppressing my thoughts about Julie and her threat; it was high time I confronted them. And we found Lovers' Leap, to the delight of Karen and Sylvia: the overhanging cliff, the

whirlpool beneath. Karen wanted me to clamber up and pose on the cliff's edge, but I couldn't make it. And it wasn't just my leg. The very thought of it made me dizzy. So my lusty sister went up by herself instead and stood on one foot with the middle finger of her right hand raised to the camera's blinking eye.

It is the opposite of Bath, that town, small, isolated, lost, forgotten; and the waters from Chalybeate Spring, there in Rock Park, are a green so violent they must have been distilled from a jealous lover's bile. There in the grove where the cuckoo sings. Or the jays, that day. There where the Romans were, where they built an auxiliary fort, not a city. Deemer would like that. He could build a fort of his own, hide out and hang in. And the German physician, Dr. Wessel Linden, in 1754, even he was daunted by the effects of the healing waters: damned near shit himself blind.

And the Bowling Green. We found that, too, on our third try. We walked past a lawn where two dozen women, all of them dressed in white, were rolling black balls across the green grass. I was in a town made up of women.

It was Karen who ruined things; she went around with her cameras, with her notebooks, with her large, deceptive brown eyes, recording the place for a cameraman who would come out from London, she claimed, in a week or two. If she could scrape up the money.

She was irked, I suspect, because I wouldn't go to bed with her. She had some cockeyed theory that I needed the spa worse than anyone, that I was a mess, that I was searching for my own salvation; I blushed at the indecencies of her archaic language. I pleaded with her, a woman of the late twentieth century, a woman so self-consciously and pretentiously ahead of the rest of us. "Get with it," I said. "Speak our language. Forget about history. Make do."

We were borne down upon by a column of schoolgirls in their obsolete costumes; Karen insisted that I step off the path. She wanted a shot of me, standing on crutches, seeming not to notice at all the girls in their black uniforms passing in front, the women in white behind me, bowling. She would capture me with the broken clouds in the far background. I leaned against the high fence. I lifted myself off my crutches.

It was then and there, waiting for Karen to wait for the light, that I swore to myself I couldn't go to Luso. Hanging there, like a dead hawk on a barbed wire fence, I'd been thinking in my moments of silence. I recognized the name, of course: Luso, a place famous for its waters. But to hell with Julie Magnuson and her threatening and her beckoning. Why would she go there? Was she trying to show me the very spa she didn't want me to find? I balked and I argued and I wondered again. Life is short enough as it is, I decided; I'll be my own man.

NOTES TOWARD
A TRANSITIONAL CHAPTER

I swore I wouldn't go. I meant it. And I meant it, even next morning, when, over cold toast, I suggested that Karen and Sylvia pack a lunch and take the car and drive to the coast for a look at a couple of castles and maybe even at St. Non's Well. Sylvia must go to Brussels in a few days and she'd have no time there for castle-hunting, what with so many metaphysical eggs to candle. She liked my suggestion. She hadn't decently heard my spiel when she was telling a waitress how to make genuine sandwiches, not any of those English substitutes. Karen, I suspect, wanted to see the pub in New Quay where Dylan Thomas drank to his own forthcoming fame; she was having intimations of immortality of her own, what with the combination of a camera and a government grant. It was becoming obvious that no mere professional photographer was up to her genius; she must do everything herself, trust to no one.

I went to a doctor's office. I'd noticed one the previous day, actually, but the initials in front of the doctor's name fooled me. He turned out to be a woman. More inclined to be a carpenter than a surgeon. But she knocked the cast off my leg.

I phoned Deemer's London office the minute I got off the train; there were messages sending me this way and that. He'd purchased, sight unseen, a roomful of clocks in Switzerland, which was hardly an original idea. But he wanted me to go dicker for a collection of teeth behind the Iron Curtain.

I used those opportunities to drop in at a half-dozen spas, all of them for the healthy I'm tempted to say. The one that interested me most was not for humans at all; rather, it was a delightful place in Hungary where hippopotami breed with great abandon in the warm and inspiring waters. Standing, watching, not a little responsive myself, I thought fondly back to my own passion, there in the Upper Hot Springs, in my distant native land.

I thought for a moment I had found the perfect place for old Jack Deemer. I imagined him looking something like a hippopotamus himself, a little heavy in the middle, a face that is less than beautiful, and yet somehow attractive to other hippopotami; I could imagine him, there in the mud and steamy water, making out. Getting it up and making out.

It was the teeth, however, that make me decide the place was not for Deemer or anyone else. I was in Budapest, where I'd seen spas that went back to the Bronze Age, where I'd looked at modern facilities that offered subaqual traction, carbon dioxide baths, irrigations, radioactive water. It was there I purchased the teeth. And damned near swore off eating.

I developed a raging tooth ache. That was the first trouble. Somewhere in the upper right quadrant of my mouth; I could never pinpoint the place. In fact, I went to a dentist, and I have reason never to trust a dentist; I might even say I loathe dentists. I found a dentist's office. And I had almost completed the requisite forms, working through a translator who assumed I was speaking Russian, when I abruptly walked out, back into the dusty street, back to my tooth ache.

The mere combination of crown and root has myriad possibilities, and that collection represented most of them. If you could get past the smell. Fish scales that over the millennia migrated into the mouth and became teeth. The horny cones from a lamprey's mouth, and horny I wasn't, at that moment. The full armature of our friendly northern pike, hinged teeth and all. The upper tooth of a rare Siberian frog. The fourth and eleventh teeth from the longish mouth of a crocodile, Egyptian, the owner insisted, reputed to have devoured a pair of American Peace Corps workers while they were fornicating.

That collector loved his collection. He'd lost his nose in a war somewhere, and he sported a rubber nose whose color didn't match his face. His own teeth were all in his mouth he told me, nose or no; and, he might have added, for I was staring into his mouth, not he, every one of them rotten.

The egg tooth of a night heron which, I insisted, is not a true tooth at all. The teeth of a horse that, my host insisted in his turn, was ridden early one Greek morning by Socrates. The forty-two teeth of a bear that existed in Wales before bears became extinct in Wales. The teeth of a camel, looking tobacco-stained; the teeth of two rats, not adequately sorted; the eighteen teeth of a walrus collected by an Arctic explorer who was looking, unsuccessfully, for Sir John Franklin. The forty teeth, not one of them even slightly worn, of a young female hippopotamus. The toe of a rhinoceros which the deceptive owner tried to pass off as a tooth; I thought of Albrecht Durer's "Rhinoceros," his magnificent portrait of a beast he had never seen, olive green to his imagination; and somehow at that moment I thought of Karen Strike, at the Max Ernst show in Calgary, drunk on champagne, climbing a palm tree; and then I thought of Karen's mouth, hot and alive on my body.

We catalogued the human teeth. We began to catalogue them, sitting there side by side, that fierce-eyed collector and me under a dust-coated light bulb. He seemed to know each skull and story. The milk teeth, the deciduous teeth, he remarked, correcting himself, in his precise and bookish English, of a baby bayoneted by the Turks. The single-rooted canines which he had, as he so delicately put it, picked up as a kind of memento and thus, accidentally, begun his collection while lying in a shell crater in a graveyard and listening to bombs explode. The pronged molars of a shepherd who was put to death for eating a sheep. The incisors and bicuspids and miscellaneous this and that of a family of pre-Bronze Age folk who had been reduced to just that, a scattering of teeth.

My host began to wax ecstatic. Teeth, he explained, because of their constituency, will survive when all else is gone. Teeth, he said, absent-mindedly picking his nose, may well be our only immortality; he looked positively saint-like as he warmed to the subject, there in his small apartment, crowded full of teeth; he was somehow master of all that immortality and only the direst of straits had brought him to his transaction.

"You are looking into the mouth of God," he whispered. And gave me a wink.

And then a fit of conscience seized me, after those teeth were boxed and tagged and shipped out of sight. It was that that replaced my tooth ache. I had left Llandrindod Wells rather abruptly, it struck me, not quite allowing Sylvia and Karen time to get back from their castles and pubs; I tried to contact Karen in Wales, shouting at a Hungarian telephone operator that I wanted Llandrindod Wells and, not getting through, trying to phone Ed Thorn in Edenwolf, Alberta, and not getting through that time either. And phoning Deemer's office and, to my own surprise, getting through, and to his secretary's surprise saying I had nothing to say, everything was fine, I was in Hungary, I was flying back to London in a few hours, I'd be getting on with my search for a spa.

Mobility is the first rule in my profession. Move fast. And three weeks after "abandoning" my two fair ladies I was back at Heathrow Airport. I hardly had time to find the TAP desk and check my bag.

And the second rule is wait. And wait I did, for two hours, thanks to a carburetor or some such thing, or a bomb scare. Who knows. I sat under my seat belt, out on the runway, listening to Portuguese and staring at the signs: NÃO FUMAR, APERTAR CINTOS.

I didn't want to think, so I thought about that shipment of teeth, already, no doubt, safely stored in a warehouse in Calgary. And I thought about that goddamned hippopotamus, Deemer.

While I puzzle out the whole world, old Deemer, alone at night, does it all again, repeats it exactly in a warehouse in Calgary; Deemer, alone, after a day of getting richer prowls through one of his warehouses full of collections. And what is he looking for? In each of the four quadrants of that mathematical city, he has a warehouse. I forward the collections as he gives direction: To SW. To SE. To NE. To NW. He has a compass in his head that tells the rest of us all and nothing. He works, as old as he is, or is reputed to be, from dawn to dusk and every day. But the nights are his mystery. When the chinooks come blowing over the mountains. When a winter storm is enough to silence the streets of the whole raging city. When the summer heat fries the green grass brown. When the moon is as big as half the sky, up there on that lost and undulating plain. Old Deemer is in one of his warehouses. He is in one of them, somewhere, and no one can guess that either, cannot guess which. He is looking and looking. Prowling and poking. Counting or cursing or crying his way, or maybe calling, who knows, fussing his way through boxes and crates, through cupboards and cases. Old Deemer. What does he do there at night? What gives him his insomnia? Is he looking for his own lost innocence, assuming once he had it? Does he ask forgiveness from the blank night? Is he a mad alchemist of the darkness, proposing to turn it all into light? Or, light failing, into gold? He who alone makes speeches or farts or undresses in front of all his stuffed tigers and his lances and his theater costumes and his painted tiles and his aphrodisiacs and his carved Buddhas and his, the world's largest, collection of wooden wheels. Once he sent me a message: Keep an eye out for a collection of feathers, Dorf. He with all that collection of collections that he bothers to show to no one. Perhaps he only winds his clocks. Or checks for temperature control. Or makes sure that no one has left on a light. Or perhaps he is appalled, each night, by what he hasn't got, by all that has escaped him, a calving iceberg, an eclipse of the sun, a single pained or singing or loving voice from the Middle Ages.

I got him his goddamned teeth. He can study those, too, at night, caries of the kingdom of which he would be acquisitor and lord. Except that it's us, homo sapiens, who have mastered the art of rot. I found that out, my head inside those velvet-lined cases. Or maybe I am only his taster after all. I am the comic imitator of what he proposes in earnest. Deemer, there, alone at night, in the four corners of his warehoused universe, acting out reality.

I thought about all that.

And I was thinking, also, that I should get off the plane, ask that my bag be sent along later; I should fly in the opposite direction. I should take my sister's advice and give up my folly.

THE COCK CROWS AND,
A SORE LEG NOTWITHSTANDING,
DORF GOES FOR A WALK

*T*he landing at Oporto, here in Portugal, filled me with a concern, naturally enough, for my life. And yet I stayed calm: we rode from the plane to the terminal in one of those crowded stand-up buses where the passengers bump each other's hips and stare out through the windows and comment to each other on the sudden, unimagined heat. I flirted briefly with a young woman from Liverpool who was looking for an adventure. My mind was my own, not Julie's. But by the time I stumbled my way through the Portuguese language and signed my way through capitalist bureaucracy and rented a Mercedes, the Liverpudlian had disappeared.

My right leg was bothering me again. I drove with a foot of lead. When I arrived in Luso I checked in at once at the Grande Hotel das Termas, *situado a meio da villa*, and went for a swim. My leg was aching beyond all reason; I was hesitant to drive in the winding, cobblestone streets. I swam, as they say, at my leisure. I ate a hearty dinner. I located a couple of bars. I went to bed early. Julie Magnuson, wherever she was in that town, assuming she was there, be damned.

I went to bed. We have a need to speak the words, I love you. Sometimes, lying in bed, I say them aloud. And I wonder to whom I speak.

This morning at five a.m. a cock crowed outside my hotel window. I got up and dressed and went for a walk; a heavy mist kept out the sunlight and the air was cool. The buildings around the hotel, softly pink and blue and yellow, lured me into walking farther. The consolation of tile roofs told me I was safe; I peeked behind high, painted walls, in at secret gardens. I needed no keys; each door, and every one, swung easily open.

And the gardens, all of them, were full of life. Thick and violent with creeper and vine and leaf and stem and branch and trunk. A violent, green wonder in contrast to the deserted streets of stone, to the softly painted walls of the houses.

I was, in a sense, lost, walking in the fog; lost and walking. But I sensed I was moving, slowly, downhill. As if into a rift or valley or basin. After having climbed and circled and going downhill, I came to the actual fountain.

Or at least I guessed I was coming to the fountain; I came, abruptly, upon two busloads of tourists. The buses were decorated with flowers. Wreaths and bouquets of flowers. The tourists, or pilgrims perhaps, tumbled out of the buses. At first they went to the stands where hawkers sold tourist objects, rosaries and drums and post cards and walking sticks; and at first I did not see the water at all. But the tourists, or pilgrims, their first impulse spent, turned from the gaudy trinkets and walked down the hill, still further, as if they were going to the bottom of something.

I followed after. I saw, from a distance at first, a small figure in a large stone trough.

The trough extends along a stone wall. From the long wall, eleven round mouths set in a horizontal row pour water into the trough. Standing beside the middle stream of water, lifting one foot to be bathed, was a smallish figure with long fair hair. A delicate figure, or so it seemed, wearing a velvet blouse that was belted; the blouse did not quite cover the upper thighs. The legs were bare.

I was, quite frankly, somewhat aroused by the prospect. Imagine my surprise, even my horror, when the woman or girl turned around and proved to be, not only a male, but a dwarf as well.

He was undoubtedly a dwarf, smooth-shaven, with long, flowing, blond hair; only his head and his genitalia seemed to be of normal size. He was handsome in the indigo blouse that had deceived me into thinking he must be a woman. He waved at someone on the stone steps, and I moved around past the flowering bush that concealed me; I heard him speak in what, I was certain, even from that distance, must be English.

Sitting on the stone steps, sitting beside the dwarf's discarded shoes and socks and trousers, was Julie Magnuson.

DORF SPECULATES:
AN EXERCISE
IN AVOIDANCE

*H*er hair was dark, swept up onto the top of her head in a careless way, in a way suggesting abandon, and into her massed hair someone had thrust a flower. Her eyebrows were darker even than those of my memory. She looked not at the dwarf, splashing in the water, but rather down at her own bosom; she was wearing a white dress, the thin straps of the dress too bright, almost savage, on the soft skin of her tanned shoulders.

She has a face that has no history. It is one of the secrets of her success. She is close to my age, I was surprised to realize, but time erases her past. Those perfect eyebrows, that perfect nose, the erotic perfection of her ears — they are totally of the present. Time creases me into sorrow, my long face its own map and maze, my hazel eyes hung sadly on a strong but sunburnt nose.

When she looked up from her own breasts to the dwarf where he stepped carefully from the water, seeming to dance alone and obsequiously the ritual dance of attendance, my despair was complete. I knew, then and there, that she had, in Luso, a lover who might provide her, even, with a slave.

My sympathies went out to the dwarf. He looked, for all the world in spite of his being male, like a miniature of Karen Strike; she with her blondish hair and her flattish breasts. I took my sad quart-sealer face, its contents showing, dill pickles or raspberry jam or preserved plums, away from desire itself. I walked, blindly now. I walked for miles, surely, cherishing each push and throb of pain into the leg that Julie had broken.

We dwell in the body, nowadays. With the world gone

hank-end and haywire too, we live in the self's body. As if to cure the body's pain is to be cured. We are all St. Augustines in this broken world; saints not of the soul but of the body, of the bloodstream and back. Deliver us from the heart.

I found a glorious bar. I spent the day drinking Cerveja, trying various brands, Super Bock, Sagres, getting my change back on a little plate, trying, for vinte escudos, a bottle of Carlsberg. All this in a bar called The Bar.

It was in my hotel, next morning, that I had my first taste of the mineral water, Agua Termal de Lusa, and with it the advice that it's good for Artritismo, Albuminuria, Doencas Dos Rins, Hipertensao, Reumatismo, etc. A young lady on the bottle's label drank along with me, just to give me assurance.

And believe me, I was thirsty. I had a killer of a hangover. I ordered a second bottle; I could feel the cure swelling inside me. Life is like that; we are all the children of a fugitive dream. It was that mineral water that lured me on.

I digress toward the main point. The days of a collector's agent are made up of mad hurrying and intolerable waiting. I had, while in Switzerland cataloguing and packing clocks, made a hurried trip across the border to Baden-Baden. In a matter of two days I lost two thousand dollars, there at the gaming tables. A great little spa, that. I'd somehow conceived the notion that, if I punished myself sufficiently, I wouldn't proceed on to Portugal. Having lost the money, I bought my one-way ticket to Oporto.

On that first day, there in paradise and hell, I made phone calls. I went back to my room and managed to get through on the telephone to Llandrindod Wells; the connection was so good, all of a sudden, that the answering voice might have been next door. I asked about Karen Strike, knowing the desk clerk had had his eye on her, would know her whereabouts. And indeed he knew. Ms. Strike was gone, yes, to take pictures of a Greek island, Cos, where the first doctor did his first little act and invented billing.

I tried to phone my dearest sister and she wasn't home; she was out, I suppose, gathering eggs. I didn't phone Deemer's office.

What could be wrong with Julie? Did Deemer, I began

to ask myself, want the spa not for himself but for Julie? What incurable affliction, I began to torment myself by asking, had driven her to this quackery? Luso is famous for its liver and its kidney cures. For its treatment of the gall bladder. For its treatment of hypertension, varicose veins, gout, and skin allergies. And was the dwarf *her* taster as I was Deemer's, stepping for her, and protecting her in the process, into the waters that might cure or kill?

NEGATIVE #3:
IN WHICH THE TRAPPER
STEPS INTO THE TRAP

On the third day of my stay in Luso I again went to the fountain in the center of the town. And that time I was prepared.

I arrived a few minutes late, apparently; the dwarf had already washed his feet at the feet of Julie. He was drying his little toes, pulling on his little shoes and tying them when I arrived.

And then the man who had dallied in the fountain's trough was suddenly the picture of brusque efficiency. He went charging off so fast on his stubby legs that Julie, for all her long stride, could only just stay behind him.

They disappeared, the two of them, into the maze of low, white, stuccoed buildings that are the spa proper. I believed I caught a glimpse of them stepping in through a pair of large, official-looking doors, disappearing.

I was hot on their heels this time. I was at the big doors and through them one minute after they closed.

In the gloom of that building, after hearing my own abrupt footsteps on the marble floor, I saw a guard rail.

Behind the rail were four women in green. There were many people pressed to the rail. Then I saw that the women in green were filling glasses with water, passing them to the people in the crowd that pressed itself to the rail. The four women worked silently. The grateful drinkers drank too in silence.

I realized that the water was dispensed free of charge. I pressed myself into the crowd. I was handed a strange, flattened glass, a tumbler with two flattened sides. I was more fascinated by the container than by the water I drank off in one long swallow.

I joined the dozens of people who sat in chairs in the hallways, presumably waiting either to be cured of something, or to feel thirst again and to drink more water. I had to chuckle to myself. We were a motley crew, some of us knitting, some reading, some merely staring into space. I was sitting beside a woman whose ankles were swollen to the exact thickness of her knees. I tried, in vain, to exchange a few words with her. I guess that's what made me leave.

The light outside the building was blinding now. I was fleeing not so much the heat as the light when I took my Mercedes and drove the short distance out of town to the forest of Buçaco. Perhaps the light reminded me of the blinding glare on the mountain, there in Yoho, where Julie sent her avalanche down upon my trust. And yet, for all that, in going to the forest I went to another mountain of sorts.

Because the forest of Buçaco is on a mountain. I went there on that third day after watching Julie and the dwarf perform their little ritual. I drove my Mercedes up onto the mountain where monks, commencing in 1628 on orders from someone, built a monastery in a virgin forest. They received their orders and jumped to it; they built a wall around the forest, declared the trees inside, the pines that were already there, the maples and laurels that were planted, to be sacred trees.

And then the trees began to arrive from the New World. And the monks planted them, too, in their bounded forest: the Mexican cypress, the white ash. And then, from other explorers: the monkey puzzles, the ginkos, the gum trees from Australia, the Himalayan cedars, the arbutus, the sequoias, the Oriental spruces.

Deep are the woods, dark, peaceful. I, again, the happy man. The original and wandering man, returned to the forest cool. Three hundred varieties of exotic trees, come to that place as if trees had up and learned to travel. I marveled, day after day, at the audacity of that monkish collection.

There is, in the middle of that forest, a stone stairway that disappears up the mountain. Not a flight, but a series of ten flights of steps. And each flight is double, really, two parallel sets of steps with a stream flowing between them from the spring high up on the mountain to the lake and its swans below. *Fone Fria.*

I was there. I was in the water at the pond's edge, under those perfect long stone stairs when I chanced to look up.

And through the myriad blossoms, down the long stone dream, a couple, unaware of my presence, was hesitating its way toward me. They were holding hands, the woman and the dwarf, so he would not fall, stepping down from ledge to ledge. The woman was tall, and even at that far distance, obviously beautiful. Portuguese, I took her to be. The man was a dwarf; perhaps this was a haven for such people, a place to cure their spirits if not their bodies, I told myself. They came down the stairs, so attentive to each other, the woman and the dwarf, stopping to look at the pools of water between the parallel and sequential flights of stairs, admiring no doubt the petals afloat on the clear water. They did not see me.

I was only watching. Idly watching. And in that idleness I saw the dwarf caress the woman's thigh. And then she looked up at the touch of the dwarf's hand to her pubis. To her, if I might say so, cunt. His hand, gentle as a butterfly's wings. That hot black blossom, underneath. And she glanced around, furtively glanced around, looked down the stairway, saw me.

I had taken off my shoes and socks and rolled up the legs of my trousers. I was wading in the largest pool, there at the bottom of all those stone stairs. With butterflies all around me.

Julie waved. She waved as she waved that day, in a time that seemed so long ago, before the avalanche struck. She waved, and there in the still air I felt the wind in front of the snow, the wind filled with white iron filings that sliced my eyes.

There was no way I could escape. I was trapped. There at the bottom of the endless stairs, standing up to my knees in the water at the edge of the little lake with the indifferent black swans; I was trapped. In a storm of butterflies. In the sickening and exciting and overwhelming odors and stench and sweetness of all those strange trees: vanilla, camphor, eucalyptus, pepper, jasmine.

My nose was its own animal, beyond my knowing. Sex is, finally, a smell. The forest, for that overwhelming and endless time while the couple came down the long and unrelenting stairs, was Julie's body.

I suppose I got my notion of dwarfs from circuses or some such things. Or from fairy tales. Or even from Wagner's musical nonsense.

Manuel de Medeiros, in fact, is a medical doctor. He is the epitome of good breeding, and comes from an ancient Portuguese family. An aristocrat from the word go. His English is so insufferably well pronounced that I feel all the time he is giving me lessons.

It turns out that we went to the same university. In some distant past we were both students in that unlikely place, the University of Iowa, in the middle of the cornfields in the middle of the American Middle West. Our years of study actually overlapped by a year. While I was being thrown out, he was getting his medical degree; it was only later that he became disillusioned with medicine, at least with traditional medicine, and returned to become a spa doctor in his native land.

We had hardly time to speak to poor dear Julie who stood there somewhat astounded at the immediate familiarity between Manny and me. She made some absurd little joke about dwarf and Dorf, and that indicated to me that Manny was not embarrassed at talking about his affliction.

I had, as I said to Julie, using our own vernacular, brushed up on the history of the local trees. I pointed out to that native of the place a few of the native species. The butterflies were so thick around they seemed *loud* in their presence; they caused me, at times, to raise my voice.

We made our leisurely way toward the parking lot by the Palace Hotel, there in the center of the forest. I felt so tall walking with the dwarf, I was awkward. I almost, at one point, took his hand as I would the hand of a child. Julie, by staying at his side, signalled that I must walk more slowly. We walked among and under the sleeping trees, past somnolent gardeners who raised and held and seemed never to use their hoes, their shears. We found, in the held heat in a clearing, a small row of cars. I was about to get into my blue Mercedes and drive away when Manny, to my surprise, changing his tone of voice, spoke directly and specifically to me.

"We can," he said, "begin the treatment in the morning."

You could have knocked me over with a feather.

They were proceeding toward the hotel, de Medeiros and Julie, to have a drink in the elegant outdoor restaurant that extends itself from that old, ornate hotel. I felt no thirst at all.

"I'll see you," I called to the two of them as I drove away.

"Six-thirty sharp, tomorrow morning," the little doctor answered.

DORF,
AN EXAMINATION

*N*ext morning at six-thirty on the button, just for my own amusement, I showed up at the dear doctor's door. I had nothing to lose, after all. I marched through that startling dawn with its rows of blue hydrangeas; the whole town was ablaze with those bursting blue heads of blossom. I glowed as brightly as they.

The doctor, to my surprise, was expecting me.

Yes, the dear ninny of a doctor wants me to drink water! None of your average water, but Luso water. Magical water. And what I'm to be cured of I haven't the foggiest notion.

What struck me first was not the proposed cure at all, but the doctor's office. Perhaps that explains why I neglected to ask what my disease might be. Dr. de Medeiros' office is the world's only accommodation to his size. I walked in and felt that I'd become an ungainly monster of some sort, ill equipped to contend with a smallish world: cupboards close to the floor, chairs too low, a hat rack on which I might catch my belt buckle, a basin with taps I had best turn on with my toes, assuming I could tell hot from cold. I am only just six feet tall, and look as if I was shorter but was stretched on the rack. The examining table was a rack intended to reverse the process. It was so close to the floor I had indeed to *crawl* onto it. The good doctor began the examination with a severely critical examination of my rectum. "Nerves," he repeated, either to me or to himself.

Yes, I'm being introduced to, prepared for, balneotherapy. I am back in the nineteenth century here, listening while Manny puts me through the cure. Water, my physician explains to me patiently, can be applied in any of its physical states: gas, liquid, or solid. But he is going to try, first, its internal application. As

part of my hydrologic management — and he uses this language
with a straight face — I'm first of all to be *rinsed*.

Every eighty-one minutes, or every nine minutes squared
to be more precise, I drink immense quantities of water. This
heavy drinking is accompanied by reminders of the original
sulfurous waters of Thermopylae, the idea of sacrifice that must
accompany the purifying bath, the necessity for sleep as a
preparation for whatever it is that must follow. I hear more
about Hercules and Aulus Cornelius Celsus and Mohammedan
laws of cleanliness than I do about medicine. The sheer
arithmetic of the endeavor is driving me to distraction. But Julie
assures me that Dr. de Medeiros is regarded as something of a
genius in his field; he is making a successful application of
hydrotherapy and balneotherapy to sexual problems that were
once supposed to be rooted in whatever the unconscious is
supposed to be.

Fortunately, the hotel is only a short distance from the spa
and I am able to walk back to the hotel and take the elevator up
to my room between treatments. Or up to Julie's room. I begin
in the morning when the mist is still here on the mountain in
every crevice and cranny. I continue until the heat of early
afternoon makes walking itself unpleasant. I march back and
forth, back and forth, measuring minutes, measuring water out
of glasses. The ladies in green have come to expect me; they
have glasses filled and waiting. I have become a proper slave to
their expectations; I am so *rinsed* that the pure sky itself looks
sullied by comparison.

But, as I was saying, I sometimes, between my drinking
bouts, visit Julie's room. I swear there are times when I have
hardly time to get from the hospital to her room and back again
in time for the next treatment. I am at once frantically busy and
totally static. My life has become so simple that the relationship
with Julie serves as a beautiful counterpart to the stillness.
Especially since that morning when I rushed into her room and
found her reading a letter that turned out to be from Jack
Deemer.

I wanted to talk to Julie about my own problems. I had
come to know a bit about spa medicine; doctors are not always

the keepers of secrets that they like to pretend to be. If my leg was at the source of my ailment, I should be given peloid therapy, mud packs, instead of all this internal rinsing that was going on.

"I doubt that it's your leg that's being treated," Julie said.

"Thank you, doctor," I said. "Then do tell me what *is* being treated."

She hesitated. "Dr. de Medeiros is concerned..." She hesitated again. "He says it's as if you have the ultimate case of jet lag...You're out of tune...."

"I'll tune that little goat," I said.

"He's a lovely man," she said. "It's as if...you took a wrong turn...missed a corner...like someone, come to this planet by accident, too late...slowly getting...it's as if..." And she hesitated, leaning back onto her left elbow on the patterned white bedspread, her face close to mine, her right hand still fondling the golden coin that was all her throat wore...."You hate the desire that makes you love —"

"If me no ifs, if you don't mind," I said. "I'm as healthy as a horse. Even with my bad leg, and that had something to do with you, you may recall."

The cards were on the table. I was very close to accusing the woman of attempted murder. But I had my reasons too, my question that she alone could answer; it was she who could explain Deemer's request; after all, she had proposed to kill me for finding the spa he had asked me to find him. I had lived into and through an avalanche to get to this occasion; I wanted an answer, straight out, balls out and no equivocation. I had to play it cool. Like that woman in Connecticut, I wanted to know not only how the key fit the door but also how the door fit the wall. I would settle for nothing less.

"I'm still looking," I said enigmatically.

It was then she reached out and touched my right foot. She said nothing.

"Do you think..." I began. And I very nearly asked her directly about Jack Deemer.

Julie patted my foot, my ankle. The ankle of my bad leg. I had slipped my shoes off. I sometimes slip off my shoes while visiting her. Sometimes, in the heat, my feet hurt; they swell and begin to ache, and in the cool of her room I can relax, my shoes on the cool floor placed neatly side by side at the foot of her bed.

"Do you think this is a place," I asked, "where one might be cured?"

"Is the place of cure a place?" she said.

I heard a sadness in her voice.

"Conventional wisdom," I said, "so dictates."

She allowed herself a sad smile. "You don't give up," she said.

"Give up what?" I said.

"Nothing," she said. She caressed my ankle. "What's wrong with you men?" she added.

"We are all," I said, "in the end, faithful. To something."

"It makes all of you dangerous," she said.

She glanced significantly at the letter which she had left exposed on the dresser, almost as if inviting me to peek. And I did just that, more to oblige than out of any curiosity. Or at least I glanced at the first sentence of one little paragraph: "Has that genius agent of mine done anything?"

That I struck back goes without saying. I was wearing myself out at my task, wrecking my health. Julie was silent, pretending to be busy with her jewelry; she wore gold as if it alone might conceal her nakedness. She was waiting, and yet she pretended that she had not noticed that I had obliged, had peeked at her letter.

"He knows I'm here?" I said.

"I told him you'd be here."

"How could you be so sure?"

"I was sure," she said. She closed her eyes for a moment under her perfect, dark eyebrows. And there was no ice, now, no freezing mist to disguise them. She couldn't meet my rebuking gaze.

She was disarmed and, while so, I played a long shot. "He's dying," I said. "Is that it? The old coot is dying." I was trying out, in that unlikely instant of Julie's hesitation, Karen's naive idea;

poor innocent Karen, arguing that a man who can have whatever he wants has only one want remaining.

"When is your next treatment?" Julie said.

"Is that it?" I said. I demanded. Brusquely and bluntly. There were no ands and no ifs about it. I would be accurate and precise. Perhaps I wanted to prove Karen wrong, wanted to be reassured. The one thing worse than having Deemer alive would be to have him dead. "He's getting scared," I said. "That's it, isn't it?"

Julie either shook her head or nodded, I couldn't tell which. We were both of us half sitting, half lying on the smooth and patterned and pure white bedspread that seemed to engulf the bed. "Dr. de Medeiros," she said, "when he arrived in Calgary ... "

I tipped back my head as if I'd been hit in the stomach.

"When he flew to Calgary," Julie said. "Manny," she added, as if I might not understand. "When he came to see us." Perhaps she saw my confusion. "Jack sent for him. He stayed with us ... "

"Us?" I said. "Us?" I lay back, full on the bed. "Us?" I said.

"He stayed with us," Julie said. "He stayed with Jack and me. It was Dr. de Medeiros who told Jack: a spa, the right spa!" She stopped. "You men are all alike," she burst out.

"Is that so?" I countered. I didn't stir where I lay.

She gestured around the room, held up her empty hands to the empty air. She sat up on the bed. "You must find another spa," she said. "Not this one, Dorf. Not this one." She was ready to talk or cry or something, I couldn't tell. "We all live by our alibis, don't we, Dorf?" But she didn't wait for an answer. "We were somewhere else when it happened. Or should have been. Or shouldn't have been." She slipped off a golden bracelet, placed it carefully on the table beside the bed. "Manny stayed with us. Perhaps he shouldn't have. He said the cure is always, finally, in the acceptance ... of desire ... "

"Your Manny," I said, "is full to his lowdown eyebrows of enemas and frigidariums and Methuselah. And old Deemer needs all three, you bet your boots. He's getting old, that's it, isn't it? He's old and he can't get it up; he wants to get it up and he has half of us, all of us, goddamnit, wearing ourselves out, killing ourselves, trying to find a goddamned spa that will give him back his stiff prick. That's it. Isn't it?" I was almost on the edge of shouting. "You are so beautiful, Julie," I cried out, "you need not one man, you need two men, ten men, all the men you can love. You can love all men, I know that. I see that in you; you are everything and capable of everything and I would grant you everything if I were Deemer. I would grant you everything, everything, because you are so beautiful, so perfect; if I were anything but Deemer's idiot agent … "

And that was when she unbuckled the buckle of my belt.

"I love you," I said.

We were passionate together. In the cool heat of the Portuguese morning. Eighty-one minutes after my last treatment by drinking whole damned litres of mineral water. We were lovers together. The insects whispered at the window's ledge; the cocks, misremembering their time, crowed in the farther distance.

We knew, deliciously, that I was overdue at the spa. We both knew. Each ticking moment was a theft, a glory stolen from the hour-keeping day. We were the lovers of love. Frankly, I took the woman. The verb is quite appropriate. Over and over and over. I was insatiable. The sun, somewhere, cast no shadow; in its own way it stood still.

When I wavered, even slightly, she lifted me back to our mutual joy. Julie took me in her mouth and I was happy. I was lifted, again and again, into a newer need. Her mouth was my only cure.

THE DOCTOR
VISITS THE PATIENT

I knew that de Medeiros must, sooner or later, out of his impatience or his curiosity, come to investigate my absence. I cannot deny that that very knowledge, kept shadowy in my aching mind, was part and parcel with my desire. I thought of de Medeiros, his long, golden hair, the hair that Karen would have had, had she let her own grow to its decency. I could imagine him against the mystery of my not appearing; I could see his confidence absenting itself, his manner changing from the polite condescension of the doctor to the impatience of the jealous lover. I could see him brushing too quickly at the sheet on the examination table, snatching a thermometer away too soon from a puckered ass. Poor, dear de Medeiros, realizing, as he hurried past the hydrangeas, past the swimming pool, into the lobby, to the button that would summon an elevator to his slow rising — he, realizing, already, that it was already too late.

What surprised me, if anything could surprise me in that perfect morning, was de Medeiros' response when he came in through the door.

He seemed nothing so much as pleased at my show of health and vigor. He gave a little cry of surprise that was more pleasure than disapproval. Julie, showing her bare bum to the doorway, not hesitating for a moment in the slow motion of her rump, responded with her continuing silence. Perhaps she tried not to hear his arrival. I too was silent, as if my tongue must count each curling hair in that chasm of my joy. The closed room was surely rank with our sweat and our musky need.

Julie was the complement of my size, there on that bed; I was not, with her, too gangly or too tall. My legs were as if discarded, at the head of the bed, I was the torso of her rapacity. Desire feeds on desire. Omphalos, somehow, is a mountain word.

The doctor, after his single cry, moved silently across the room. He walked around to my side of the bed. He was hardly tall enough to reach across the bed and tug at my sweaty hair. And yet he did so. And, silently, gently, he checked my temperature, putting his mouth to my forehead, then touched a hand to my naked buttocks.

"Mr. Dorfen," the doctor said, gently now, gently, softly, "you are late for your appointment."

Apparently I said I was sorry.

"Sorry, nothing," the doctor said. He gave my backside a little whack with the palm of his little right hand.

Julie, not I, started at the soft blow. I thought she was hurt at my being hurt, and I tried to assure her, my returning tongue feverish to her wet surrender.

"You're quite a naughty fellow," Manny said. He gave me a good whack this time, followed by another.

I was caught there between the two of them, between the doctor's impatience, real or feigned, and Julie's patient insistence. I was caught between the doctor's recurring voice, his small tight mutterings, in Portuguese now, some oaths perhaps, and Julie's motion, her mouth's silent need that would have all of me in a single taking. And I might have stayed there, always and forever, in my mind, had not Julie herself spoken, the soft obscenities of her need that made the doctor leave my side, move to her wanting; and when, then, beyond my closed eyes, I heard him, I imagined she had on panties, strawberry red, and he took them off, and still she had on panties, the color of mint this time; and I spoke the colors aloud then, spoke aloud the names of those colors, and Julie asked me to speak, but more the slowly to make my speech; and she was between us then, between Manny and me; and she took each named delight as her special own, her tongue's challenge; she had a tongue to each tasting; and I was the dazzled narrator, held to her touch by a raveling promise; it was cinnamon peach that made her nuzzle until I hurt; and blueberry drew her away, the taste of that bruised color; and I heard him, Manny; I imagined he took off another pair, a bitter shade of lime, and still she wore beneath that lime need, against his taking, more panties and more, until he could never find her; the color of pistachio, I named aloud, let its slow name into Julie's damp ear; we were our own small anarchy; pistachio, I tried, a spartan sweetness, and corrected it away, or would have; but Julie whispered her own words now, her own; it was not Sparta she would have but the bite of Turkish coffee; she said the name and let herself repeat it, again and again, my mind in its own mind, tearing itself apart; and Manny had found his seeking; and I pushed to her hot, demanding hand, the whispered heat of her taking; the pillowed call; we gave attendance, Manny and I, to the sly ritual of her pleasure; we the attendant rut, doubled and one, the drowning of our voices into the long and meditated cry, the delicious scream of her outraged pleasure.

BLUE

*I*t was on that fateful morning that the three of us became inseparable. There is a doom in language. We talked. And, having talked, having spoken, we touched, our fingers joining into the conversation. We touched each other's hands, shook hands even at my instigation, as a kind of congratulation.

Julie was in her bliss. No doubt she recalled our earlier pleasures together in the pool in Banff. And there, too, that time, the presence of another, the presence of Karen busy with her research only excited us further.

It was the marvelous possibilities of our little triangle that gave me no rest from desire. I felt not the slightest touch of jealousy. Indeed, by pretending just slightly that Manny was Karen, with his head of perfect blond hair, I was able to add a further dimension to our already outrageous joy. I truly felt no jealousy. I was able to write in my journal exactly on each day those two blind words: he ... I. And what did it matter, the slightest difference? We were together and as one. We were two as one and three as one and each of us, one as three, isosceles in our splendor. We were our own geometry and arithmetic too; we could add and subtract with perfect abandon.

It was not until I realized that the doctor thought of our arrangement as part of a "cure" that I became slightly irked. I recognized and allowed for the man's need to deceive himself, but yet, even so, I thought it showed a lack of self-knowledge on his part. I was in his office, lying down, stark naked on his ridiculously low table, my anus once again under perusal when he asked me to describe what I had done the previous afternoon.

"But you were there," I protested.

"Let us assume, Mr. Dorfen," the doctor insisted, "that you are describing the event or events to your doctor."

At first I was baffled into a kind of silence. The doctor tried to help me along. He tapped gently at my spine.

"Did you drink water as directed yesterday?" he asked.

"I feel like a sluice gate," I said.

"Did it make you feel better?"

I had to admit it. "I felt open to the world. I was in contact with the world. Life flowed and I was part of its flowing."

"And what did you do then? How did this experience of 'a flowing life' manifest itself?"

"I counted hydrangeas," I said.

"Tell us more," the doctor said. Where he got the "us" I don't know. "Elaborate," he said.

"There's nothing much to tell you. I was waiting to meet with two of my friends. They'd gone out to dinner. While they were gone I began to count blue hydrangeas."

"Did you share this experience with your friends?"

"The whole town became a mystery, a kind of bowl. My friends were up on the mountain and I was here in the valley below. The valley became a kind of bowl, or a vase for me, filled with hydrangeas. I counted those in the streets, along the footpaths, easily enough. But then I felt I must peek into gardens, into vineyards and private lanes, into private courtyards even. I must peek, I must count."

I began to sense that the doctor wasn't pleased. He pressed me further. Frankly, I began to suspect that he wanted a lurid account of what we did together, he and Julie and I; he, in his boar-like mounting while her mouth gave assurance that what she wanted most was to be with me. He could not live up to that insatiable expectation, poor Manny; sometimes he could only watch our pleasure. Perhaps old Deemer himself is only Julie's shadow, an agent of her total desire, and has sent us all here for his own sleep. And we, in a bed we think is secret: all of us in a spendthrift heap, me on the bottom as the underpinning of love itself, Julie alive to my bunched muscles, Manny on top like a frenetic *campino* on his mount, flailing his small imagination. I was lying there, belly down on his table; I hadn't a stitch on. I could feel he was staring at me, at my stretched and normal body.

I felt I was disappointing him. He was waiting for something else. I had a longing, right then, to be away from the man, to be out in the streets in the sunlight, counting hydrangeas. They are so enduring and yet so fragile; they are fed on the soil's iron, those puffs, those small explosions of pleasure. And of course they are beyond all collecting. Because they are all so exactly alike.

"My friends," I said, "neglected to tell me they sometimes make love together with a strange man who drives a blue Mercedes-Benz." I began to sense I was finding a way out of the corner I was almost in. "The thought of it offends me," I said, "the three of them, together in one bed, all of them nuzzling and cooing, touching, whispering obscene words, tasting and sniffing and licking and biting."

The doctor started to move. I heard him; I saw him, possibly, from the corner of my eye. He began to raise his hand. His small right hand. Then he lowered it again.

"You identify this friend of yours through his automobile," the doctor said. "Have you no other way of identifying him?"

"The automobile," I said, "is his only means of defense. Is it not peculiar, doctor, that the vehicle which kills so many thousands of persons each week, each day, I suppose, is also a vehicle for liberation of the spirit; it becomes, for us, almost the only avenue to what used to be called the soul."

I shifted on his examination table. I had, for whatever reasons, the slightest beginning of an erection. Smallish man that de Medeiros was, he was no doubt offended that I would exclude him from a major experience, communal and private, of this our time.

"Automobiles and hydrangeas," he observed, "are not objects that most minds would place in such necessary conjunction."

"On the contrary, my good doctor," I said. "Anyone who himself drives a car must have a sense of the erotic invitation offered by the hydrangeas that line these dusty streets of Luso." I was hitting him, I realized, where he lived; Luso to him was a quaint and lovely place of ancient medical practices, an escape from the vital reality of our daily speed. *"Mineral water,"* I said to him. "Isn't that a strange conjunction?"

"You were saying," he said.

"Precisely," I said. "The flower and the machine. They must marry, or we are all dead. Perhaps that great oilman, Jack Deemer, came to understand as much in his plundering of fossil fuels from the bowels of the earth. Understanding, then, he comes to you and me, two kinds of wise men, for advice. He waits to hear from us. Or we are all dead."

The doctor left me where I lay, a single shaft of sunlight crossing my bare buttocks, and sat down on a miniature stool near my head.

"You see, my dear wise doctor," I said, "I am only the collector's agent. I only act out the collector's desire. The desire is his."

"I am only the doctor," Manny said. "The disease is the patient's. Is that what I'm supposed to say?"

"Not at all," I said. "Unless you wish also to separate the cure from the disease."

"The flower and the machine," the doctor said, "in conjunction, announce only their dissimilarities."

"Not if they are both blue," I said.

Manny chuckled, in spite of himself. "You've got me there," he said.

"Blue," I said, "is the point that turns the mere opposition of two points into a triangle, and only in a triangle does desire know itself. Blue is a true point of healing. Consider the sky above us."

"You're sounding blue yourself today," Manny said. He was so pleased with himself when he managed to make a pun in English. "Put on your trousers and go drink more of that pure and colorless water."

THE MAP OF
WHAT MUST BE

*M*y happiness was struck a violent blow on the morning of the fourteenth day of my treatment. I was humoring the doctor to the best of my ability. We were, the three of us, de Medeiros and Julie and I, constant companions from mid-afternoon until the time of their late dinner.

My nights I was able to spend by myself, yes. Sometimes I made journal entries; the idea of a journal, planted in my mind by Karen Strike's generosity, had taken seed and grown. For those few brief and fleeting nights I had been able and free to record, each night, each day's activities, even while the night-flying butterflies teased at the page itself. What I find in those journal entries now, confronting them, is the recurring pain that all lovers must feel. I was happy; I was happy, indeed; and yet the nature of love is such that to be happy is, paradoxically, to know suffering. I had the doctor to humor. I had Julie's moods to contend with.

She was nothing if not mercurial. One hour she would make such a feast of our bodies that Manny and I retreated or fled with relief to our various tasks, he to see an extra patient, I to drink water. The next hour Julie was so cold and unaware, so intrigued by her own speculations that she seemed to have turned to stone. She imagined eyes in the very trees themselves; she could imagine the birds in the air were spying on her. We must, Manny and I, in the space of the clock's turning, pleasure her every need and practise a secrecy that was as absolute as ice.

It was on the evening of the thirteenth day that she said to me, feigning a certain casualness, "You write none of this in your journal, I trust."

"Trust, indeed, yes," I said. "Trust me to the ends of the earth. But I cannot lie to my journal either."

"You have written of this?" she said. "Of *this*?"

We were lying together on her bed, all three of us, in such a tangle of arms and legs that I could not recognize my own limbs let alone identify the this of her this. Manny had, in his passion, bit her violently on her right thigh, and I was kissing it better, warming the bruise with my breath. And when I inhaled, breathing deeply in so as again to blow gently onto her bruise, I filled my head with the heat of her desire, rankly sweet, like iron newly lifted from a bog.

"I will show my journal to no one, fear not," I said. "Not even to the likes of Jack Deemer himself, collect what he might." I breathed warmly onto Julie's blue bruise. "And I begin to wonder if this is not the spa he most seeks in the wide world."

We were in such a hot tangle that all conversation ceased for a while. I let the fingers of my right hand find the toes, each one and separately, of Julie's right foot. The one and very foot that pushed her through the Portuguese night when she and Manny borrowed my car; it was appropriate that I should spend those same nights tending my journal as a gardener tends his sprouts and his blossoms.

With my left hand I lifted my member into firing position, so to speak; it pleased Julie to watch my giving myself a good healthy stroke or two. It gave me pleasure to give her pleasure.

This time she closed her eyes. "I'm afraid, sometimes," she said. "I never used to be afraid of anything."

De Medeiros was busy chewing at one of her ears. He mumbled something about health. He was a nut on the subject of health; in the midst of our most abandoned love play he would spout solemn lectures on his dear balneotherapy, explaining how the Roman customs were taken over by Byzantium, transferred then through Islam to this very Portugal in which we now delighted; we were Romans, after all, whatever our degrees of remove. These speculations from a man who boasted that he had not once, ever, entered a body of water larger than a tub. And, I might have reminded him, there were occasions when he hadn't done that for a day or two either.

"The doctor," I remarked finally, wearying of the lectures that intruded on my insatiable lust, "might take note from his patient." I was, in appearance at least, speaking to the ceiling of that high room, for Julie had taken it into her head to, as she so coyly put it, ride her broomstick. "He should try counting hydrangeas," I said. "Such careful ordering clears the mind."

Dear Julie forced my mouth silent with her tongue.

It was the very next morning, as I tried to sit down on the edge of the doctor's absurd low examination table without falling flat on the marble floor, that I got the shock of my life.

Dr. de Medeiros was wearing his stethoscope around his neck, as a badge of authority no doubt. Except that its size made him ridiculous, dangling down in front of him the way it did, almost touching his toes.

"Mr. Dorfen," he began — we had a delightful way of switching from informality to formality when we moved from Julie's bedroom to the spa — "I have made further arrangements for you."

"How so?" I said. I was truly astonished.

He was prepared, I saw, to write me out a prescription of some sort.

I anticipated, in my intuitive way, what was, so to speak, up. I tried to be reasonable with and about the stupid little man; I tried to resist any feeling of hostility I might justifiably feel. He was, after all, acting out of good intentions, even out of what he took to be a version of medical understanding. What he failed to understand was intimacy itself; he who encouraged the rest of us toward it. To be intimate. To intimate. I took pains to try and explain to the poor fellow that the two usages are alike, first in their delicacy, then in their making something *known*.

"To touch is to talk," I said. "Intimacy is, finally, an intimacy of telling. Therefore we must *be* together."

"You must try to stay calm," the doctor said, incoherently.

"Calm, my ass," I said.

He raised the end of his stethoscope as if he would press it to his own little chest.

"And speaking of intimacies," he said. "You must never, on pain of death, at another time speak of this time."

"I know what I know," I said.

"Do you understand what I'm saying?" he said.

"I know," I said. I tried to stoop to his level. "I know what intimacy is. I know the touch of touch, the taste of taste, the smell of smell." I was tempted to shake a finger at him. "I know that we all, like those blue hydrangeas, desire our way back to the source of all desire, the sun itself. That is why grass grows up. That is why men stand. That is why the stag leaps, the ungainly heron flies."

"Do tell," the doctor said.

"I have wings in my mind," I said. "I drive a car. You don't. I have been at the real edge of escaping dumb humanity."

"You are," de Medeiros said, "beyond me. I'm sorry."

And I said what I did not mean to say. "I'm sorry too," I said.

And then, he, abruptly, sternly almost, began to explain that I was indeed beyond his ability to cure. I can only say I was dumbfounded. He shook his head, sadly. I almost felt a tenderness for the man in his defeat. "There's a woman," he said. "You should go see her. She's a healer in Greece. Near Salonika. I've gone myself and talked with her, but talking is no substitute for what she can do. We call her, forgive us," he smiled and grimaced at the same time, "the smelly woman. We have difficulty pronouncing her name so we call her instead," and he repeated it, smiling again, grimacing again, "the smelly woman." He was writing instructions on his pad, showing me how to find her; instead of a prescription he drew on his pad a ridiculous map. "You can't possibly miss her," he said. He went into great detail on the map, labeling bus stops and train stations and monuments and crossroads. I stuffed the piece of paper into a back pocket and buttoned the flap and walked with the silent doctor to the fountains where we might both have a drink.

AN INVITATION TO A DEPARTURE

*Y*es, it is five days exactly since the good doctor sprung his little surprise on me. I am too sick; he cannot cure me. A marvelous sense of humor possesses the man. Instead of laughing at him, instead of pointing out to him that, being healthy, I need no cure, I begged him to try one more time. I asked him, begged him, for one more of our morning audiences. I had become quite dependent on the fellow, I have to admit; I'd come to enjoy the brief examination, the long silence, the glasses of water punctuated by my reflections on the absurdity of life and love, on the insignificance of death itself. I told him as much. He would only shake his head.

"We can all have lunch together," he said, indicating that Julie was included in our plans. "And a drink."

We sat down together that same day, five days ago, the three of us together at this very table, here in the out-of-doors restaurant of the Palace Hotel on this stone veranda, in the forest of Buçaco, overlooking the plotted gardens that at once mystify and center the dreamer; here we sat together and ate our lunch and sipped our wine and talked.

It was at this table that I sprung a surprise of my own. I invited Julie to accompany me to the Algarve. We should, I suggested, spend a few days down south there, on the Atlantic shore, away from all this. So that I might get away from the doctor's irresistible magic, I said, and think about what I must do next.

It was a late lunch we were having. I had had tortille of potatoes for my first course. Julie and Manny had both had fish soup with toast. I was being served filets of sea wolf pompadour style. Yes, I have no difficulty remembering. Julie and Manny, together, had already been served their sauteed capon with red wine.

Manny nodded his blond curls into his capon, as if he must be deeply meditating on what I had said. The restaurant people knew him well and had discreetly led him to a chair that was higher than mine. Yet even so his chin was in his plate.

I shrugged as if indifferent to the silence around me. Julie flicked her dark gaze at Manny. Manny took his face off his dish and studied a path in the elaborate garden beyond the stone arch that framed earth and sky. It was only into that forest, a few hundred yards I would guess, and farther down the mountain that I had first spotted the indecencies of the conspiring couple.

"I've never been to the Algarve," Julie said.

"Nor I," I said. It would be new to us, to both of us.

"I was to Nazaré," I said, "up from Lisbon, one time, to buy a collection of dolls for Jack Deemer." I paused, letting my own silence speak. "You may have seen some of the dolls in his house. In the petticoats and panties of the women of Nazaré. I was told they were much appreciated in his house."

"I'll go with you for the weekend," Julie said. "Then, if you plan to fly on from Lisbon, we can drop your car there and I'll catch a bus back here to Luso." She glanced around at the hotel, the garden, the forested lift of mountain. "And to Buçaco," she added.

"Splendid," I said. "A perfect plan."

THE ALGARVE

We left early next morning for the south coast of Portugal, Julie and I. And what a glorious drive we made of it in my rented blue Mercedes. We were determined to make the whole run by evening, and I drove with my foot well down on the gas through all that glory of looming green and the painted red earth. South of Lisbon, once we had crossed the Salazar Bridge, once we were over the Tagus and had left behind us Setubal, we were into groves of cork oak.

Have we not all dreamed the cork forests of Portugal? And yet they are more than any dreaming, those park-like groves of ancient evergreens. Like a child counting telephone poles or cows or white houses, I wanted to count trees; those great thick trunks and heavy branches, stripped to an orange or reddish brown, to a brown so deep and rich it seemed like blood gone brown in light.

My driving was so reckless, in my care for the trees, that Julie reprimanded me.

"But wait," I laughed. "It was you who promised me a death. If I dare to find a spa for Jack Deemer."

And, still laughing, I counted off the whizzing trees. Gauguin himself would have envied each tree its shades of brown. And the large white numerals, strangely human, unnatural, painted onto the stripped sections of each tree spoke back to me. What code, what puzzle, invited us southward, there? Those mere numbers, inviting an understanding. And yet the trees, so carefully spaced in their hugeness, offered no hiding. We were in that forest, Julie and I, and we were in awe, and I knew she was happy.

Sometimes, while I drove, she would touch her little finger, the smallest finger of her left hand, gently to the lobe of my left ear. She would lift the lobe as if to open a secret place. And the cork trees reached up their still brown branches to their own green leaves. And the stacked cork, there by the blurred road-side, hugged itself brown and warm to the earth. And Julie touched my trousers open.

Her head, there on my lap, so vulnerable, so exposed, so loving.

South, then, out of the forests and onto a high reaching plain of grass and grazing and far trees that held themselves like fallen green clouds above the sad earth. It was too much like my own prairies. I drove hard. I drove up into the Serra de Caldeirao, those last mountains that held us back from the coast, those stripped and scalded peaks and their clinging trees, the eucalyptus trees, the pine, the cork oak and the holm; and then my own wild turning, into descent. And the first glimpse, far beyond us, far below, of the soft Atlantic shore.

I remember the birds. I remember the birds in the trees in the town above the golden beach. We found a hotel in Armação de Pera, a fishing village on the largest beach on the Algarve shore. It was the Hotel Garbe. At sundown the birds came back to the trees, to the looming trees we could see from the balcony of our suite. They came back loudly in a cloud as if each leaf of each tree might conceal a bird. We heard the trees. And the boys with their slingshots waited.

I was careful not to burn. In such a blast of daytime heat we had no choice but to stay in our suite a good deal of the time. It opened out onto the cliff; we could stroll out onto the cliff's edge, lean over a low parapet and, dizzily, look down onto the somnolent bathers on the sand, out over the blue Atlantic water.

"This is your chance," I said.

"What chance?" she pretended.

"You could push me," I said. "Just push me, and pretend I fell."

She laughed.

And then we retreated to the palm and the cactus that gave us privacy.

Indeed, there was a danger that I would not get a suntan at all. We were hardly seated at breakfast when Julie was setting all the delicious, crusted rolls in front of me, indicating that I must eat in a hurry, finish the pot of coffee, then hurry back to bed. It was like that, there, the Algarve in mutinous blossom. In blinding blossom. And the Atlantic chill of the morning was a provocateur to all kinds of surreptitious seeking after the heat of our own bodies.

Sometimes, lying on one side of Julie, I would conceive a great passion to be lying on the other. I needed to be twice myself. Her nose snuggled softly to my shoulder, I needed to be lying at her back. Or watching how she stepped into her panties, her head bent toward me, her dark hair confusing her sight, I would step behind her, slip them down again.

Hers must have been the warmest ass in the world. I could lie for hours behind her, pressing my body against the lovely squirminess of her restless bum. She would ease me into a hot and sticky laziness. Sometimes we spoke of Manny, missing his presence, his little edge of violence in our peaceful bed. I missed even his chatter about health and water and the needs of his patients and his plans to rush off to conferences here and there, in Oporto, in Japan, in the farthest reaches of China. And then, having spoken of Manny, we would plan our own little expeditions; a few miles east on the highway to look for leather in Albufeira, a few kilometers west so that we might admire the pottery of Porches.

It was the sharing, that giving and receiving, not only our passionate love, that made her disappearance all the more inexplicable. We were together all the day long; we walked to see the gypsies camped on the edge of the village; we counted their wagons and their horses and their dogs, watched their fires begin to glow in the falling light, listened to their songs. Julie held my hand, and threatened to run away. And I would not let her go. And we went to eat shrimp and lobster and grilled sardines, there in an open-air restaurant, up on a high cliff. The Panorama Grill it was called. Those blond cliffs, undercut by the licking sea, and a high footpath where the cliff broke straight and emptily down to the swept sand.

We had decided to stay one extra night. Julie had agreed to my suggestion.

I wanted to give her a birthday present. She had confessed, in a moment of abandon, while I touched my face to the pool of sweat on her belly, while I let my tongue follow the row of small black hairs that led down and then down and down, she was to be, on the day next, my own age. Julie made something of a secret of her age. I wore her bristly bush on my mouth as I spoke. I promised her a gift. We would stay an extra day. We would drive to the farthest point, to the Sagres Peninsula, to Cape St. Vincent itself where Prince Henry the Navigator, collecting together his cartographers and his mariners, prepared the way for that greatest collector's agent of all, a certain Mr. Columbus.

On that same night, and even as we made our plans, we walked on the sandy beach in the shoreline dark, in the light from the town above us on the cliff. We walked, together, dreaming our own compass, our own western point.

One night we were walking on the sandy beach in the darkness under the bright town. We held hands and flirted with the moving edge of the ocean, daring it to swamp our sandals, laughing, kissing under the water-hollowed rocks, daring the blank ocean to swallow us into its ravishing surface. Yes, and far out on the water the lights of the fishing boats made a path; the boats were stationed in a row on the darkness and their lights made a golden path. As if we might walk and laugh and kiss forever, into the closed eye of the horizon.

Next morning I awoke to find she had locked the door that joined our rooms. Hers was the front bedroom opening onto the cliff overlooking the beach. Mine was a womb-like affair in the interior. I had to enter her room to enter mine. My room had columns in it, strange tall columns and contrivances of light that made the smallish room seem immeasurably secure; Julie had thought it would be good for me. I knocked on the door that separated and joined our rooms. After the ferocity of our love-making she liked to sleep alone, knowing I would, in my insatiable way, not allow her a decent night's rest. I knocked at her locked door. There was no answer. I had been ready, in the quickening of my desire, to bruise her awake with a rough yet loving kiss into our special day. Instead, there in that windowless room, trying again the locked door, I remembered again the avalanche, my opening my eyes to the thin light, my knocking a space in front of my face for air to find my nostrils.

The lock was a simple one; I had thoughts, for a moment, that I might tickle it open. But while I was thinking my shoulder hit the door. I smashed my shoulder against the door.

Her bed was empty. And yet it was still possible she had absent-mindedly locked the door, if only to protect me; she might have gone for an early morning walk back to the beach where we had together planned the day. I checked to see what clothing she might have worn to go outside in the warm and yet cool dawn.

It was then I knew she had departed. Her closet was empty. Her suitcases were gone.

Needless to say, I had a terrible morning of it. I went to the desk and asked clumsy and mysterious questions; but at least I determined that she had not checked out. Then I went to the parking lot.

My blue Mercedes was gone. I remembered then that she had borrowed the keys the previous afternoon, had borrowed them to get something from the car and had not returned them. Should I run to the police? But hardly to report a stolen car, the woman I was sleeping with proven a thief. No, I couldn't be that ruthless. I rushed back twice, three times to our suite expecting she would be there again, having played some little trick on me. She would be there, laughing. But the silence of the rooms laughed instead. I went outside, peered over the cliff's edge as if to find her, terribly squashed and broken, lying on the sand. But only the towels and backs and umbrellas of the day's innocent sun-worshippers greeted my blurred vision.

Perhaps I was wrong in what I did; perhaps I reacted too hastily. But I simply packed my bag and checked out of the hotel, paid all the bills and took a taxi to where I might catch one of those splendid Portuguese express buses, and I caught it and rode directly north to Lisbon and there rented a Mini 1000 and came racing here to Luso.

Julie has vanished. I rushed back here to the place to which I was certain she would return. Her precious fool of a doctor and his water cure.

I cannot find hide nor hair of Manuel de Medeiros. I sit here now at this table in the Palace Hotel, the very table where the three of us agreed that Julie and I must spend a week end on a southern beach, deciding a future. I sit here having *Bacalhau à Lisbonense* and a bottle of adequate Portuguese white wine and I am alone.

What can I do but guess at what happened? I took Julie away from her pizzle-faced doctor; yes, I claimed her away to a southern coast in the very car which she either stole from me or which was used by another to steal her away. Did Julie's dwarf, in his jealousy, follow us to the Algarve, there capture Julie, steal her out of her own bed and force her to drive him away in my car? He could not himself drive, I know that for certain.

He might have spirited her away like one of Deemer's dolls, taken from their home in Nazaré by Deemer's money. I had half a mind to make a pilgrimage of my own, as the Portuguese have for these eight centuries, to that town and its cliff and its chapel. Deemer had liked especially one doll, and for obvious reasons, I suppose: Our Lady of Nazaré, holding in her arms a man on a horse. Dom Fuas Roupinho, companion to King Afonso I, who galloped to the cliff's edge, there in the sea-mist, pursuing a stag; the stag tumbling into the misted space, stepping out onto nothing and finding the nothing there and falling and turning and falling; the warrior saved, stopped in his tracks, only by a miracle; and his mind, for the rest of his life, galloping to the cliff's edge, stopping, galloping again to the cliff's edge.

De Medeiros had gone clean out of sight. Detained, a nervous secretary insisted in impossible English, in Lisbon. A story I couldn't buy for a moment.

"Tell him," I instructed his secretary, "I'm looking for him. And I'll find him, come hell or high water. You got that?"

She nodded, yes.

I had come to like the little fellow. That we were for a time rivals in love, and that I had triumphed, seemed hardly an adequate cause for such violent behavior. The doctor and not the patient in need of a cure.

I was at my wit's end. Needless to say I headed for a phone.

Is not the telephone its own version of intimate need? I must, as usual, get hold of Karen Strike, ask her to show me the way to the phantasmic spa. First I spent an hour in the forest of Buçaco, walking up and down the long stone stairs, counting butterflies. Count that man fortunate who has butterflies to count. I felt my way with feet that were hardly my own, imagining short legs. Then I climbed reluctantly into my little car and drove back to Lisbon and found a telephone operator who could speak English. And then, to my further bewilderment, Deemer's efficient secretary knew exactly where I might find the gifted Ms. Strike, Our Lady of the Camera.

SANCTUARY

We tore each other's clothes off when we met there on Cos, Karen and I. Perhaps I exaggerate slightly. She was wearing a bikini. Perhaps I write this down for her eyes only, reminding her by my slight exaggeration that my heart hurt at our finding each other, there on the Greek island where Hippocrates made his medical reputation. Karen wanted me to stay and look around; she had in tow a big German who owned a sailboat and who wore something only larger than a G-string over his balls; he was forever muttering to me, *"Danke, Danke,"* an expression which he somehow managed to make sound like "donkey."

I had chartered a small helicopter to fly me to Karen's latest folly. All the way from Athens. Mr. Deemer's accountants, I assured her, will blanch at this one.

"But Cos might be the place Deemer wants," Karen said. She has that kind of inventive imagination. Show her a tourist trap and she'll trap herself. "Come take a look. We can rent bicycles."

I was more likely to be run over by a bicycle than to rent one, there on that quay; it was overrun by people come on bicycles to see the whirlybird. We were in the town of Chora, its green gardens and its puzzle of walls, its oleanders and olive trees and its palms and the coast of nearby Turkey still fresh in my mind from our steep descent. We had tumbled down from the sky, and I'd almost upchucked. I was still feeling queasy.

"Two miles out of town," Karen said. "The sick of the known world," she added, laying it on a bit herself, "went there to take the waters. Nero himself, as I will suggest in my film." She tugged again at my neck. "Come see the sanctuary of Aesculapion at least. The old pillars like pricks in a row. You'll be impressed. The sacred grove full of blossoms that make you dizzy."

"Just what I need," I said.

The German nodded his head and his balls. "*Ja,*" he said.

I told them both I had no need of a sanctuary, thank you, though God knows Deemer could use one; he needed somewhere to wash his hands. Like Nero, yes. And then I was reckless enough to explain to Karen exactly why I was there; I have heard of a spa, I explained. I was trying to be both patient and precise. It's in the north of Greece, in Macedonia. Not a tourist attraction, a *real* spa. And I promised Karen she would get materials that would make her documentary a prize-winner at Cannes and a money-tree to boot. I explained at great length, apparently. I mentioned a smelly woman, but could not give details when asked, for obvious reasons, or for reasons that should have seemed obvious enough.

"Are you okay?" Karen said.

"Fit as a fiddle," I said. "Try me."

"Horny old man," she said. "That shirt looks like you've slept in it for a week."

"Only two days," I said. "I had to stop in Lisbon on the way."

"Oh," she said, "by the way," as if the mention of my traveling only then made her remember, "I received a telegram yesterday. For you."

"For *me?*" I said. I was shaken, somehow. "No one knows where I am."

"From a doctor," Karen said. "Madeira or something." She looked to her German for confirmation and he shook his equipment again and said "*Ja*" again.

I grunted quizzically.

"Madeira said if you arrive on Cos you should contact him at once."

"A friend of mine," I explained. "He lives in Portugal, as you might have guessed. I had hoped to see him. He's worried about my health."

"You look a wreck, Dorf," Karen insisted. "Your eyes, they've been torpedoed, they're sinking."

We were standing next to one thousand Calymnos sponges that were set to dry and that smelled the worse for being out of water. I was waiting for my pilot to come off a fishing boat where he was visiting a friend and no doubt getting into the ouzo. The bicycles pushed around us like bees in a hive.

"And you've lost weight," Karen said.

"Send him an answer," I suggested, "since he's taken the trouble to find me. Send him a message: Physician, heal thyself. And ask him…"

I stopped.

It was none of her goddamned business what I did in Portugal. Women can be insanely jealous.

"There's a plane tree here," Karen said, "that sheltered Hippocrates himself. It's a huge, monstrous thing that covers a whole town square." She gave what is sometimes described as a winning smile. She was tanned, I swear, the color of a stripped cork oak; her chopped-off blonde hair was streaked from salt and sun. Her chief item of clothing was her cameras.

She wanted some footage of me, exploring Hippocrates' plane tree. A tree itself as healing place; it seems she had interested Jack Deemer in her pictures and she wanted to give him a surprise. She'd phoned his office. Karen being a success, while her follower nodded various parts of his body and quoted Hugo von Hoffmansthal on the charms of Greece.

I suppose in a sense I captured Karen, took her prisoner, kidnapped her by pretending to let her lead the way. I gave her three hours in which to get her pictures taken and her sailor drunk on retsina. She agreed to the departure on the condition that we stop for a few restful days on still another island.

"You haven't been sleeping," she said. "Who was she?" And she winked at both her sailor and me across our streetside table and our empty wine bottles. "Not another woman, I hope, like that Julie of yours."

It is only the ironies that make sense. We had time, I said, for one more bottle; then we must hurry. My pilot was paid by the hour. We had skies to ride, seas to cross. The blood does quicken, there on Cos. I almost hated to leave.

"Just don't ask any favors," I said to Karen. I tried to move my right hand and forearm the way Greeks do, a quick, stirring motion, suggesting volumes unspoken, unspeakable.

I smiled at the naked German sailor.

IN WHICH DORF CLAIMS TO UNDERSTAND
AN OCTOPUS

*A*nd we found her island, down there below us in the Aegean, among the Cyclades. We saw the terraced slopes of the stark hills, the abandoned fields, the impossible white of the hilltop and seaside chapels of Sifnos.

What am I to say? What is there to say, ever? After love, one is weary.

We landed. My helicopter pilot found a stretch of wet sand between a beach and a chapel. We took our bags and cameras and walked among sun-baked bodies, Karen and I. Bodies in the last, late slant of light, clay figures put out to dry. We stepped more than walked, Karen leading the way. And I wasn't surprised when she met an "old friend" at a sidewalk cafe under the trees, there at the water's edge in the tiny port of Kamares. I wasn't surprised at all.

I learned to go naked in this world, there on the island of Sifnos, and for all that I am wistfully grateful. Karen's friend, a graduate student who claimed to be studying Homer but who had neglected to bring his books, shared a stone windmill, shares it still, even now shares it every summer with four of Karen's fellow teachers from Mount Royal College, there in Calgary. Strangers from home, you might say.

They are content to live together, all five of them; each summer they are friends, a family, and each summer they know what their summer will bring, what horrors it will enable them to escape. They abandon the idea of knowledge. They have no need for names. They drink together, loaf in sidewalk cafes together, wash clothes together, talk and laugh together, quarrel together, shit and piss together, sleep together, buy goat meat and eggs and tomatoes and olives and squid and bread and eggplants and green beans together, sunburn together, walk naked on this sated earth together.

What is there to add?

Karen and I took rooms in Artemon, the village adjoining the windmill. The windmill has no sails; it is a circular stone structure that rides the crest of a high hill and holds out four stiff arms. We took a bus, late each morning, all seven of us together. We stood in the crowded bus and jostled and joked our way along a ridge-top path that claimed to be a road. We risked our lives each morning down the crooked ridge to the village of Kastro. And when the driver finally gave up, at the edge of a cliff where the village also hesitates, we shouldered our packs full of melon and feta and bread and retsina and ouzo, and we scrambled our way down to a small white chapel, to an outreach of naked rock on the sea's rim.

I was with that group, always, the graduate student and those five women. Or I was alone. I was thinking back to Portugal. The temptation of somewhere else that is our home, these times. It took me a full three days to learn to be as naked as the others, there on that grey-brown rock in the chapel's protection. And after that there was no stopping me.

I took to eating feta and bread and drinking retsina while in my birthday suit. As did we all. Karen, stretched out naked on the rocks, half swilled on ouzo, developed the habit of saying, "Let's get drunk and fuck." This, with her eyes shut. As if she addressed the remark to no one in particular, or to anyone. The dear pot-bellied graduate student quite abandoned his talk of Odysseus' travels and took to sitting at Karen's right hand, listening as if she must be some new Buddha, flat on her back, about to unveil the secrets of the maudlin universe.

Karen's female friends, two or three of whom proved to have quite marvelous bodies of their own, were constantly inviting me to go for a swim. This, especially, when I, provoked by the blistering sun, developed something of an erection. "Watch out for sunstroke, Dorf," one of them would say. And offer to cover me with a towel that advertised an Alberta beer.

We are all exiles, sometimes even from our own hands. Even to strike back is to seek.

I found a fellow sufferer one afternoon while swimming alone, diving alone on the opposite side of the chapel from the attentive scholar and his bevy of ladies. I dove into the pulsing water and found a beautiful shell. A large shell, old and encrusted. A conch, perhaps. I have never bought a collection of shells for Deemer.

I lifted the shell from the sea's bottom, held it in one hand, carefully swam to the surface. I surfaced and looked into my shell.

And the octopus was there inside.

We have all of us, now, learned to rejoice in silence. And silently. I swam ashore and clambered up and then eased myself onto the heat of the rocks.

Octopus vulgaris. A renowned adaptation to the cruelty of life and its abrupt endings. That vulnerable creature. Invertebrate. No fins. No shell. The configuration of zero. Deny and refuse. Only its complex eyes. Its eight wavering arms. Its remarkable mind.

I was sitting there in the sun, using my own body to shade the octopus in its borrowed shell, when the graduate student and Karen came around the corner of the chapel, no doubt to act on Karen's often repeated injunction. Except that now they were followed by four other naked bodies as well.

I was naked, perfectly and unashamedly naked myself, and I wanted my friends to share with me my discovery. "In the male octopus," I said, loudly and precisely, sounding learned to assure the graduate student, holding out in one hand the shell as I did so, "the right third arm is modified to function as a sex organ, what is usually referred to as the *hectocotylus* ..."

I raised the third finger of my right hand. I wanted my friends to share my discovery, and instead they screamed. They saw the octopus and screamed. Such a scampering of bare asses I have seldom witnessed. A herd of frightened buttocks. They screamed like harridans, all my friends, including the portly graduate student; they shouted at me to go away and they made animal noises and in the revulsion that they managed to communicate I dropped the shell and its occupant.

That the octopus fell onto my groin, there were I sat on the barren rocks, was pure accident. What startled me was not the fall itself, but rather my own calm. The octopus fastened itself to my damp body. It was unimaginably cool, a cool poem I later explained to the ignorant student, not a study of a poem but the poem itself, finding me. And the octopus had found me, not I it. The adhesive suckers on the eight arms of that octopus adhered. They stuck to me. I tried gently to lift the octopus off my scrotum and my retracting penis, out of my pubic hair, out of the discovered crack of my ass. And the suckers adhered.

Is not life itself our own vexed adhesion to what we do not comprehend? Perhaps I did not sit there long, but in the long-seeming and cool and fast embrace of that octopus I had time to count arms, so to speak, the holdings I thought had plagued me: Deemer, Julie, de Medeiros, Karen perhaps, my sisters, my children, my devotion to work. And I realized the octopus-embrace of that troubled being was all I had. It was all I was. Those reachings to each other, tremulous, confused, mistaken, are as much the divine intimacies of nature as were the infinite small kisses of that octopus.

I might have sat there, at peace with myself, forever, had not the meddling graduate student come with a sack of water. He had filled a large green plastic bag with water from the sea, and unceremoniously dumped the water between my legs. I jumped about six feet.

And then I saw, realized, understood, that the octopus knew instinctively where to find the sea. Over the dry rocks it moved, over the washed pebbles at the water's edge, directly toward the water. And in that moving I saw the harmony of the octopus, its perfect accord with the violence that threatened it everywhere. I saw its motion, its stealth, its courage, its accurate sense of purpose. Its eight arms all at once working and necessary. I saw its vulnerable beauty, its subtle change of color. I saw it disappear, perfectly, into the safe sea.

NEGATIVE #4:
DORF UPDATES
HIS JOURNAL

*T*he Aegean was perfectly calm. Absolutely calm. There wasn't a ripple anywhere from the bow of the "Saint George" to the horizon; even our wake was a passing mirage on the certainty of the sea's calm. And there wasn't so much as a trace of cloud in the sky. Karen, in that light, that heat, decided she must work on her tan again. She was always "working on" her tan, if nothing else. She slipped the top of her bikini under her MAKE DO T-shirt; then she wiggled and squirmed her way out of the T-shirt and handed it up to me where I sat high in the stern of a lifeboat, above that monstrous crowd of passengers, being mariner and scribe.

I had fished my journal out of my bags. I wrapped Karen's T-shirt around my head, then adjusted my position so that the shade of my enlarged head cast a shadow over the white page. I became a kind of octopus.

I sat alone in the lifeboat's stern, glancing to seaward, then down to the page. I was writing and scratching out and writing, trying to explain to myself however it was that Julie Magnuson disappeared from our Algarve hotel. I took it as a reflection on me, not an indication of her headstrong ways. It was for that reason, in my absent-mindedness during those six hours, that I got too much sun. Even while Karen, below me on the crowded deck, pretending to sun herself, drank too much Loutraki water and too much wine.

I was the last person on the "Saint George" to notice we were sliding into the harbor, there in Piraeus. "Hey, navigator, wake up!" Karen shouted. We began to don our clothes again. It was the clothing, the awfulness of shirts and skirts, of mere trousers and stocking and shoes, that turned us against the impaled desire of the voyage. We pressed abruptly into the animal passage down the gangplank, onto mere land. We heard, distantly at first, the raucous guarantees of the waiting cab drivers.

And after all that, starting to shiver, I imagined sleep. But I wouldn't accept Karen's suggestion that we spend the night at a party in Athens and catch a flight next day. "No," I said, "no, let's take the train. In the morning, when we wake up, we'll be in Salonika; we'll be rested; we'll both feel a lot better."

We went to the station, there in Athens. A good connection. We lugged our bags out onto the platform where the rows of young travelers lie on their sleeping bags, lie resting or sleeping, waiting like so many casualties for trains to God knows where. We all need a spa I told Karen.

The trouble was we couldn't get a berth on that crowded train. We sat in a compartment for eight, ten of us, under the small racks heaped with our luggage. The heat continued all night. Cheek by jowl we sat. Karen had a hangover that would have killed an ox, and wanted to throw up, and didn't want to throw up. While I shook, and then dozed, and then shook again. And four soldiers, on their way back to the Turkish frontier, all of them together, lusted after Karen in their various dialects. And the smell of tobacco and sweat and souvlaki combined with the wine-stink of Karen's irregular breath when she put her head on my shoulder. And a little girl, traveling with her ancient grandparents, carrying her pet chicken in a brown paper bag, let the chicken amuse itself by pecking at my right knee. And a youngish man from Crete, transporting fifteen canaries in a large cage, placed the cage on the floor exactly where my feet might comfortably have been.

The inside walls of the birdcage were lined with sheets of newspaper. The Cretan, as the night became hotter, poked more holes into the daily news. But it was I who peeked through the poked holes; it was I who indicated one of the canaries was dying or dead; I tilted my head and let my tongue hang out.

That's the way it was. We rode. And swayed. And joggled. And somewhere in far places we stopped, and waited, and started again. The Cretan, who spoke some English, assured me we had passed Mount Olympus and the beautiful valley of the Lapisa. "A verdant valley," he said. "Verdant," he said, his word, against the corroding heat of the night. "No shit," I said. Our bodies rattled. We might all be going to Laspi. And I wrote in my journal. Only I did not write this time, Karen asleep on my shoulder, the train jolting my hand; I printed in capital letters, printed a passing message to the stilled world outside

DAWN COMES TO THE MORNING STOP THE BAY THAT IS CALLED THERMAIKOS AND THE BAY THAT IS HOTLY THERE TWO BOYS SELLING SOUVLAKI YOGURT ICE CREAM STOP THE SWEAT OF OUR TOSSED BODIES AND OUTSIDE NOW WHILE OTHERS SLEEP THE VINEYARDS GREEN THE COTTON PLANTS THE ROWS AND ROWS OF STOP SO GREEN THE FIELDS OF EGGPLANTS BEANS AND MELONS OR OF WHEAT THE DAILY LIFE OR LIVING STOP ITS DAILY STOP AND THE VINED CUCUMBERS THE FIRST APARTMENTS AND CITY BYZANTINE THE WALL AND CROUCHING TOWER STOP

in my journal. Those are the words I found in my journal. As if to send a telegram. And we took a cab to the bus depot on Langathas Avenue, there in Thessaloniki. "Let's throw away our passports," I said to Karen. "You must be nuts," she groaned. And we found a kiosk selling aspirin. And the ten o'clock bus to Kavala

AND STARTING THEN STOP FROM SALONIKA INTO THE GRAVEYARD DISTRICT WHERE THE DEAD LIVE IN EXCELLENT ORDER AND OUT INTO FIELDS OF PASTA WHEAT AND KAREN TRYING TO STAY AWAKE AND NOT SUCCEEDING AND TRYING NOT TO SLEEP AND NOT SUCCEEDING STOP SOLDIERS ON A LONG BEACH PLAYING A WAR HITTING THE BEACH

IN LANDING CRAFT AND HELICOPTERS CLOSE
ABOVE AND SUNBATHERS WATCHING STOP
AND UP OVER STOP DOWN THE HILL STOP
THE SPANNING AQUEDUCT OF ROMAN TIME A
RIVER RAISED TO SKY BLUE OVER STOP THE
OLD WALL OF THE OLD CITY UP OVER THE
WHITE HOUSES OVER THE HARBORED BOATS
AND THEN DE MEDEIROS DO NOT STOP SO
MUCH AS STOP TRY TO FOLLOW HERE OR
CATCH

and I had, all day, all through the day of Karen's hangover, the
notion that I was writing telegrams. She did not speak, could
hardly get her tongue out of her mouth, or in, and I wrote and
wrote. We could not get a room in the Galaxy Hotel. "What
happened to our hurry?" Karen managed to whisper. The old
aqueduct of Sultan Soleyman the Magnificent snakes its long
way over the city, high on its pillars and arches. We found a
cheap room underneath where no one asked for our passports.
Karen slept the sleep of the damned. And woke up needing
coffee.

BATHED IN THE BASIN DOWN THE HALL STOP
AND WALKED TO HARBOR WHERE ISLAND
FERRYBOATS WAIT TO THASSOS LET'S GO I
SAID STOP YOU IDIOT KAREN TO ME STOP
WHICH RESTAURANT THE OUTDOOR TABLES
THERE THE CITY ARRANGED ABOVE OUR
COFFEE SO AN ANCIENT THEATER IN STONY
TIERS AND STOP THE FISHING BOATS AND
SQUID AND OCTOPUS AND THE LONG NETS
SAFFRON AND OR RIPE AS YELLOW RED AND
DRYING IN THE SUN AN OLD MAN MENDING
STOP BASKETS OF THE SMELL OF FISH RED
MULLET AND SUPPER IN A TAVERNA STOP
KEFTETHES AND FRENCH FRIES A SLICE OF
FETA STOP THE WAITER ASKING TWICE NO
WINE STOP NO AND I LAY AWAKE OUR TWO

BEDS MOST OF THE NIGHT ONE ROOM THE HEAT STOP HOPING STOP A TORRENTIAL RAIN A MINOR STOP EARTHQUAKE STOP

And we got up with the sun, out of our two small beds. We washed the sweat off our faces. We nursed our Greek coffee and ate fresh bread with butter and honey.

And still we were too early at the bus depot. Trying to find someone who might explain the schedule to us, we had the good fortune to meet a Greek who had once worked in Calgary. "Ah," he said. "Calgary. The paradise of which I dreamed."

"You went there?" Karen said.

"Yes," he said.

"But you left," Karen said.

"Yes," he said.

"Then it wasn't paradise?"

"Yes," he said.

Karen was confused. I saw she was looking at his biceps, not listening to what he had to say. I was compelled to break in and ask about Laspi.

"Ah," he said, "Laspi. Yes."

It was that Greek, a sailor from Calgary, who told us where to get off the bus, where to take a cab to Laspi. His name was Dimitrios Galanopoulos, which he wrote, when we could find no other paper, on a page in my journal. But he gave no address, no telephone number. He insisted on explaining everything to Karen, not to me, even though I asked all the questions. His mother went to Laspi once each year; she was, each year, in the course of a week, cured of a skin disease which I took from his description to be nothing more than eczema.

We boarded the bus. We charged out into the countryside as if the bus was a tank, we the invaders. Except that all of a sudden the driver stopped, signaled us to get off. We stood there, at a "Y" in the road in Crenides, Karen and I, not knowing which way to go. Karen wanted to turn back.

"I'm carrying your ton of equipment," I said. "Relax." And then I saw a cab, two men in the back seat, two faces looking like the pox returned from the Middle Ages. "Here we go," I said, and I shouted, waved, damned near got run over when the cab backed up.

We crowded our way into that cab with its two corpses. We rode with those two ruins through ruins of another kind, marble and brick and stone. And Karen liked that part of the ride. She loved it. She hung halfway out of a window, either to see the sites or to get away from the smell. I couldn't tell which.

We swung off the paved road onto gravel and dirt. We were let out by the cabbie on the dusty track just at the edge of the spa. He refused to drive in under the cluster of tall trees that marked the entrance to our destination. He refused. And he was gone by the time Karen and I bent down and somehow managed to pick up all our bags. We stumbled in at the lane, following the two sprightly old corpses that disappeared ahead of us.

DORF, ARRIVED,
DOES NOT REALIZE
HE HAS ARRIVED

*A*nd then we saw the tents. They were scattered in among the trees. We might have come to a refugee camp, not a spa. Ragged children played in the thin shade, in the dust; there was hardly a blade of grass to be found. Beyond the tents, we could see, were a few makeshift tables and benches. We walked through the scattering of tents, old tents and small, staked to the bare ground, tied for support to the listless trees. Laundry hung on the tent ropes to dry. Ragged clothing. Ragged towels.

At the tables there were men, men only, playing cards or eating; and there were a few men, also, who sat or stood and only watched the men who played or ate. The children watched us from behind each other. The men did not look at us at all.

"What the hell are we doing here?" Karen said.

"This is it," I said.

"This is it all right," Karen said.

"We've found it," I said. "Hang in." I hadn't slept in days; I was just getting over my sunstroke. Even the mulberry trees, in that camp, were suffering from the heat. The dust that we stirred just hung in the air, too weary to fall. "Let's make some inquiries," I said.

I did my damnedest to ask about the smelly woman. But there wasn't so much as one adult woman around, no one to whom I could speak or point or plead. I got a bit excited, I guess, and that drew the attention of two or three of the men who weren't eating tomatoes or playing cards. I tried to describe the woman I was seeking. I had no language. I held my nose and made a noise. That at least made the children laugh. They thought I was imitating a donkey. They backed away from me, laughing; I could see that Karen was trying to pretend she didn't know me.

Actually, the place did stink. It smelled of something infinitely old and decomposed. And it wasn't a bad smell. In all that dust and heat the smell was of something damp and earthy. Something marshy and cool.

A high wooden fence, apparently knocked together during the night by a blind carpenter, shut off the second side of the small triangular space in which the tables were set up. On the third was a low building, almost a shed, from which an elderly man limped periodically, bringing out food and soft drinks and wine to the men at the tables. Even he, I noticed, gave the high, unpainted fence a wide berth.

It was that man who brought us the food. Abruptly we were presented with bowls of eggs, tomatoes, onion slices, olives, bread, peaches, pears. It was indicated to us that we were to sit down. We were overwhelmed with food. And just as abruptly as the food arrived, I was hungry. I was starving hungry. I dug in.

"Look at the flies," Karen said. "Flies, flies, flies everywhere. Can't you *see* the flies?"

"The flies be damned," I said, stuffing my mouth with the best tomato I ever tasted in my whole life. "Eat up."

"This Coke is vile," Karen said.

I indicated to the man that I wanted wine. I pointed to another man's bottle.

That other man, now, insisted that I have some of his wine. He pushed his bottle at me, would not take no for an answer. I brushed the flies away. I took a swig from the bottle. It was great wine. I said as much both to Karen and to the bottle's owner. He took a swig. Karen wouldn't touch the bottle. I took a swig.

We had pretty much finished that bottle, the stranger and I, by the time mine arrived on a tin tray with two sticky glasses. We proceeded directly from his empty bottle to my full bottle. Karen was pretending to be a teetotaler, drinking instead her vile Coke.

I would have been content to sit there forever, eating and drinking. The olives were perfect. The big white slices of onion were perfect. Now the children were losing their shyness or their fear and they came closer, forming a neat circle around me while I ate. I made faces while I gulped down the food, showing my pleasure. The children giggled and laughed.

It was because of those children that I didn't notice the other men had finished eating, had put away their playing cards. One man leaned toward me, lifted his wrist in front of me, tapped significantly at the face of his old wristwatch.

And just at that moment a door in the high wooden fence banged open.

I should have been ready for that, I guess.

Out came a stream of women. Through that door, that gate. Out came women, and then more women, their heads wrapped in towels or their wet hair shining. Their cheeks aglow with the world's first wonder, their skirts and blouses and shawls and towels the original colors of the rainbow itself.

Oh, they were a strange crew too. Some of those women came hobbling through the door on sticks. Some had real canes. Some were supported by others, led by others, a blind woman holding hands with a woman who was equally blind. Out they came. There were tall women, short women, old women and young; there were girls too young for suffering, hardly women at all. There were bent old hags, stooped and broken and twisted women. There were fat women who pushed their fat before them, through the gate, women who hauled it behind. There were gaunt women too, racks of bones. Bloated women. Blotched women and scarred women and a woman who was bald. They came through that door, that gate, in no great rush, some of them hardly making it at all. They were the sick and the suffering, the injured and the hurt. But something had happened behind that fence. They were all of them newly washed and shining, spick and span, even their old clothes looked reassured. Their old-fashioned skirts and their faded blouses and their worn-out shoes. They were brand-new women, newly created, newly hatched from the cosmic egg or whatever, hot off the press of creation, as newly minted as silver coins.

And then I realized that the noise of those shining women had closed my ears. What a din they made in their laughter, their talk. I was being told something by the limping old man who stood at my shoulder. He had a bad knee. He gave me a tap or a poke.

Karen poked me from the other side. "Dorf," she was saying. Shouting in my ear. "You aren't going to *do* it?"

Just that abruptly, the men were caught up in a command that had not been spoken. I was caught up in it myself. I had hardly time to push my wine bottle at Karen. A man stopped me, pointed at me and then at Karen's Greek-island bag. She had in it, over the top of it, a towel. I snatched up the towel and joined the line of men and fumbled in my pockets for some loose change.

AND NOW DORF IS IN
FOR A SURPRISE

We lined up at the gate, all of us men. And what a sight we made of it. We were a walking ad for the washday blues. We were a road-construction gang, ten threshing crews from the dirty thirties. We were the people who miss every bus on a wet and muddy street with a lot of traffic passing. We were a soup line. We were the ragtag survivors of Napoleon's visit to Moscow.

We were the bearers of human ache.

And a joshing good time we had of it; those men were proud of me. We laughed and joked. I didn't understand a single damned word of what they were saying, but I knew and I understood. We were brothers in our misery. We chuckled. We smiled. We were shy, too, with each other. Someone tried to pay my drachmas for me to the limping man at the gate; a tiny old man with scars all over his face and four coins in his hand wanted to pay my way and I let him do it, both of us pleased by that.

Inside the gate I saw the blackest black pit I have ever seen in my life. It was about as far across as I could throw a baseball. On our side was the fence. All around the other sides was a growth of tall plants, some kind of marsh grass or bamboo, hugely tall grass that obscured the landscape, that concealed and contained, entirely, the pit.

There were nails in the plank wall. There was a row of nails at about head height. Each man went to a nail and hung up his towel and began to undress; we were on a narrow strip of high ground between the wall and the mud itself.

Those bodies were something to remember. They were, first of all, a shocking white. Except for the hands and faces and necks and the pubic hair. I was the only person there with a tan.

And they were every shape but the right one, those bodies. The shanks too thin, the bellies gone slack. The hands gnarled, the feet splayed; shoulders broken down over sunken chests. Yes, I stood there, reluctant to take off my clothes, and I knew what work and disease and age will do for the human body.

I hooked my towel onto its nail. I took off my shoes and socks. I hung my pants over the towel, my shirt over the pants. I took off my shorts.

A metal ladder, coated in dry mud, led steeply down from our high bank and into the pit. The first man, backing his way down the ladder, holding onto the metal rails, eased his feet, then his legs, into the thick mud. He gave a loud sigh of relief.

The mud was buoyant. It wasn't so much mud as a thick black paste of the kind I had seen in pigpens. Except there was a whole pond of it, flat and shining in the blind light and unwittingly waiting for all of us.

There were cables strung across the pit. I hadn't seen them at first; they were sagged down into the mud itself. The first man took hold of a cable and began to pull himself along it out toward the center of the pit.

Now the men were crowding their way down the ladder into the mud, pushing each other, hastening each other, talking, laughing.

I was the only man left outside. There I stood, bare-assed naked, at the top of the ladder, my prick hanging out. I couldn't do it. I couldn't quite immerse myself in that stinking thick mud where all the sick and the maimed did their suffering and their hoping. And their pissing and their bleeding and their farting. I couldn't do it.

A huge old man, huge and fat, with stringy long hair, a figure that hardly seemed human, raised up a fat arm out of the mud. The arm, pure black with mud. He waved to me, signaled to me to come in. Then, with his mud-covered hand, he drew a design on his face. He drew a circle on his face with his face inside the circle. Then he put a dab of mud above each eye. Only it wasn't a dab of mud. There, around each dab, around each of his eyes, he drew an eye.

And then the others began to imitate their leader. The

others began to turn their heads into masks, into sculptures, into faces that were faces other than their own. They were doing that for me, I realized. To give me courage. I looked down at all those floating heads on the mud, and suddenly they were beautiful; those men were strong and powerful and handsome again. They were, some of them, tragic, some comic; some were wisely old; some were young, but intelligently young. And the oldest man, the one who was first to signal me, drew a pattern on his head. Over the thin and straggly hair of his head. He drew a pattern that neither he nor I could see. Then he tipped his head toward me.

He had pictured an opening on his head. A cunt. As if he was to be born out of his own head. As if he had figured a way to escape the world. Or enter it. The thickened lines that were the lips, that opened and closed.

And I knew what I had to do. I went down the ladder. I went down, not with my ass foremost as the others had; I managed, hanging onto the rail, to approach that mud prick first.

I have never been so shriveled and shrunk, I must admit, in my whole life. Put a string on it, as we used to say in Edenwolf, when the weather was thirty below. But I went down the ladder. I put my left toe into the mud. And it felt good, that stinking, thick mud. I had both feet in the mud, then I looked down and saw my left knee disappear. And I pushed my right knee after it. And the mud came up my goose-pimpled thighs. And the bush of me was in the mud, and a shiver went through my whole body.

I was belly deep in the mud, armpit deep. I had to suck in my breath against the outside pressure of mud. I took hold of one of the cables. I began to pull myself out into the pool or pit of mud. Someone took hold of my arm to help me, touched my clean shoulder with a muddy hand, and left his hand there, the mark of it. Then someone else was helping. The silence was complete. They handed me along, pushed me, helped me along until the first person who had signaled me out of my hesitation was a head facing my own, there in the middle of the mud; two rheumy, pus-encrusted eyes, inside the eyes that were large, owlish, totemic.

He was the man with the cunt on his head. He raised up his right hand. He raised up his muddy hand and the hand was full of mud. He put the handful of mud on my head. My clean hair, somewhat bushy in the heat but always neatly groomed, always clean, was abruptly full of mud. The mud felt good on my head.

The man facing me took in each hand a handful of mud. He raised both of his hands to my head. Again, he put the mud on my head. I held still. Again he raised up mud and put it on my head. He was not only placing the mud there, he was somehow shaping it. He took my two hands, then, out of the mud, and with his hands he raised mine, made me touch the top of my head.

He had made a dunce cap on my head, that man. A pointed cap of good, rich mud. He spoke a word. In Greek, of course. You have never heard such a cheer as the one I got from those men. They accepted me. I was joined with them. I drew a mask on my face. A simple mask. Circles around my eyes. Circles around my ears. A happy smile around my mouth. Some of the men raised up their muddy hands out of the thick mud and ponderously and slowly they clapped, laughing at the same time. I had drawn my mask and I was one of the floating heads.

We were floating heads, all of us, joined in the mud, joined to the mud. In that mud, there, up to my neck, to my chin, I realized, for the first time in my life, my mud self. I was in touch with the world. My heart was warm inside me; the world was my body. My whole body became a heart, a heart beating in the mud world. I dabbed two mud tears, one under each real eye, inside each eye's circle. That was my weeping. My body was deep in the mud and yet afloat, buoyed into its being of mud by the mud of being, under the hot Greek sun in the mud it shared with the other bodies. Deeply, I farted, steady and strong, shitting a little, possibly, and a smile grew inside the smile I had painted on my new face.

THE ARCHEOLOGY
OF HOPE:
AND THESE THE SHARDS
FROM A JOURNAL
THAT WILLIAM WILLIAM DORFEN KEPT
BUT DID NOT KEEP

I can only say I nearly cried when the whistle blew.

We crawled up that ladder, each and every one of us reluctant. We went in single file toward a building, or a roof rather, without walls, that turned out to be the washhouse.

I hated that blast of cold, clear water. We went through a series of showers in single file, moving forward all the while, slowly, heads bowed under the blast while we rubbed our own bodies with soap, rubbed each other's bodies, catching a spot of mud here or there, on a back, on a hip, and I hated that water for what it was doing. I dried myself, dressed. I went through the gate with that straggling row of men, all of us shining and loud, yet all of us hating the mere world, too, for waiting, outside the gate.

And believe me, Karen was waiting.

We had a knock-down argument. Karen had got hold of a taxi while I was in the mud. She'd caught a cabbie who was bringing another customer, and she'd put our bags in the cab and was waiting for me while the cabbie kept his motor running.

"We're staying," I said.

"You're out of your tree," she said.

"I've never been so sane," I said. "This is it."

"It's a miracle your doctor hasn't locked you up," she said.

"What doctor?"

"That doctor."

"I don't have a doctor," I said. "I don't need a doctor."

"Madeira," she said.

"Not *Madeira*," I said. "De Medeiros. Dr. de Medeiros, one of the finest spa doctors of this century, possibly the best, renowned for his cures for various malfunctions. Perhaps you should see him about your inability to tell a cock from a flagpole."

"I look at you," she said. She made a feint, as if to kick me where most I live. "You don't do anything but run away."

"I spend my life seeking," I said, "and I don't avoid what I find."

"You don't even avoid what you avoid. You just let things happen."

"Try me," I said.

"Try *this*," she said. And she seized the handle of the door, damned near tore the old car door off its rusty hinges. The cabbie flinched, hearing metal squeal.

"Once more," I announced. I turned away from the open door. "Once more, and then, once more again."

"Go *wallow*," she said.

Karen deserted me. She left me alone in Laspi for the day. We'd noticed a lot of ruins along the road, acres of cracked marble, crumbling brick, broken stone, on our drive to my spa. Everything that she loves in life. She prefers the dead to the merely wounded. She'd lectured me and the two corpses with us on the way out, pointing to a city that we couldn't see. No ingrown toenails there. Only rubble. "Philippi," she'd explained. "Mining-center, once, to the Pangaeus goldfields and basis to the conquering of all Persia. Built right here by Philip II of Macedon."

I'd made the mistake of saying, "Oh, him. The father of Alexander the Great. Deemer would be fascinated."

I was content in the knowledge that within a mere two hours it would again be the men's turn to go into the profound and immeasurable mud. I had time to sit and relax. I found an empty bench under a mulberry tree. At first I sat down; then I lay down, stretched out on the bench with my wallet opened over my face to keep out the light that filtered down through the leaves. The world was my oyster; I had not even the annoyance of language to deal with; there wasn't a word I could exchange with those kind people. No one knew so much as my name. No telegrams, there, from Manny, from Deemer, from anyone. I was delighted, even, at Karen's sense of repugnance. She could waste all her film on the splendid ruins of Philip's golden city, its pillars that held up nothing, its stairways into the blank sky, its mosaic floors hidden beneath the weeds, its marvelously preserved latrines.

I slept like a log. When the men woke me to go back into the mud I was refreshed beyond all expectations. I was into the mud this time, no hesitating, and the man who had lured me earlier only smiled now, smiled his bad teeth white in approval; that fat old man indicated that I was to cover my face this time. No designs, no caps, no mappings. I covered the top of my head. I let the mud run its slow course down from my head and hair, around my ears, into my eyebrows now. And when the mud was too slow, I dabbed and daubed; I plastered mud to my cheeks and chin; I began to build my neck shut, sloping the rich mud carefully from the ears in a curve down to my shoulders. I built myself of mud, and sturdily too. There was a texture to the creating mud; it had a fiber in it, after all, a quality of shredded grass, of rotted roots and leaves; and the fiber held the dark mud's flow. My protector, there in the mud, gave his approval with a nod that almost submerged his own huge head into our consuming mud. The other men, around me, were pleased. They looked like senators, their floating heads become the living busts of the Romans who conquered the Greeks. They looked like the bishops who followed the Romans. They spoke, learnedly and considerately, to each other, those floating heads. Those transformed men.

To tell the truth, I forgot about time. I was vaguely aware, responsibly aware, that Karen must return. I made arrangements. I was playing cards with a group of men when she showed up, lugging her cameras and looking sweaty and scalded.

"Kah-lee-SPEH-rah," I said, carefully. "Good evening."

"How's that?" she said.

"I'm not ready to leave," I said.

"Nor am I," she said.

I damned near dropped my cards. Karen Strike had agreed with something I wanted to do.

"Are you all right?" I said.

"Never felt better," she said. "You should come see the ruins tomorrow." She pointed vaguely out past the high wooden fence. "Right there," she said, "Antony won a great battle. And Brutus and Cassius lost." She was ready to shed tears of joy, thinking of the red ground littered with dying men. "And I was in the place," she said, "in Philippi," as if her Philippi still existed, "where St. Paul was thrown in the jug. For the first Christian preaching, ever, in Europe." Her face glowed, not with a prisoner's pain, but with a captor's fierce pleasure. "A terrible hole of stone and dark."

"We pay the price," I said, "for our ideas."

Karen was too busy with her ignorant fantasies to hear that little clue to my frame of mind.

"Tomorrow," she said, "the ancient theater. There's a motel of sorts, I noticed, just down the road."

"Not necessary, my dear," I said.

I gave my cards to the man who was sitting beside me; I pointed, indicating he should take my coins as well as my cards; I stood up from the table.

And then Karen was horrified again. This time at the sight of the two bunks I had managed to rent while she was taking pictures of broken pottery. Two cots, side by side, with maybe eight inches of space between them, in what she referred to as the hogpen. The gentle old man in charge, recognizing her squeamishness, pinned up a ragged army blanket onto a wire so that we might have a cubicle to ourselves, or at least a stall.

A lot of people slept in that old building that during the day was mostly used for preparing food and serving drinks. The cots were jammed together, with hardly space between for people to undress or to put down their few sacks and cardboard boxes. In the night we heard the old being old, the sick being sick, the lame being lame on their way to the back door, the vomiters vomiting, the scratchers scratching, the coughers coughing and hacking and spitting into tin cans, the criers crying, the possessed speaking to their ghosts and phantoms and possessors. It was like that. By three in the morning I had sort of got used to it. The place was more or less quiet. I whispered as much to Karen, and she agreed. Then I suggested that we both of us get into one cot, either hers or mine, I didn't mind which. Then it was her turn to throw a little fit, expressing her revulsion, wondering how I could do anything but weep in the situation we were in. "Look at these people," she whispered.

"I heard them," I said. "Some of them were making love."

"You must be looney," she said.

"I'm feeling muddily human," I whispered in return. Across the space between our cots. Leaning there, into the dark, wanting to be touched, discovered, held. "Deep down, I mean."

"Mildly?" she asked.

"Muddily," I said. "I want my daughters to find me here."

Karen likes her history mean. She was dying to stay there with me, but instead of admitting as much she said she would sit it out, endure, wait for me to come to my senses, wait to show my two daughters not the mud but the antiquities.

I refused to argue. I pretended to be sleeping.

Actually, I did doze off for a little.

I woke up just in time for the men's first visit to the mud.

TO ACT
AS A MAN OF ACTION:
AND PHILIP II

*D*uring the next few days I became something of a cardsharp,
there in Laspi, but a sharp of a very special sort. The patient men
taught me the game while the women were taking their turn in
the mud. We played a game that was almost pinochle, something
I'd played as a kid in Edenwolf, except that I couldn't remember
all the rules. We gambled for small coins. There at the tables,
out of doors, in the sunlight, in Laspi. We gambled and I lost. It
was not at all like my disastrous losses in Baden-Baden at those
gaming tables where rich women brought out folded bills from
between their perfumed breasts and elegant men learned to
sweat in public. Hour after hour I went on losing, but only out
of a natural generosity. I was grateful to those suffering men for
allowing me into their midst.

My two daughters, as I had arranged from Sifnos, were
scheduled to fly in shortly. Into Salonika from the States; to
spend their annual vacation with their errant father. Karen said
she would go into Salonika and meet their flight if I agreed to
leave Laspi one day after their arrival. Or two days at most. She
wanted to show them Philip's theater and take them to a play
right there on the ancient site; she wanted them to see the
temples or tombs or whatever, and the ruins of the Christian
basilica that was built on the Greek and Roman ruins, and the
ruins that were built on the ruins of the ruins.

"Any traces of a Roman spa?" I asked.

"Of course," she said. "A heap of treasures that even
Deemer couldn't steal. You should spend a few minutes having
a look."

She pretended a defiance, but she had been tempted all the same. I heard that in her voice; she was bitten, caught; she had, like Deemer, learned a longing.

Karen was become obsessed and, had I been a more dishonorable man, I would have had her in my power. She had got through her head, finally, the terrible excitement of Deemer's standstill quest. Philip II had gone out and gathered in his world; Deemer would stay put and do the same. Karen was pleased with the parallel, and bored me with it while we lay on our cots whispering against the anguish around us. She had to see the museum in Salonika, she claimed, where the treasures from the royal graves at Vergina are kept, the treasures from Philip's own grave, the gold chest and the queen's diadem and the silver vessels, the ivory heads and the milk-washed bones. The carved portrait of Alexander's father, the sad and bearded face, the crooked eye, the wise and weary man.

"He looked like you," I suggested. "Except that you don't have the beard. Or the eye."

She left at mid-morning for her rendezvous with my daughters. It would take her the good part of the day to get to Salonika, a full day to meet my daughters and see the museum and return. And I missed her, I must confess. I lay alone in our little cubicle in the hogpen, that night, listening to the distress of those who slept or tried to sleep around me. The whimperings of pain. The sighs that name a troubled rest. The anonymous screams from nowhere. The furtive cries of love.

I was my own man. I had decided, by dawn, what I must do next. Therefore, next morning, when the fateful whistle blew and the men's first visit to the pit was over, I did what I must do.

I crawled out of the mud at the whistle's command, then simply left my clothes and my towel on their allotted nail. I didn't bother to go to the washhouse. I stepped through the magic gate and walked out into the sunshine.

My friends were rather surprised at first, and could hardly refrain from smiling. The women were lined up to enter into the mud; they were, in their nodding and pointing, both tolerant and supportive of what they took to be a slight aberration, even a little folly. The children came from far and near to have a gawk at me; they left their games, their tents; they left their plates of food and their cold drinks; up out of the ditches they came, down from the trees. They had never been through the gate, and thought I must be a marvel. And yet, in the politeness of their Greek upbringing, they were at once present and silent, at most only yielding to a concealed giggle.

The mud was quick to develop its own crust in that sun. I became a strolling mud pie, a knight coated in muddy armor, a wilful clod of the earth itself; I might grow grass, grow bushes, flowers; I might become my own vegetable garden, sprouting beans and radishes; I might ask to be planted, and harvested too; I might become my own four seasons, my plowed and seeded spring, my scarecrow fall. My own green flame in the summer heat. My own stiff wintering.

The men were afraid, briefly at least, that I wouldn't wish to play cards. Such, however, was not the case. I had left my coins on the table the previous night, beside the worn deck of cards that we used. We sat down, we players, in our accustomed places; the audience gathered around. I rubbed the tips of my fingers smooth. Carefully and precisely, I dealt the cards.

JINN AND JAN ARRIVE
AND HAVE A LOOK
AT THEIR FATHER

*T*hat day was, in many ways, the happiest day of my life. I played cards with my dearest friends out in the darling sun. And I was cool, for all the heat. I was feted; and I feasted and I drank. When the hour came round I returned with my friends to the mud pit. And there we sang songs too, and were happy; I hummed along. We returned to our cards. Again, I rubbed my fingertips smooth. I could hardly speak a word of Greek, except for *"Te kanis,"* and yet we spoke to each other, all of us, through hearts and diamonds and spades and clubs, through the passing back and forth of small coins, through nods and friendly grimaces. We had a language that whole nations might envy. We formed alliances, resisted oppressors, paid tribute, exacted tribute in return, learned to win and were forced to surrender.

Imagine my disappointment, then, when a cab came racing through dust, almost to our table's edge. Imagine my heart, beating inside its muddy home; and Karen Strike, leaping from the cab. And then no one. And then my two and beautiful daughters.

The museum, Karen explained, was closed for the day. And she added appropriate oaths.

The hand had been dealt and was in progress. I couldn't at the moment stand up from the table. We had spread an old piece of flowered oilcloth over the plank table. That made it easy to brush away the dried mud that fell from my arms.

"Dad?" my younger daughter asked. Jinn. She had only turned fourteen, and in her adolescence was both young and old. "What are you doing?"

I might have answered, "Playing cards," but I said nothing.

She had that gentle way about her. She stood there, so tall for her age, her long blonde hair flowing over her shoulders, her blouse a western shirt though she had never spent a day of her life in my west, her jeans so crisply tight she must have grown inside them. Her sneakers were brand-new; she seemed embarrassed when I noticed.

I was decently coated in mud from the top of my head to my toenails.

I tried to be reasonable with the children. But the young are slow to recognize that a slight eccentricity, a slight off-centeredness, is precisely what brings the mind and the senses into focus. They crave, instead, an appalling conformity.

My older daughter, Jan, somehow recovered her tongue; she had fallen silent, as a girl of sixteen might. She was wearing a dress. A dress of some recent fashion, all in cotton and cut quite low enough to show she no longer thought herself a girl.

"Dad," she said. "Where are your clothes?"

It seemed a reasonable enough question. And yet I found it vaguely distrustful, and I took some small offense, I suppose. I was trying to play cards.

"Let me finish this hand," I said.

The people I was playing with, of course, could not understand a word of what was going on. They were sitting stiffly still, the men, staring, though not impolitely, at the two young women who presumed to address me in such a familiar and yet solicitous manner.

"What would mom say?" Jinn said.

It was apparently that simple question that prompted me to my abrupt and, apparently, unlikely action. What happened was, I either put down or dropped my cards, I am not certain which, and I leapt up. Abruptly and rudely, I'm embarrassed to say. I quite simply up and made a run for it.

It seems I leapt to my feet and went running straight for the magic gate; I banged my way through the gate, rules be damned, and made a beeline for the ladder and then, the said ladder be damned too, I made a flying leap into the mud.

There were, I would guess, nearly eighty women in the mud at the time. Eighty heads afloat on the mud's dark surface.

How they reacted to all that flying and flopping, I don't exactly know, but quite a melee developed. Human responses being as divided as they are, some of the women were against my arrival, some were for it.

A fracas developed. There in the mud, those women, expecting no gift from the sky, assumed that I, in landing on my belly in the mud, threw mud at them. They responded by throwing mud at me. But, since I had landed in such a way as to divide the group into two camps, so to speak, in throwing mud at me they came to throw mud at each other.

Two things happened.

I was somehow reminded, by the women's reaction, of the reaction of my former wife after I fired a shot or two at her lover through the screen door of her kitchen and accidentally hit the clay pot suspended over her sink holding up a fern of some sort to too much light, the fern and the cracked pot both, then, falling upon four antique Wedgwood saucers and four antique Wedgwood cups that chanced to be in the sink at the time.

Almost simultaneously with this recollection I noticed that the man who had been in the mud when first I entered was in the mud this time too. In his attempt to rise up out of the mud and stop the melee, he was climbing the ladder. He had climbed up onto the first visible rung of the ladder; he turned to face us.

He reached out his arms. He raised his arms, revealing two smallish, mud-coated breasts; or at least the breasts were smallish, considering the size of the man. And yet, struggling as I was to keep from being suffocated or drowned or merely struck dead by flying mud, I recognized that the breasts were not simply male breasts, large or small on a large and stout man, but, rather, or possibly, smallish female breasts. That man, there, was the smelly woman. Mud covered all of her body. She had coached me, day after day, in the appreciation of mud. Or he had. Manny de Medeiros, as usual, had not adequately prepared me for the experience.

I struggled toward the smelly woman. The din around my ears made any attempt at crying out a stupid gesture, the merest folly. I thought of the birds of the Algarve coast, singing the air solid with sound. I tried to struggle. Not having a cable to hang onto, while I slithered and strove, the mud simply yielded to my frantic flailing.

I realized I was being touched. As if the mud had concealed secret creatures.

Twenty hands at least, quite possibly more, found and touched my vulnerable body in that deepest mud. The hands of those women. Twenty and then more. Some in secretive delight, some in mere curiosity. Some in surest abandon.

Women with arthritis who were still, nevertheless, able to reach out. Women with back pains from lives of lifting and chopping and digging and carrying children and feeding men. Women who couldn't get pregnant. Women who feared they might have cancerous lumps or nodes or sores. Women with migraines. Women who didn't want to grow old. Women who were dying and didn't know why. Women with rashes and bruises. Women with swollen feet and stiff knees and tumors and lesions, with aching teeth and falling hair and crooked spines.

They touched me, those women. All I could see was their floating heads. Their mud-bespattered and beautiful heads, their radiant faces, there in the flying mud. I could not see their secret hands.

That I have not had an orgasm since is not of the slightest concern to me. Other privileged people have seen God or won a sweepstake. But I, there in the Laspi mud, was caressed with passion, and I, with passion, came. I came indeed. The stroking and rubbing hands, in their friendly need, turned me over. The smelly woman stopped in her trying to stop them, returned to the mud herself. I was afloat on my back; I was covered in mud, not an inch of me showed. But the touching and the fondling hands, the hands in the mud, in their loving, found all; they touched my neck and my arched back, my slightly bent knees, my thighs; they touched with eager care my pinched buttocks, my lips and ears, my mud-nuzzling groin. My balls were cradled in a dozen different hands, my innocent cock was stroked and seized and caressed and admired and reviled and yanked and twisted and encouraged and skinned alive by a dozen mud-bespattered and playful women. I can only say I had the greatest orgasm of my life. I was, briefly and perfectly, my own fountain. I cried out, no words, no names, only a pure cry of total joy and total pain.

SALONIKA

It was my daughter Jinn who first noticed the police were pursuing me. This was after we left Laspi; we were in Salonika at the time. Or at least I was.

Karen and Jinn and Jan ran from pillar to post, from Roman ruin to Byzantine church, as if they were looking for life itself. I couldn't believe their folly. Round and round they went, day and night, while I sat at a cafe table, there in Salonika, drinking ouzo and eating octopus and appreciating the idea of mud.

I had come to the still center, there in the cradle of civilization, I, the thinking man, the man who reasoned his way free of action; there I sat, alone, thinking; poor old Dorf, they said, Karen, my two daughters even; but I was learning to relax, not to be myself but to let myself be; yes, he sat in a taverna up in the old city, Castra, eating fried feta or pastitsio; he sat up there on the mountainside looking out over the city that rumbled below, the port; he knocked back his retsina; he walked down Aristotle Street, down past the Street of Alexander the Great, down to Aristotelou Square, to Tottes, his favorite open-air cafe, by the long promenade that parallels the fouled waters of Thermaikos Bay.

And there at the first table, the table nearest the water, nearest the road that separates the square from the promenade, I simply sat. Four chairs gave square arrangement to the small, round, zinc-covered table, each chair made of iron, painted white, padded a bright yellow. A brick and marble design of circles and squares, under the table, gave comfort to my feet. A tree to my left lent special shade to my special table. I, each and every afternoon, sat in my chair under that tree, my back to the platoons of tables and chairs and gaudy umbrellas arranged in careful luxury around the square.

I sat and watched the cars and the bay and the endless flow of people along the promenade. It is a place where the world goes by; all the living, and possibly the dead too. I had Greek coffee and Greek brandy; I stared out at the wide bay, at and over and beyond the American warships, their long guns tilted up at the unoffending sky; I thought mud thoughts.

I earned my first degree, the only one I completed, in art and philosophy from the University of Alberta. I was studying Heraclitus even while Jack Deemer was out in the bush murdering a partner and making his barbarian fortune. I spoke of that irony to my daughters over tiny cups of Greek coffee. Call it Turkish if you will. Jan liked the little cups, if not their contents; she began a collection right there in Salonika.

I explained to her and to Jinn, and to Karen when she wasn't watching the crotches of the young men who swaggered by; *fango,* I explained: *fango,* as the Italians call it, is either thermal mud or mineral peloids. And I am of the opinion that mud itself, not its thermal properties, is the therapeutic factor in mud, let pelotherapists say what they will. And, given a choice of one of the peats, either high moor or low, against an estuary mud, I will always choose the latter. One thinks immediately of the great peats of Marienbad, of Brückenau, of Kohlgrub, of Luragawa, of Nenndorf; and still not one is likely to surpass a sedimented mud of Cuxhaven or Harrogate. And, I explained to my listeners, in ancient Egypt mud was frequently rubbed on the skin and dried in the sun, as it is in Odessa to this very day.

They went for a walk again, down to the White Tower, Jan and Jinn and Karen, down the long, wide promenade, through the gauntlet of approving eyes.

"Jinn," I called after them. To distant ears. "In the mudbaths of Battaglia, at Héviz in Hungary, in the famous mud of Piešťany, northeast, there, of Bratislava, on the River Vah, one can be cured..."

All that to deaf ears. To far, deaf, retreating ears ... "Of rheumatic disorders. Of diseases of the nerves."

And the waiter came to my table. I pretended I wanted the bill. I paid. And I didn't leave. "Everything," I said. "Everything can be fixed up."

And I opened the menu again, the beautiful Tottes menu with the rich and elegant lady on the cover, her hatted head in profile, she not watching at all, like Julie Magnuson, not ever needing to turn her eyes onto the accusing world. And I considered: bitter ice cream with chocolate and crème de cacao. Or a peppermint shake. Or scoops and more scoops of ice cream, with pineapple and whipped cream and cherries and almonds, with peaches and the liqueur of love. I was hungry again. I turned to look for the waiter who had assumed I was leaving.

And that's when I saw her. It had to be her. It had to be Estuary. My old friend Estuary, from Banff, from everywhere, from nowhere, endlessly seeking the spa that would soothe if not cure. She was seated alone two tables back from where I was sitting; she was at a table exactly like my own, eating pastry. She was so busy with the pastry and her fork and a glass of milk that she didn't see me. One hand was on her lap, concealed in her pale blue skirt. She was sitting with her legs just slightly spread; I could see, in the small cave under her skirt, the hot green flare of her panties. She had pulled up her skirt, wrinkled the skirt on her lap, to conceal one hand. Her panties were a bursting green.

I looked again at the menu. Fireflies danced in my memory of that glowing dark. It had to be Estuary. Is distance itself, mere distance, the mere and empty gap, the first cause of desire? Estuary, seeking. And waiting, too. I held to my small patch of shade, the tree beside me, its bark light brown and a wrinkled grey, its trunk become four large branches, intertwined with each other, shading me out of the blistering sun. The sweat rolled over my eyes. I was surrounded by shadows. I must stay mud cool.

I ordered another coffee, Greek coffee, with that mud in the bottom of the cup, that brown, deep, radiating mud. I could not forget Laspi. I could not betray my smelly woman, whatever her commands, her silences ... She, he, that man or woman in the mud, that hermaphroditic creature. She ... if it matters ... he

... I should have listened ... was a floating head ... I couldn't so much as stretch my neck. I was become my own statue at my own table, under my own special tree. The shadows moved in the leafy tree. I heard them. The smelly woman gave her command. She, at once contained in the mud, emerging from the mud, containing the mud, giving the mud its center and its loud halloo; she was the mudhole goddess of all the muddy springs. Kirishima. St. Amand-les-Eaux. Beppu. Laspi ... I could not turn my anchored skull. She was and she was not language and idea, dream and reality, good and evil, Satan and God. This little world is just another mudhole in the universe.

"Jan," I called. "Jinn. I wanted nothing. I wanted only to be ... a curator." All that, to my retreating daughters. To Karen. "I only fired the gun ... because ..."

And I tried to explain to the smelly woman. I tried to confess, when she approached my cot in that ramshackle shed where I was rubbing off the mud, in Laspi. Scraping it off. I had retreated to our stall, the stall I shared with Karen, even if she would not join me. She only waited outside, holding my daughters' hands, now and then.

The smelly woman came to the stall, she stood on the other side of the blanket that hung on a sagging wire, and I tried to tell her how it was, how I had been for those few years, in upstate New York, the curator of a county museum. After I did not earn my degree from the University of Iowa for the thesis I wrote on cash registers as works of art. I had done tons of work on every kind of cash register ever manufactured. Gilded machines and silvered machines, at once both angular and curved with bells that sang to the finger touch, automatic signs that said NO CHARGE, or, in red and black, YOU PAY, with a blank after for the abrupt appearance of staid and strict numbers. Scrolled drawers and secret locks and mechanisms that confounded merchant and miser and picklock alike with their total precision. Beauty and money become each other's alibis; and it was that same thesis, flung out of court, so to speak, that landed me my first real curator's appointment. In apple-knockers' country, in maple syrup country, in the hills where a cash register gave birth to IBM. I liked that appointment and might have stayed forever in the hardwood forests and the lifting ridges of the Susquahanna River plateau, had not fate and a horny dentist intervened. And it was that thesis, failed, that cinched my job with Deemer.

I thought she was listening, the smelly woman. She had doused herself in something that smelled like carbolic acid. I couldn't see her. I thought she was hearing my confession, my tale, my small account, my evidence. I knew she understood no English. It didn't matter.

And then she reached over the blanket and its sagging wire; silently, she reached over one huge arm, slightly hairy, clean, abnormally white, and she touched the top of my head. I was rubbing the dried mud off my breasts. I stopped talking.

"You must go away," the smelly woman said. She said that, recited it, as if she could say it in six languages, had memorized that statement in six languages for all the tourists who came to gawk, and did not herself know what her saying meant. Her voice was without emotion.

But then she drew, invisibly, slowly, with one finger, the pattern of an opening on the top of my head.

I had expected Estuary to recognize me. A car pulled off the road into a parking space in front of my special table. It was, by some grotesque accident, a Mercedes; it was a quite old Mercedes, aimed straight at my table, or at my tree. Its old hubcaps bore each a blue circle containing that strange design, a triangle undone, its three sides pointing each away from the other, yet all of them meeting, joined, at once fleeing and united. The old man at the wheel was so small the car seemed, at first glance, without a driver. I turned away from the driverless car. I had nothing to hide; I had gone to my Embassy, in Lisbon; and when I tried to report the disappearance, the absence, I was told by a government clerk who only raised his

empty hands that he had no time to listen. I turned to meet
Estuary; I would meet her patient eyes, the rank, green glow of
her panties, in that fainting sun.

But Estuary was not there. Her table was deserted.

The waves. The gulls. The battleships.
It is a great fault, to know how to love.

DORF, IN THE MANNER OF SOMEONE OUTSIDE
THE LAW, SEEKS SANCTUARY

Ο ΝΤΟΡΦ, ΕΝΕΡΓΩΝΤΑΣ ΣΑΝ ΠΑΡΑΝΟΜΟΣ, ΖΗΤΑ ΑΣΥΛΟ.

*A*nd then, sitting there at my table in Tottes, listening, I heard about a collection. A collection of the skeletons of creatures from the sea. Everything from a sea horse to a dolphin. With, thrown in for good measure, what was purported to be 'the authentic skeleton of a mermaid. Deemer, I knew, would want every bone and smell and forgery of that collection; promise him one forgery in a collection and he would buy it all.

And then I discovered that I couldn't do it. I couldn't leave the city to go to whatever Turkish port was home to that treasure. Just as I couldn't write in my journal. I carried it with me, set it down on the table when I sat down. But instead of writing so much as a word, I ordered more coffee, more brandy, more retsina, more fried squid. I was looking rather heavy; even the breasts of my once gaunt body were showing signs of fullness.

Karen and Jinn and Jan were doing my traveling for me, and I paid without batting an eye. Karen included a spa or two or three in their travels, hoping to spur me into still another visit. But I wouldn't take the bait. She was become a nut on the very notion of spas, taking pictures of every glass of warm water in Macedonia. It was almost indecent, her frantic haste to take a snapshot or a moving picture of any damned dribble or drop of water that might be claimed to cure the feeblest tremble or tic; I came to feel a compassion for the woman.

And, as if that wasn't enough, I had to look at the results. That's what trapped me, in a way.

We were in my room in the Electra Palace Hotel, there on Aristotelou Square, just up from Tottes. She had scrounged or borrowed or stolen a projector; we were about to look at pale shadows on the pale wall, when my daughter stuck her head in the door.

"The cops," Jinn said. "I think they're looking for you, dad. They're downstairs at the desk asking about passports."

"Thank you, daughter," I said.

Then she noticed all of Karen's equipment.

"Looking at dirty movies?" Jinn asked.

"Looking for a man named Dorf," I said.

"I know where he is," Jinn said. "Want me to find him for you?"

"Karen thinks she's going to show me," I said. "But she has no pictures of the mud."

Jinn blew me a kiss across the room.

The prescience of the young is something of a miracle. My daughter Jinn, for whatever reasons, had guessed right. She gave me the word and skinned out; she and her sister had met a couple of bellboys who wanted to practise their English.

I might have fled immediately; I supposed I was to be brought up on some ridiculous charge of indecent exposure, given my few hours of freedom in Laspi. Word like that spreads. What was applauded on Sifnos was to be judged a criminal offense when caked in mud.

I might have fled immediately; I was ready to head out, lay low for a day or two; the cops would have other fish to fry. But I hadn't seen any of Karen's pictures. And what I wanted to see in her pictures were the pictures of myself. Billy Dorfen in Llandrindod Wells. Billy Dorfen up a tree on the island of Cos. That's the way it is, and dear Karen will always be in demand. Considering that, she should at least learn how to thread film through a projector without hanging herself in the tangle.

When the knock came at the door, I did something I will always be proud of. I knew the knock was not that of either of my daughters. I went out onto the balcony and pulled down the long venetian blind behind me. I heard through the blind the policemen enter into the room; I heard one of them try, in halting English, to interrogate Karen.

And then I crept along the balustrade that edged my balcony, half straddling the cement rail, half walking on it. I edged my way along, looking six stories down at the street, the open square. I worked my way around a partition to the next balcony. But the door to that room was closed. I had a great view, hanging out over the zero of my intent. My special table was deserted at the far edge of the busy square. Edging my way, crouched against the uneven wind, I indeed thought I was making the heroic escape I should have made from Julie's avalanche. It was the fourth balcony that led into my daughters' room. I went into their room, out timidly into the hall, fearfully down all the stairs, avoiding elevators.

Standing somewhat shaken on the pavement outside the hotel, I knew I needed the consolation of a spa. Karen had mentioned a place that she and my daughters had tried to look into, right there in Salonika; they'd offered to take me with them. At the time I'd refused to leave my cafe table, there in Tottes.

I was suffering from recollections of an earlier occasion, when three policemen came to my door and I was foolish enough to let them in. That, on a sunny afternoon, in upstate New York. The dentist, not my wife, had sent them.

I high-tailed it straight up Aristotle Street, away from the sea. Uphill and inland. I went to the food market; the place in Salonika where one might lose the devil himself. I went first into the huge building that is the Mounthianos Market.

The fish market, first. That silvery, dark place, with those broken shapes from the sea. I caught my breath at the sea-stink there. I stopped to admire an ice field covered with lobsters. I went into the gloom. Plucked chickens hung in rows where I bumped my face into a headless torso. My eyes, adjusting. And the honey beige of dorado, the dark of sea bass on the diamond chips of ice. And crates of red mullet. And I listened to and did not understand and recognized the obscene cries of the fishmongers; the proud heads of women, glancing away, glancing back again; those stout men in their rubber boots and their plastic aprons, hosing down their fish, heaping fish onto ice, ice onto fish. Shrimp in their subtle shells. And the heaped sardines, not so big as the Portuguese sardines, fresh off a charcoal burner, the crisp skin breaking under your teeth.

The crowd was a hurrying, waiting crowd.

I went across the street, across Ermou, and into the open market; in among the pyramids of peaches and tomatoes. And the fresh-ground coffee at my nose. And in among the coned heaps of olives, green olives and black, and shriveled olives to find with a pin, and olives that looked like failed plums. And kegs and blocks and barrels of feta, the quickening smell of brine and goat. And eggs and more eggs, and more stalls selling eggs until I knew my sister controlled the whole world with her egg cartel, and more cheese, Dutch cheeses, Italian cheeses, and ripe and soft and flowing cheeses; and an old woman selling rice by the sack and out of sacks, and the shouting and the calling of the hawkers, the din of voices, the raised scales, the balanced scales all around me, the scooped rice, the rounded weights; and the green of the heaped melons, the sweet smell of small round melons practising up to be suns, and cucumbers and squash and the special green of green peppers and the long stare of an eggplant.

And a man stopping me, scaring me with his hand; and his wanting to weigh me. His signaling me to step onto his scales. And I stepped on and was weighed and gave him a coin and heard in Greek my public weight and did not understand. I was weighed.

And the jugs and tins and the bottles of cooking oil, and the shoeshine men pointing at my scuffed brown shoes, and the heaped pots and pans and the stacked plates, the bowls, the cups, the engraving smell of detergents, the sweet of soaps, and a wall of knives and the flour and salt and sugar; and the sudden blast of spices in a hot doorway, like a loaded gun, catching my whole head; nutmeg, cumin, cayenne pepper, oregano; I went from stall to stall; I turned corners and circled back and stood between two beggars, a mute playing a guitar, a woman holding a child, and I watched the alleys through which I had fled.

I had, I was confident, covered my tracks and lost my pursuers. I turned onto Egnatia Street and headed west; I went westward along the road the Romans built when they were joining Rome to Constantinople. I marched along that ancient street.

The hunted man. The city that hides the hunted men. Collectors.

I thought of the hammam. Perhaps I had thought of it all along. A possible sanctuary. And for that reason my guard was down. I went along that busy street seeking the odd dome of the hammam. That far, arching, squat dome, clay-colored and sun-baked and lifting into the sky the green patches of its own weeds. That promise of neglect. I turned up a winding street into a jumble of shops that sold car parts, the scattered and collected remnants of dozens of cars, hundreds of wrecked cars, sorted now, almost neatly, into hubcaps and bumpers and water pumps and engine blocks and piston rings. There, and now, in the shadow of that building that has stood through the city's violence for five hundred years, a bathhouse. A hammam. *The Palm Tree.*

I paid my money and went in. I was led to a room where I might undress and hang my clothes on nails. A single, small towel. On the narrow bed. In the tiny, cell-like room, a small table and a small chair and a narrow bed; a bed, white sheets, where I might rest, after my bathing.

I found my way along a narrow, dark corridor; a long and turning corridor that smelled only of damp and rotting wood. I hung my towel on a nail in the narrow, dark anteroom and went in through the rotted wooden door.

No.

Not quite.

I went to the wooden door, yes. I looked into the marble room beyond the door; it was, even then, even there, an echo and a replication of Turkish splendors of the past. It was a room of marble. Four high walls of marble, a marble bench against each wall. On each bench, at intervals, marble fountains. And on the marble benches, sitting near the fountains, were naked men, old men, young men; men who caught water in elegant bronze bowls and tipped the steaming water over their own bodies, over their bellies and arms, over their thighs. Over their heads, and with care. Lovingly, over their private parts.

I was about to enter into the sanctuary when the hand touched my shoulder.

How the police guessed that I would go to the hammam, how they got there so easily, I was never to find out.

There were three policemen attending to my surprise. Three of them, fully clothed, wearing their short-sleeved green-khaki shirts, wearing their stiff epaulets, their gross and numbered shoulder patches; three of them, dressed as if the open door might announce a blast of icy air.

"You are Mr. Dorfer?" one of the policemen said. "Billiam Billiam."

The other two policemen nodded, not so much to me as for me.

"Dead," the policeman said, the one who spoke for all three. "Please, I am sorry," he said. "In Portogalia."

I was doing nothing. I was saying nothing.

"In the automobile," the policeman said. "The lady was found. Very long dead. In Portogalia."

He raised his left hand up high, held it parallel to the marble floor. "Cliff," he said. Then, abruptly, he tipped his hand down, let it swoop as if to seize my genitals. Involuntarily, I stepped back, almost through the wooden doorway.

One of the attendant policemen caught me by the naked left arm, as if suspecting I planned to escape the sad news.

"Boom!" the policeman said, the one who was speaking. "Boom!" he said. Loudly. Then he added, "Wreck!" And that too in a voice that made me start. And then he pointed directly between my eyes.

"You car," he said to me.

"It was not *my* car," I said. "It was a rented car."

"You car," he said. "Come you now with us to talk." He heard what he'd said and changed it. "You come now with us to talk."

QUESTIONS OF INNOCENCE
AND GUILT: DORF
HEARS THE DEAD WAITING

*T*he notion that I might have been implicated in the death of Julie Magnuson is so preposterous as to call for no further comment. I need only explain that when I got back to Calgary I found my apartment had been broken into and ransacked from doorknob to toilet tank; I was more aggrieved than aggrieving.

I had flown back home in a great huff and hurry, precisely so I might show the flag, so to speak, and clear my good name. Karen was kind enough to take my daughters for a week-long stay on Sifnos, where she no doubt had a few lovers, as well as her Mount Royal College friends in their windmill, awaiting her return; God knows, she was eager enough to get away from Salonika.

Thanks to Canadian Pacific I was in the air an hour after the ferry sailed for Sifnos. And I was writing, writing in my journal, hour after hour, the events of recent days still vivid and fresh in my mind. I made my precious notes, up there in the Atlantic sky, for later transcription into a more coherent form. I drank only two Cinzanos.

I suspect I was traced through my daughters. The human emotions, again, were my weakness; love lays a trap. Unwittingly, I sprung it. The fuzz, in blind obedience of another sort, hassled me in that hammam.

All the cops actually wanted was for me to fill out a lengthy report concerning the car. Automobiles, after all, are possessions of the system and must be protected. Julie Magnuson had been found by men going out to strip the cork oak that her car, in falling, hit. She had been dead for quite some time, apparently, undiscovered by the laggard highway patrols. Alone and dead in a blue Mercedes-Benz. In the forest at the foot of a cliff, in the hills northwest of Faro, in the south of Portogalia; in the very opposite direction, that is, from the direction we'd planned to drive on our proposed extra day on the Algarve.

We had planned to drive west, not east, that appalling morning when I discovered her absence. I suppose I cracked, in a way, right then, made some bad judgments. Whether she stole the car or whether both she and the car were stolen by a third party remains to be determined. The car was rented in my name, granted, and the insurance company was being troublesome about it, even though we pay insurance precisely to avoid all such hassle. I made it quite clear I was ready to answer any questions whatsoever, to the proper authorities, of course, and not to a trio of Greek dicks who were doing nothing but repeating what they'd heard from Interpol.

But the state of my apartment threw a different light on matters. I had expected the redcoats on their horses or whatever to come pounding on my door with their B-movie questions about suicide or accident or, as they like to put it, foul play. Instead, I found the door itself had been jimmied, my papers scattered from hell to kingdom come; my clothes were torn apart, coats and jackets literally shredded, my files scattered, letters ripped open, drawers pulled onto the floor like tongues torn from silent mouths. I had half a mind to call the police myself instead of waiting for their visit.

Julie's mangled and decomposed body had been returned to Calgary. The Greek cops told me that much. What they didn't tell me was a crucial and cruel fact: the gravediggers of the City of Calgary were out on strike.

I left my vandalized apartment, managed to start my old Dodge and went rushing downtown to the main library. This while I was suffering jetlag of the worst sort. I found two dozen horrifying pictures of coffins in the *Herald*. The city fathers, in their wisdom, had rented no end of ice arenas and made artificial ice and now arranged the accruing caskets in patterns and rows on the mirror-like ice. I found all kinds of hair-raising pictures, and one little item of actual reporting. Julie Magnuson, the brief column of print suggested, had missed a turn driving on a narrow, bad, curving mountain road at night; the lights had been on in the car. I might have told them something about morning fogs; but, then again, I hadn't been asked.

The story had no doubt been dictated by Jack Deemer himself. I was beginning to understand the plot that connives the world into visible being; the necessary plot that makes us seek each other, if only to do violence to the meeting. Deemer thinks he can take the law into his own hands, and that just because he's managed to collect a trace of the discarded world into his warehouses; he thinks it's his money and his silent manipulation that make the collection. Too bad for him is all I can say; it's my scrounging and my snooping and my talking, talking, talking that make his famous collection. Money is cheap. I'm the poor fool who must go out and dicker and plead and lie and cheat and swindle and count and pack and ship. The collection itself only confirms the discontinuity of this scattered world; it's my talk that puts it together. I rave the world into coherence for Deemer; he sits there on his little hill called a mountain, Mount Royal; he sits there, silent, and now by God he wants to collect the law too.

I checked the phone, there in my rifled apartment, when I got back from the library. The phone was still working. Of course they wouldn't destroy that and arouse the curiosity of Alberta Government Telephones. At least I was able to order a pizza; sitting here…I beg your pardon, there…in the midst of confusion, I ate a whole damned pizza by myself, tomato and green pepper and pepperoni and anchovies; yes, as if the salt and sun of Salonika still fed my lost happiness.

Julie is somewhere in a coffin in a skating arena among the numerous skating arenas in the City of Calgary. The honorable dead rest in rows and patterns on every sheet of enclosed ice in the city; every skating arena and every sheet of curling ice in the city and in the neighboring towns has been turned into a chilly little, perfect little graveyard. Somewhere in this gridded city. Here, in this last, in this latest of the great cities of the New World, so-called, after the rise of this civilization, there in its tropical center. The great Mayan places: Chichén Itzá, Uxmal, Tulum. Those other cities, as sun-scarred and ambitious and intent as this one. As measured and mounded. As secretly into theft and gold, as murderously into the worship of death. The decorated knife, the climb to the sacrificial top, the hearts torn from the hot corpses. The calculated measurement, the ecstatic scream. Tikal. Calakmul. Gone now. Those other cities. Gone.

Gone. Gone. Gone. Gone. Gone.

I took a hot shower. I stayed in the shower until my skin wrinkled, turned pink, turned a deathly white. Those other cities. Mayan. Incan. Aztec. That long and endless flowering into death. The pyramid to the climbing and the falling sun. The sharpened axe. The cupped and splattered blood. I stayed in the shower; I didn't want to come out, ever. The New World, always, waiting outside the plastic curtain, waiting outside the door. The coffins, in rows, on the ice. Hardly so much as a scratch on the ice. The coffins, mirrored. The neat rows, the careful spacing. Death, like love, is a great arranger. This collector, too, has a corrosive sense of style.

NEGATIVE #5: DORF
ATTEMPTING TO FIND A COFFIN
MAKES A DISCOVERY

*A*nd if the *Herald* had all those pictures, all you had to do, I realized, was carry a camera.

I got up early in the morning when the city too was asleep. When the city was, in its ritual way, dead. The sun comes up early and strong on the horizon; the sleepers of the city writhe in their sweaty beds, grope, one last time, or reach, or recoil. And I was their watcher. That booming city, in the quiet of the first-dawn light, that sunburnt city has its nightmares too. I watched the cars scurry out into the horizontal light of dawn; I saw the cars in their haste and bunching; their small eyes busting faint holes into the faded dark; I heard their hunger and their whine and fear; and rather did I want, then, to be alone on a high road over the city, in Bragg Creek, on the other side of Nose Hill; that precious moment, then, when you stop to change drivers, or to get out and pee.

In the magic of that morning I learned that some of the city's watchmen mistake a black leather bag for a camera. And they don't have many visitors. They too are lonesome. And after a while I even dared to make specific inquiries, speak a name.

I found the coffin. In the northwest quadrant of the city. The arena was large and hollow and new. And empty and not empty, at the same time.

I sat on the top wooden bench, looking down. The rich do well, even in death. Their caskets speak a fine profit. The poor, I noticed, had somehow huddled together, their plainer boxes smaller too, and fitted into a smaller space.

I went from my seat, climbed over a low wooden wall into one of the penalty boxes. I sat in a hockey player's penalty box.

As a kid I hadn't made the team. I was big enough, but, even then, too awkward. My hands and feet went different ways. The puck had a mind of its own, the cross-checking broke my body in two.

Julie Magnuson, as I should have guessed, was at center ice. I had to laugh, in spite of myself. I heard my own laughter in the beams overhead. I lay down on the bench, in the penalty box, so no one would see me. I lay there, flat out like that, for a long time. It was cold in that arena.

There were only two bouquets on Julie's casket. I had expected more. That's why I was slow to find it. I stood there, thinking, not thinking, staring into the bouquets instead of at anything else. My Lady of Portugal. My lady of the fast car. There and not there. A pastoral of bones. A broken face, a broken dream. Airtight, that sealing. I had found her and I had not found her. Love is such, a terror and a silence. That broken face that once, unbroken, kissed mine.

There were two bouquets, but both of them seemed the gifts of lovers, not a tribute to the dead. One of the two, of course, was from Jack Deemer. That five-grand bouquet must have weighed a ton. Someone had stripped a tropical forest, shipped in a tropical garden. I expected to find a parrot somewhere on a palm. Or a couple of monkeys hanging by their tails. That was an Aztec bouquet from a floating garden in Montezuma's city, the only flowers that Cortes ever noticed and sniffed and then purchased instead of stealing.

The smaller bouquet was all of blue flowers. Mountain blue. Wild flowers, meadow and slope flowers, high country flowers. Delicate blossoms, bluer than blue. Lungwort. Monkshood. Jacob's ladder, I suppose. Dog violet. One alpine harebell in the lot. They were all of them stuck into the mouth of a beer bottle. There was something in the bottle, too. Water, I suppose. Or beer, perhaps; I didn't try it.

I couldn't see a card anywhere. I was stupid enough to pick up the bottle.

I needed two hands to hold that bottle and its little bouquet. I was sniffling, with the cold in that arena. I hadn't worn enough clothes.

It was a bottle with one of those labels on it that we played with as kids, trying to find the bird on the fencepost, counting the birds, looking for rabbits and teepees and trains and oldfashioned airplanes that hardly flew, seeing who could find the most people. An impossible collection.

Dorf, it said on the bottle. *Dorf.* Written in a careful, even precise, hand. As if I had sent the bouquet. Or as if it might be addressed to me.

It took me a full minute to clear my eyes. I could hear the dead in that hollow place; they were all listening.

There were two other words. Over my name, there on that beer bottle label. Not under it. They were written, as was my name, in marking pencil ink. Two words. *Deadman Spring.*

My hands shook.

There was nothing else on the label. Two words, the name of a place, apparently. Then my name. Then a small picture of a fish under the words, one of those simple designs we learned to make in school, a line that goes sweeping down, then up. A line that goes soaring up, then down, crossing the other. A quick stroke to complete the tail. An eye, a mouth. It was Fish, I knew, who had sent the message. Or the flowers. Or the flowers and the message.

And what the hell isn't a message in this world we live in?

And what is?

DORF SEEKS WESTWARD
AGAIN, INTO THE MOUNTAINS,
IGNORING THE LESSONS OF THE PAST

I made a number of phone calls. Deadman Spring, it turns out, is a spa. I phoned everybody but Fish himself. I phoned a realtor and learned that Deadman Spring is a little ramshackle run-down spa with a mineral hot spring that runs from deep inside a cave into a small swimming pool. The whole damned thing was up for sale, lock, stock and barrel; the owner was going belly up, waiting for customers to drive west through the Rocky Mountains into the next mountain trench, into the next range of mountains. He was in debt up to his ears, waiting for customers to drive past three of the finest hot springs in the country to his hole in a mountainside.

To say that I left Calgary in something of a hurry would be true. It was as if I had read on that pilsener bottle a command from Julie herself. I resented having to stop to buy gas. I didn't have time to look for Fish when I drove through Banff. I only glanced up, once or twice, at the slopes where the avalanche came down.

And Deadman Spring exceeds my fondest hope. Here on an edge, between a lake and a mountain. You can hardly see, hardly find the place where the spa is, hardly know where to turn off the lakeshore road, swing up, find the parking lot. This is my Buçaco forest. These native trees. The Engelmann spruce. The western larch. The hemlock, the alder, the birch, the pine. The Douglas fir. The avalanche-streaked forest, the snow-raked forest, reaching green to a glacier's lip. The lake that is black in late afternoon, the sun behind the mountain.

I've arranged, on Deemer's behalf, a down payment; his lawyers are clearing the title and writing cheques; the owner is in Vancouver, even now, buying himself a trawler or some such thing. I was permitted to walk right in and tear down the FOR SALE sign; I set the staff to work, painting the pool's edge, trimming the ragged hedges.

It is, curiously, a double-mouthed cave that gives issue to the hot spring. Two gaping black holes in the forest and rock. The juniper mouth; the lichen, grey and green, on the scoured rock. Both tunnels go back far into the limestone; then both, somewhat abruptly, turn; the two tunnels turn toward each other into a darkness that is so absolute it defies the imagination. In that same darkness the two tunnels meet. They meet where hot mineral water gushes out from overhead, then falls across a bench-like ledge and into the water at one's feet.

The water in the joined tunnels is hot and steaming and just deep enough so that when I wade in, or when I wade around on the horseshoe-shaped journey, as is the custom, I find the water lapping at my testicles. An exquisite pleasure.

The two tunnels are in fact one. The bottom of the tunnel is in some places bare rock, in others a surprise of fine sand, in others still a coarse gravel that forces one to curl one's toes and tremble forward, holding one's breath and wishing to fly or develop fins. There is not an ounce of mud to be found. I am in no disharmony, here, with my Laspi friends.

The tunnel is lit by a string of inadequate lights that is somehow tacked to the arching rock roof and its dark eruptions of stalactites, somehow held to the swellings and protrusions of the multi-colored rock walls, the grey and brown rock that bursts like bruised flesh into shades of purple and yellow, green and red and black. The two entrances have low dams built across them, bench-high dams, to maintain the level of water inside the cave; the water flows over each of the two small concrete dams, into the light outside, into a swimming pool that is large enough and deep enough and hot and green enough to contain a pair of mating hippopotami.

The catch has been, for the succession of poor devils trying to make a living out of this spa, its location. The spa is on the shore of a long lake, a lake that runs for many miles north and south in this mountain trench. The best approach is via a ferry that crosses the lake a few miles south of the spa. But the first hangup is the ferry itself, its slowness, its size, its entailing a long wait; only the most determined customers persist, taking the turnoff highway to the ferry landing, then the ferry, then the road that winds north, clinging to the slope between the lake and the mountain. And yet I find in my journal a catalogue of revelations. Here in this monkish place of mine: two porcupines, a black bear, rumors of a grizzly, a rare glimpse of a pine marten, talk of a cougar that killed a calf, a plague of chipmunks.

I am reminded of those other men in other forests and mountains: Oertel and Priessnitz and Kneipp in a lost Europe, in the century just past, finding they were humble men with great gifts, whatever their detractors might say of water cures and therapeutic nihilism and the dangers of unabridged nature.

I have come to the green smell of things, fish in the evening waters, birds in the morning sky.

A GIFT IS GIVEN, A GIFT RECEIVED:
IN WHICH DORF RECOGNIZES THE ANCIENT
TRADITIONS OF HYDROTHERAPY

*I*t was almost noon on July 14, if my notes are to be trusted, when a man came to me where I was sitting at the back of my cave, letting the flow of hot mineral water, as it fell from overhead, lave my aching right leg. It is bothering me again, my knee. All my work around the spa is doing it; I am forever hauling and lugging boards and planks and sheets of plywood, carrying buckets of plaster and cans of paint, hacking trails into the forest of my little Buçaco.

"I have no name," the stranger said.

The overhead lights were so dim I could hardly see his face. The rushing water made its steady noise around my ears. I had almost relaxed. "Sir," I said. Both with deliberation and gentleness. "Everyone has a name."

"Not quite so easy," said the man with no name.

I remembered, then, how de Medeiros had been so careful with the injured of this lunatic world. I was weary myself from collecting dollar bills at the entrance to my establishment, from supervising the help and handing out towels and chatting with swimmers and bathers. Sometimes I station myself at one of the cave's entrances, giving customers a chance to talk to me, to comment or to complain to the tall, gaunt figure of myself clad only in a blue swimsuit. But this time I had retreated to the water's source, to be alone, to give myself a rest.

"I have no name," the stranger repeated. "I come here often," he added. He indicated the cave, the water.

I tried to reason with him, joke with him. Everyone has a name. How can one not have a name?

And yet it struck me as reasonable enough; it could

happen, I realized; out of all the billions of people. One of them might have slipped by, might have missed being named. I thought of Julie, for some reason, with a face that was a face, but no longer to be recognized as her own. Was she still herself, then? And what about names if even faces were on shaky ground? I began to marvel that so few people had been missed. I looked at the stranger and was filled with wonder. He was there, standing before me, like a fish that has no name, that is only a fish, like a bird that is only a bird. I was, in my knowledge, lonely.

"I myself have an extra name," I said.

I hadn't expected to say that.

There were three people gathered there, maybe four, listening to us now. Three or four at the most.

"What is your extra name?" the man who had no name asked.

"I am named," I said, "Billy Billy." And at that moment I remembered that my grandfather's mother who had come to visit us when I was a wee child had been something of a witch. She could, it was told to us secretly late at night, take the form of a cat. My father disappeared for two days; he drove her in his buggy to have a sweat bath at Meeting Creek, where the Indians bathed, before the homesteaders drove them out. She was my paternal great-grandmother, but her name was not Dorfen; it was Dorfendorf. And I said to the man who had no name, "I am William William Dorfendorf."

Somehow I had two lives. I had one that I could give away. I saw that. Maybe that is the human condition. We have each two lives. We have each one that must be given away. One hears the rain and one knows that it is not one's self that is hearing the rain.

Dorfendorf. That was my paternal great-grandmother's name, and that only by marriage. Women are allowed to name their doubled lives. The solitude is male.

"Then you can spare a name for me," the man who had no name said. Or that's what Billy said. For he had decided his name would be Billy.

Somewhere in the history of that mountain valley he had

failed to receive a name. How people referred to him I never asked. I merely announced my name and he announced, having received and welcomed the gift, that his name was Billy. He had a name.

"Do you want me to change it to Willie?" he said.

"Billy is fine with me," I said. "Stick to Billy."

That same Billy had been blind in his right eye ever since he was hurt in a sawmill accident. He was a man hardly my age, perhaps a shade younger. I'm not going to pretend he could suddenly see with his bad eye. No, not at all, that wasn't it. It's just that all of a sudden he was able to say he didn't give a damn. He had a life to live; he would look at it with his one good eye. He said that and a couple of people clapped. "Good for you, Billy," they said.

And I realized what I had done. I hadn't really cured the guy; I never thought I cured anyone. It's just that I'd given him a nudge in the right direction. I was as astonished and terrified as he was; more terrified, I suspect. And, I guess, just a little bit pleased with myself, too. I wasn't into de Medeiros' category. I wasn't the smelly woman of Laspi. But I was no slouch either.

My little success created something of a stir, I have to confess. Within two days I could tell the difference at the box office. It turns out I have something of a knack for this water cure business. For getting people to let the water take hold. My unpleasant experiences of the past few months have been to good avail. At least I have come to a kind of objectivity, and I am another man, cured of past follies. I am able to talk to the bruised and hurting people who come to these waters. And come they do to this ragtail place, from the outside. They come across the lake on the ferry and they stay in the local campgrounds, the local motels, the trailer courts; some people even camp in the forest and make themselves trails to my cave. They are the mere blind and the mere lame, come to soak out the hurt.

A VISITOR ARRIVES AND DORF
IS, TO SAY THE LEAST,
DISCOMBOBULATED

I magine my unease, my suspicions, when Karen Strike arrived on my doorstep. Or at the ticket window.

It was noon and I was selling tickets while the lame old woman who runs the window for me was having lunch. The bus was late. It was one of our busier days. Karen Strike was one customer we didn't exactly need.

She was wearing shorts so short the pubic hairs came curling out on either side of the flimsy cloth. I was tempted to remind her that mine is a spa of some decorum. But I guessed, from the look of sheer exhaustion on her face, she had come to be treated, which circumstance, I knew before I opened my mouth, she would stoutly deny. She is a woman who hates love. I am a man who, in the mystery of what self is, can give away a name and still have it.

"I doubt that we can treat you here," I said. Perhaps I was baiting her a little. "Those who arrive helpless and go away cured are those who arrive with a willingness to cure themselves."

Karen hauled her wallet out of her Greek-island bag. "How much is it, Dorf?" she said. "This time."

"The waters," I said, "are here for all. Use them as you will. I'll give you a pass, don't worry about the money. I recommend an hour of soaking, to be followed by an hour of rest and silence, this to be repeated as the day goes on."

"Deemer sent me," Karen said. "Got it, Dorf?"

"To take the treatment," I said, "I trust."

"To take pictures," she said.

It was that and simply that, her smart-aleck bravado that

"I was preparing myself," I said, "for my trip to Laspi. I told you that at the time."

"Deemer is planning a trip too," Karen said. "I'm telling you that right now."

But then a woman came up to see me, one of my patients; she had, while preparing the bath in her trailer, there, up the valley in a fishing camp, scalded her child. The baby was in the hospital and doing fine. But the mother was going bonkers.

I thought of my own daughters, helpless in my arms, when they were babies. How I'd watch them in the bath. How I'd tiptoe into their rooms when they were sleeping and listen for their breath. I knew about that, and I was going to say so. But without expecting to I said, "I scalded myself once. I haven't told you that."

The mother looked surprised.

"I scalded my prick," I said. We were there inside the cave. I could tell her. I was wearing my blue swimsuit. I clutched myself by the balls. "You better believe it."

Karen laughed. That made the mother laugh too.

"Jump into that hot water," I said. I pointed her deeper into the cave.

And even Karen proved to have a heart, along with her cameras, if not a tongue. She followed us silently now; she followed after me and my patient. It was a motley crew she found in there where the water falls gushing hot, as if from the rock itself; as if it falls from the mountain, from the sky. And a motley crew we were: farmers from the prairies with arms missing, fed into machines; women from the mountain towns who were half mad from gossiping, from being gossiped about; truckers whose piles were killing them, who just of a sudden swung off the Trans-Canada, headed for Deadman Spring.

We hardly spoke, Karen and I, after her announcement that Jack Deemer was on his way. But I was not entirely displeased. Deadman Spring was humming; people drove away one morning and came back the next, bringing friends with bad backs, people with liver ailments and skin trouble and breathing problems. A tourist from Toronto who had fallen off a horse. Two members of the constabulary who drank some bad moonshine. People who were just plain fed up and sick of it all and listening for something besides the sound of their own emptiness.

Karen and I went on together, working, not talking, while she took her pictures. And then two visitors came in, not just tired and sore, but wiped, wrecked; a huge towering bearded Mennonite and a tall gentle man with a large head of curly grey hair and sad hazel eyes and a mouth that wanted love; authors, they claimed to be. I was uncertain as to why they came; maybe to be cured. And then on the second night of their visit, late, deep in the cave, they cornered me and wanted to talk; the Mennonite was looking for a moral presence and was fascinated by crime; the other was looking for the source of life itself, and couldn't keep his eyes off Karen. I had to watch him. God knows, she is not life's source, but that writer, there in the dim light, let his hands disappear into the water as if they were close enough to the source to have taken on a life of their own. Two octopus hands, finding Karen's buttocks. Touching and rubbing, caressing, slipping her bikini bottom an inch lower than it already was. Even the Mennonite was offended; he had a grip on reality; he knew what history is and he didn't like Karen's slash and burn approach to the old trees; she was forever interrupting with her theories of how to make a realistic film, a documentary that is at the same time art. "Distort," she said. Selection is distortion, and distortion breaks the truth into visibility. The historian and I disputed, agreed, talked about the design that is not created but, rather, creates us; and all the while the other fellow was up to his ears in water, there beside Karen, dead silent, letting a finger do his talking. There were only the four of us, speculating, late at night. We'd closed the place. We sat in the water, all of us, our heads afloat; that powerful Mennonite, his voice echoing like muffled gunfire, and I, agreeing on the night's hushed grandeur, its filling the world with shape. While that other bird, a poet I take it, was all the while slipping Karen's bikini aside, or down, or off, or pretending to assist while she removed it herself; his hands, as warm as the water. He was a mute, I began to think. When we stood up to leave, to walk out of the cave, Karen didn't have a stitch on. And nor did the poet.

"Feels *good*," Karen said. "It just feels good. To be naked, here, in this water. In this cave."

Next morning, when they showed up again, that pair of voyeurs, pencils in hand, so to speak, I ordered them off the premises. I am sympathetic to all the dispossessed and the failed and the scoundrels and the castaways and the charlatans who show up in my cave. But I chucked those two out, showed them the gate, for turning other people's misery into their own little puffed-up reputations. And Karen was ready to kill me. I was only saved by a strange bus.

The ferry had landed. We knew that. We were in the habit of watching down the valley to where the snaking road is visible. We watched for traffic to increase, bringing the possibility of more customers.

But none was half so excited as I on that occasion. For I recognized the bus that the others said was strange. It was the bus that Fish always drove. He has presumed to put his own markings on the bus he drives; he flies a crimson pennant as if his bus is a ship at sea.

Karen was nothing but nerves; she had to have her film in the can, she claimed, by the middle of October. She had to finish her shooting. "Get your cameras," I told her. "All of them. Line them up."

And while she labored, the bus labored too. It came up the road, pennant flying; it made the sharp left turn, came through the gate.

But Fish didn't stop in the parking lot. He drove right up to the NO PARKING signs and the ticket office. The door of the bus opened. If ever my confidence had a scare, it was at that moment. I remembered only too well the boast that Fish had made about knowing Deemer. I saw Fish at the wheel of the old bus looking as crazy and as cocky as ever under his rakish tour-driver's cap. He recognized me, and he grinned his shit-eating grin.

I was expecting a large old man to come down the steps of the bus. Or a tall old man with thick eyebrows. Or even a man who was old and skinny with a small rifle for a cane and the voice of a barking dog. It wasn't really clear in my mind. I had seen no other head than Fish's own in the bus' windows. Expectation alters perception. I looked for an invisible Deemer.

Instead, it was the dwarfish figure of Dr. Manuel de Medeiros that came down the steps, out of the bus, into the blazing July sunshine.

He was wearing the same indigo blouse he wore in Luso. Apparently it was the only thing he owned. His long blond hair fell richly, fully, over the shoulders of his blouse; he was a walking lesson for Karen and her cameras, in how to appear in public. He had added something, however; he wore a gold earring in his left ear. He was carrying a basket.

Actually, we shook hands. Dr. de Medeiros and I, we shook hands, formally. I forgot to introduce Karen.

Each of us pretended to be delighted to see the other. I was holding, in my left hand, a large paintbrush. I accidentally dropped it, giving myself, in the process, a green shoe.

"I'll take care of everything," Manny said. He was under the impression he was seven feet tall. He didn't even bother to stand straight. He glanced up at Karen.

"Is that so?" I said.

"Mr. Deemer will be here shortly," Manny said. "May I look around?"

"Won't you come in and look around?" I said.

"I don't mind if I do," Manny said. He turned and signaled Fish to drive away.

NEGATIVE #6:
AND THE LOVED, TOO,
HAVE LOVERS

I went hollering and waving after that bus. I went as hard as I could go, gimpy leg be damned. And Fish didn't slow down; instead, he seemed to step on the gas a little. But he was trying to turn and trying to miss a dozen parked cars and vans and trying to close the door, and I managed to get up onto the bottom step, blocking the door, keeping it from closing. I was not actually blocking the door open; I was caught in it; I couldn't move forward or backward.

"So," Fish said. He had that look on his face as if he might break out laughing. "You fool. You couldn't even resist the corpse."

"Let me in," I shouted. Or I shouted, but in a whisper. I was caught in the door. "They wrecked my apartment," I said. As if that might explain, might make him relent.

"You dummy. I knew you'd show up. For the corpse and the flowers."

"You wrecked my apartment," I said. "You fucker."

We were careening out onto the highway.

"It was necessary," Fish said, pulling at the big steering wheel, "to make inquiries. You made me leave the mountains."

"I was coming back," I said.

"You had fallen silent," Fish said. "You dummy."

"Yes," I said.

"Always talk," he said. "Don't you know that?"

"I had to keep silent," I said. I tried to shout, but I couldn't. Maybe I had to hurt Fish, shock him, insult him for leaving the mountains, for violating his own code. "She never mentioned you," I said. "Not once."

"Did you kill her?" Fish said.

I saw, then, his anger, behind his beard. Or maybe it was fear. His fear for himself, for me, for the dead woman even. For the way the past is not the past, the dream not the dream. And even the facts not quite the facts. He wasn't watching the road at all. He was ready to kill both of us.

"Maybe it was an accident," I said.

"Julie Magnuson didn't have accidents."

"I was her lover," I shouted. I could hardly speak, after running; I was being squeezed in the door. I thought, absurdly, of the old lady in Connecticut, her doors safely mounted in the middle of the room, each door isolate and innocent; I should have loved that woman, I knew, even then; she kissed me, once. Behind a door.

"I was her *first* lover," Fish said. "*Me*," he added. "I was."

I wanted to say something. But Fish gave a whole god-damned lecture, a sermon, a pious little diatribe on his own implicit virtue, the virtue of the first lover, shifting gears all the while, dodging out of the way of a logging truck, hitting the gravel shoulder and then finding the road again. "We were kids together. Deemer and me. Out there in the Coal Branch." He looked puzzled, surprised, at his own confession. That great gap in the Alberta wilderness, there, east of the mountains, on the other side, where, for a few decades, the coal towns filled the forest with talk and hockey games and fist fights and gardens that froze in the late summer, and elk and moose walked out in front of iron locomotives, and men forgot they had wives somewhere else and took to drink and cards and to other women, and the train wheels sang in the silver night, and money glowed in the dark. And then, one day, as if a curtain fell, someone struck oil on the open plains. "It's all gone now. Abandoned. Bulldozed down to the bare ground. Burned. Destroyed. Erased."

"She didn't love a one of us," I said. I shouted at Fish. I wanted, suddenly, to console him. I shouted by way of consolation. We can only forgive. And learn to remember, fitfully, with gratitude. "She didn't love me. She didn't love you. She didn't love Deemer either. In the end."

"Or maybe she loved all of us," Fish said.

And then he pulled open the door. Fish opened the door of the bus and I went rolling out of the doorway, down into the ditch, into the grass and the dandelion leaves and the thistles beside the road.

DR. DE MEDEIROS
CONDUCTS AN
EXAMINATION

I went limping back to the spa and de Medeiros took one look at me, covered in dust and grass stains and traces of blood, and he told me to lie down on the floor of the office of the spa; he poked at my ribs and looked at my jaw. "Nothing wrong," he said, "that wasn't wrong before." But I wasn't satisfied. I insisted on undressing. I asked him to check me over from the top of my skull to the soles of my feet.

"Check me over, Doc," I said. "I think you'll find me cured."

I was a wreck; it's a miracle I wasn't killed. I had to go sit in the mineral waters. I spent the rest of the day there, soaking in the water at one of the entrances to the cave. I'd haul myself up onto the concrete dam and catch some sun, then drop back into the water. I was missing a few patches of skin.

My old friend, Manny, from the hour of his arrival, began to treat me like a usurper in my own camp. I was handicapped by my tumble. But I went out of my way to be a considerate host. I arranged a room for him in a motel that was close enough so that he might walk. He couldn't drive a car, I knew. And yet I knew also that, in rugged Portugal, he was able to walk up a mountain and down, following Julie Magnuson.

Poor Manny thought that he alone was able to effect any cure of the griefs and sufferings of this mortal world. He stationed himself in the deep interior of my cave and they flocked inside, after him, the curious and the hangers-on. People stared as if he was...I hate to write this down, commit it to paper; but, frankly, they looked upon him as something of an oddity. I did my best to treat him as a friend and guest.

On the third morning after his arrival, however, he did

overstep the bounds. I waded, limping, to the interior of my cave and found the little man as busy as usual, chattering with Karen, giving his free medical advice, so-called, to any who would listen. He even pretended, briefly, to lend Karen a helping hand; he was able to scamper up into the rock hollow where the water fell out. But, that done, he began again to address the admiring multitude, this including two girls in nothing but brassieres and wet, clinging panties who claimed to suffer from boils. Hardly a new affliction. But it might have been a wonder to the entire medical profession to hear Manny. I was offended by his posturing and, for that reason I suppose, against my better judgment, I made reference to the disappearance of our mutual friend.

"We must have a talk one day," Manny said.

"Why not right now?" I said.

"We should wait until we're all here."

I raised the fingers of my left hand as if to count them off. "How can we all be here," I said, "when one of us is cold stone dead?"

"From a car accident?" Manny said.

"Accident," I said, watching closely in the bad light, "is hardly the right word. Is it?"

"We must have a talk," Manny said.

"We're talking," I said.

"When we're all here," Manny said. "We will most certainly talk."

"Is someone missing?" I said, with mock naivete.

"Mr. Deemer would like to be here," Manny said.

"Is he ever not here?" I said.

"How so?" Manny said.

"He has his minions," I said. "Doesn't he?"

"He has his inhuman needs," Manny said.

I was stopped by the sadness in Manny's voice. If it was a sadness. Or a kind of pain. Or only a doctor's evasiveness.

"Inhuman?" I asked.

Manny paused. "Or only human," he added. He shrugged. He looked small under his bush of blond hair that went frizzy in the damp. "You should learn to trust me," he added.

Karen was more than a little willing to eavesdrop, and for that reason I became evasive. I tried, as best I could, to indicate to Manny that Karen was eager to catch us out in confessions of past deeds. We owed it to Julie to protect her privacy; what she did or didn't do in Portugal, what happened or didn't happen, was none of Karen's affair.

And yet we were, the three of us, there for those few minutes, desperate lovers. Karen and Manny and I. We were caught in the complicity that is all love, that all love is. Perhaps it is only, and always too, the third party that makes all parties real. The third eye in the god's forehead. The confirmation into being that is the destruction too.

We were caught, each in a desperate posture. Karen, setting up her lights as if she would photograph truth, not only catch it in its moment but preserve it as well. Manny, incurable, presuming to cure all those around him, offering his small hands, his gentle voice; that Manny who might drown simply by stumbling, unable to swim a stroke, his head only just above water when he dared to walk. And I, watching. I, pretending to be more than a watcher.

And maybe it is, after all, only a spectator game, this living.

The three of us. Waiting for a man who presumes to capture and collect the treasures of the whole world, of the universe, given half a chance, and who kept us there, waiting. And yet in our very waiting we had our power too, our ultimate defiance, our little victory; we forced him to approach us. And possibly that emptiness, that absence, that nothing at the center of the cave where water falls from solid rock, is enough, is everything.

What could we say to each other? Our listeners faded away, pushed their various ways through the water to a short nap, to a cold beer, to a breath of the day's air. They went into the two directions of that one tunnel. It was their leaving that made us guilty. We were fled from. Karen and Manny and I, we stayed. We had and knew that intimate time, that time when lovers, spent, hear in the bare walls their spent cries, hear back from the silence, and wonder what they have done, what wonders they have seized, what horrors made their bodies shudder.

We were like that. And when I tried to think of Jack Deemer, of his arrival, his intrusion into our possible world, I thought of Julie Magnuson instead. She who had found her spa, her health. Her immortality too, in a way. Her paradise. She had got exactly to where she was going.

"Did you?" Manny said.

"Did you what?" I should have answered.

Karen had dropped one of her lights so that its razor beam cut at my face. She turned it off so I might speak. I hesitated for a long time, unable to see at all. Karen's hair is short, and I remember her blonde hair, her face. On top of the stepladder she had towed into the cave.

"No," I said.

"No one is going to believe you," Manny said.

His voice was hardly there at all above the sound of the water. His voice was as warm as the water.

"No," I said. Repeated. Or said, as if repeating what I had, the first time, heard.

And it was that *no* that turned them against me. Had I been fool enough to say yes, had I said yes, we would have, there, the three of us in the complicities of love, continued lovers.

"Your alibi," Karen said, "had better be airtight."

A CHAPTER IN WHICH
NOTHING HAPPENS

*D*eemer did not arrive. Jack Deemer was waited for, expected. Anticipated, should I say? Longed for? And yet he did not cross over on the ferry that slid, far away and hardly moving, like a white snail across the lake. He did not turn in off the road; he did not come to the freshly painted buildings or to the cleaned pool.

I was too busy to be concerned; it was the others who fretted. I helped my new friend, Billy, the lumberjack fellow with one good eye, who lost the other while guiding a saw. And the woman who scalded her baby. She took a liking to me, I think. And I helped a woman who could only make love while saying the rosary; she was an attractive older woman from some little town in Alberta, Big Indian; she brought me a pot of honey and I thought of Greece, of the thyme-fed bees, of poppy fields.

And there were two men who became dear friends of mine, older men, two philosophers from my own Calgary, Wingy Wing-Wing who had spent some time on the Amazon and knew about witchcraft, and his friend Guy de Pooh Guy; they liked to sit with a thermos of hot coffee in the hot cave, each gently massaging himself; they did nothing and they asked nothing; they were simply there. There was nothing wrong with them except they hated work. Too much lotus, Karen told them. But they didn't especially want to be cured.

I couldn't persuade them for love or money to lend poor Karen a hand. And the dwarf was too short to be stringing wires. She had imagined ten different ways to end her film and was prepared and willing to contrive any one of them. And I was the slave who moved the lights, my scrapes and injuries be damned; I bruised my bruises.

You could cut the tension with a knife. The moment we were all inside the cave, we imagined what was happening at the gate. Deemer would seem to be failing us. And our only response was to watch for his arrival with more intent. With a kind of raw concentration, as if by our united will we would force to happen what must happen.

Karen and Manny liked to be left alone. They liked for all the rest of us to be out on the watch.

"You two are becoming quite close friends," I once remarked to Karen.

"He's a lovely man," she said. "It's as if…"

"As if what?" I said.

"Nothing," she said. She was moving a shield of some sort, one that would reflect light to where she wanted it to go. "It's as if," she said, "he doesn't have to *wait*, the way the rest of us do. You know what I mean?"

"No," I said. "Not at all."

I was too busy to feel jealousy. I simply didn't like the loss of efficiency, the dwarf's trumped up excuses and evasions that sent the rest of us after chimeras and left him with Karen. I was quite used to finding couples behind an outcrop of rock in the long tunnel, kissing or necking or slipping, briefly, out of their swimsuits to whatever end I didn't ask. But Manny and Karen were thick as thieves; I saw their little fandango of lust for what it was. I should have thanked them for excluding me. But Karen would only have laughed; Karen, always, tangled in the machinery of her final design. I realized I had missed my chance; when the two of them quizzed me I should have been ready. "Did *you*?" I should have said. "And aren't you delighted that you did? With Julie out of the way, you can move on to a new admirer. At least I am faithful."

The three-legged dog of destiny.

DEADMAN SPRING ABOUT TO FULFIL
ITS PROMISE, NATURE ITSELF
AWAITS THE MOMENT

*M*atters changed abruptly at 9:45 on the evening of August 1. Ordinarily I closed the spa at ten sharp. Word came into the cave at 9:45 that a limousine had arrived. The largest crowd of the day was likely to be present during the hour before closing time. It was my friend Billy, watching out for me, who reported the limousine. A few minutes later the lady with the rosary in her trembling hands brought word that a stranger had gone into the change rooms, insisting that he be in there with no one present but de Medeiros and a person I recognized, from the description of the grey beard and the evasive eyes, as Fish.

My loyal friends, Wing-Wing and Pooh, forever fingering themselves and doing nothing, became excited, rushed outside and in and out and in again, bringing contradictory reports of the man who must be Deemer. They had such distinguishing names, those two slow messengers of malingering time, but they looked so exactly alike I could never tell them apart. They, neither of them, quite got into the change rooms to see the visitor. One report had him tall and gnarled and bearded; another had him stout, even portly, and wearing a gold earring.

Then they were reported, the three approaching figures, as coming past the open-air pool directly toward the cave; they were reported as stepping over the low dam at the south entrance of the cave; they were approaching through the long cave, stopping to praise the waters, stopping to marvel at the bare rock itself; they were approaching the rather sharp bend that would lead them to me and to my speech of acknowledgment and reception.

I had spent some days preparing for this moment. It would

not be unfair, I realized, to say I had spent a lifetime composing that precious moment of success. We are each and all the fortune-tellers of our own apotheoses. I wished my daughters might be present to see my vision realized, Jinn and Jan, one so open to wonder, the other wondering all the while. I had once told them, there in Salonika, of my octopus, and Jinn had understood my reading of the deep sea's text; Jan had told me, in her biological way, I had misread the animal's intelligence and intent.

Deemer had come to find me. I was ready to be found. He had come to find my finding. And that was ready too; the rocks listened; the water was stilled.

We were a crowd of forty souls, I would guess, there in that cave. A smallish gathering, surely enough. And yet we each through suffering had earned that place. We had brought our broken bodies there. We had spirits that needed mending. I wished no credit for what I had done; I wished only to be allowed, encouraged, to go on doing what I, apparently, did well. I made small claims for myself. What I cherished most was my being cherished.

The mind anticipates the occasion, always. I suppose I tried to guess what Deemer might be in the flesh. That legendary man who had collected Borneo and Tibet and Lake Titicaca, tablets in languages that couldn't be read, a fragment of the moon, and Bronze Age spearheads, into his four warehouses. A herd of stuffed elephants, it was claimed, though that was not my purchase. The skin impressions of a dinosaur. Samples of sand from each of the world's deserts.

I thought he might be too big, too huge, to enter into my cave. As if he could not be distinct from all he had acquired. I thought he might be so small, in the face of his collections, he could come in on a boat, a small boat, a miniature Egyptian barge towed by Fish, attended by de Medeiros. Or like the sun itself, at dawn, made far away by a single raucous crow, a standing heron, a flight of geese, he would at best touch the horizon.

Perhaps I have lived too long in this world and the time has come for my leaving. Like Karen, posted between her two high-mounted cameras, I expect magnificent endings. I hear no irony in Beethoven's conclusive thunder. I seek for Van Gogh's ear and not the missing man.

It was Fish who first came into view. Or perhaps de Medeiros was ahead of him, so low in the water I had missed his floating head. If that was the case, then Karen had missed him too. She saw she had already, almost, missed the moment she had been waiting for; in abrupt haste she threw all her switches.

There was a flash of light. It was more than a flash; it was a time of such illumination that all was clear white in the cave, bone white; the rocks overhead were white; the water was the blinding white of a mirror under an exploding sun; the figures in the cave, those of us who waited, those who approached, were etched in a white whiter than white, as if a shadow itself, instead of being dark, was whiter than its shadowed obduration.

And the three men coming toward us, I swear they were not men at all but three skeletons; in that pure light the flesh was invisible. I saw three skeletons, the miniature figure of de Medeiros, the leading figure that must have been Fish, the larger walking skeleton that could only be Deemer himself; I saw all that before the darkness and the screaming.

ECSTASY
EXTASIE
EKSTASIS

*A*nd it was I alone who at first tried to restore, assert order. I thought we must have all been electrocuted, dead, already, there, for Karen's folly and greed. She is no doubt Deemer's ultimate inheritor. And then I was moving, reaching, trying to keep people from drowning each other, from killing each other in their terror.

After that flash of light the cave was so black that light might have ceased to exist in the universe. We were the spun universe itself, swirled into its final black hole.

And it was then that a strange thing began to happen. Our original terror began to turn to original delight. The terror turned to a secret delight for the people in the cave. We began to move again. Touching now. We began to touch in the total dark; we began to touch. We must find each other. Toes and fingers, touching. Skin itself was the perceiving element. We were searching, yes, for anyone who might have been stunned, for anyone who might have fallen. But it was more than that, much more.

We must simply find each other. We must touch into being and then be touched. In the midst of all, I knew it: Deemer could only be pleased. Much more than pleased. He could and must be ecstatic at my success. Not until then did I realize that even Karen's extreme stupidity was part of my success.

The warmth of the water aroused us, after the brush with bone; the darkness too was arousing. The being in the enclosed cave excited the touching searchers into each other's arms. I had succeeded, even, in mastering my own claustrophobia; I felt I might easily stay there, in that cave, with Jack Deemer and his friends; I might stay and never return to mere day, to mere dark night.

We were calling names. We were naming each other. The sweet ritual of our names assured us into the perfection of the dark.

"Dorfen."

"Dorf."

"Are you here?"

"Karen."

"Mr. Deemer."

"Karen."

"De Medeiros."

And a myriad other names, sweet and lovely names; a naming into our names.

"Dorfen," the voice called. Not a question. A loving statement of my name.

"Billy."

"Yes."

"The other Billy."

"Yes."

"And Fish."

"Yes."

"And Karen."

"Yes."

And the yessing word began to punctuate, meld all our naming, into assent.

"Billy Billy Dorfen."

"Yes, don't worry. Yes."

The flesh is fornicator with its called name. We speak the soft arousal of lilted words. Thus, the tongue, and the tongue, distantly touching. The ear that will never sleep.

"Manny."

And Karen's voice, again. "Manny."

And "Yes," he said.

And the smelly woman, there in Laspi; Manny had sent me to her. And he had been right to do so. But she had been calling all the while.

I heard names. I could hear names. I heard the cave's sweet

namings. Joe. Arnie. Kay. Pat. And the laughter of the findings. Yes. The bodies, bumping bodies. Carol. David. Yes. Dennis. Diane. Trojan. Esterhazy. Yes. Jock. Yes. Mandel. Yes. Mick. Fat Annie. Estienne. The rub and caress, the fingers, finding an arm, a face, a breast. Pete. Yes. Hjartarson. Yes. Lorne. Doris. Ricou. Garbonzo. Yes. Gerry. Lou. Jane. The surprise of hips touching hips in the unseeable dark. And the waiting. And the turning. Yes. The hand to the belly's sudden gasp. The lovely maze of our naming. And the wet, invisible embrace. Cook. Vermeer. Pausanias. Pauline. Our naming ourselves into new names. Vasco da Gama. And the yes and the yes. And Karen, no doubt, somewhere in the cave, locked in hot intercourse with anonymous arms. But we named our strangeness away. Ekerpah. Lionel. Jehovius. Wah. And the laughing. And we were happy. And our plundered bodies warm as the water's warmth, we could only yield what was already yielded. The all embrace of all of us. The meet and parting of pubic hair, the water's lap, the hands. The failed joints, the pain that forgot its pain. We were our own abandon. We traded limbs; we traded shoulders and arms and mouths; we traded buttocks and thighs. The cave permitted us. The dark permitted us. I found, there, in the naked dark, a sharp nipple.

And lost it too.

I was pushed to my knees in the water. I did not either strive or resist; to struggle was to drown. I was an old hippopotamus, gone in far, gone deep, this time. Darkly deep in the black of that cave.

"Julie."

I heard that voice. It was not my own. It was not a call, even. Unless it was I who called.

"Dorf."

I dared not answer. For fear of drowning. I was only a floating head in that darkness, my lips touching the water's edge.

I had been seized, caught from behind, surprised, ambushed, captured, taken.

I believe I passed out in a kind of ecstasy at my success. I had found Deemer his perfect spa. I fell forward as I was pushed. I had found the spa and Deemer was there and I was falling, dangerously, down into those gifted waters that might now drown me dead.

I heard her name. And that time I had called it. And "Don't," I added, "kill me." And then I was at her falling; she had come to the cliff's edge. I was held tight, there in the cave. Someone had seized me in his arms. I assumed it to be a gesture of love and that was why I did not resist. Julie, there, on the cliff's edge, held by her lover. Or held by love. I could not shout. And then the car leapt forward, the blue Mercedes, leapt like a cat, a cougar, over and off the cliff; it fell, the long car, beginning to spin; those broken rocks, those sun-cracked rocks, and the tree, the huge cork oak, like a period, on a blank page.

Billy, that I have earned a vacation; it was Billy who lent me
this cabin.

And it is Billy who tells me now: Karen must fake the
end of her documentary. She has persuaded her little gang
to restage the arrival. She has the three of them, her men,
over and over, wade into the tunnel, approach the source of
the cave's healing waters. Deemer is delighted; he has become
a child again, an actor, thrilled at the marvelous task of
playing himself. He is happy. Reshooting. Again, he
approaches; again, he approaches.

I am trying to make sense of my journal, since I was
sometimes remiss, sometimes left little gaps here and there.
I make a correction, where necessary. I type all and everything onto legal size rag paper, not dropping so much as a
letter; I happen to be something of a fanatic at a typewriter
and it shows to good cause as the manuscript grows in this
cardboard box to the left of my typewriter and the open
journal; the heaped pages; each carefully numbered, each
proofread for the merest error, then slipped carefully over
its predecessor so that all I must do, when the manuscript is
complete, is reverse the order of the pages, make the top
sheet the bottom, the bottom the top.

There is, of course, the mystery of Julie. Trying to
work that out, trying to clarify where I have inadequate
information, I am sometimes driven to taking my long walks
down the beach with rifle in hand; I have knocked holes in
all the tin cans for three miles in either direction. I'm tempted
to show the manuscript to a publisher. *Dorfendorf's Journal.* A
manual of health. I think of Vincent Priessnitz, there in
Graefenberg in the century past, a humble farmer, rejecting
all of medicine, finding the strength of water. Let Karen put
in some headings, some chapter titles to trap the unwary
eye and lure the customer; she with her gift for compromise.

There's a commune of aging hippies, three miles south
along the lake; they ran me off their land for shooting a
hole in a catsup tin; there's a religious camp three miles
north, and the forest is so full of deception I find I cannot

walk up there without stepping on the fornicating young.
But in between, for these six miles of shoreline, I am, with
my family of ospreys and a small herd of deer and one old
black bear, the happiest of creatures. Thank heavens poor
Billy, with his one good eye, had enough cartridges on hand
to turn his cabin into a fortress of some sort. I refuse of
course to shoot bird or beast; this is a peaceable kingdom.
One hooded merganser swims up the shore. The crows
caw. Two mallards stitch the water. The bats come out at
night to feed.

August 9

I was at work in the pre-dawn quiet, watching the red spill
of light, watching the ospreys now and then, now and then
finding a place in the manuscript where I must make an
emendation. The original notes, Karen's birthday journal
to me, are only the negatives which now I develop. I was
busy, minding my own business, when I heard the faraway
whine of a motor. It was not Billy come to drop off fresh
vegetables, bread, milk, a steak or two. I know the sound of
his outboard.

It moved slowly up the lake, the awkward boat. A
machine in the water for escaping from the water. A man in
the bow, two more in the stern. All of them staring, not
seeing the water at all, avoiding it. I was so distinctly relieved
when the boat with its crowd vanished to northward that I
can only conclude I am by nature a hermit.

August 10

My two baby ospreys came within an inch of leaping into the
air today. They stretched and stretched and made their
ferocious baby noises on the very lip of the chasm of air.

The man who owns this cabin is surely a fortunate

man, whatever his protestations, and what can he find at the
spa, across the lake, that keeps him there?

Already I sense the turn of autumn. I see it in the color
of the sky. In a few weeks now the kokanee salmon will be
swimming up these local creeks. I can imagine the renewing
end of things, the fish, red and green, caught in their own
spawning and dying; the crows and eagles come to feast on
the dying fish, the bears fattening for winter, a reckless
coyote perhaps, feasting close to the bears. All this in the
long cycle of our anonymous days. And I took it away from
Billy by offering him a name. It is better to have no name,
perhaps. To give no names to the passing days. And to let
the birds in their departing, the fish, in their descent and
their long climb, count the years.

August 11

I have so much, today, enjoyed rereading what I wrote
about Portugal and Julie and de Medeiros. We three
together, there in the happy place, the tended blue hydrangeas of the Luso streets, the man-made forest that is Buçaco.
Nature itself, made unnatural.

But the three of us together, Manny and Julie and I,
we were our total natural selves, unblemished by the stifled
burp and the sewer pipes and the starched necks of society.
We were what we were and we were. It should always be so.
I had not seen a cork oak, ever, stripped of its bark, stripped
to its burnt orange beauty, its brown cry.

August 12

Billy was here today with an assignment from Deemer.
Scrawled, scratched, on the back of a long strip of tickets. I
must to the spa at once, Mr. Deemer tells me, and now.
He has learned of a collection of lanterns, somewhere on

Cape Hatteras; an antique dealer has got them together from attics, from abandoned barns, from shipwrecks. From far China and new Japan...And each lantern, for all its time or place, a cage with a light inside.

I hesitate to write what I must write, but write it down, I must....I was, by any legal definition, that final night, there, in Deadman Spring...I cannot write the word. Violated will have to do. By whom, I cannot guess. Violence is anonymous. We live dumbly, now. And dumb I remain. I practise only to forgive.

Billy brought food and milk. Zucchini and new potatoes from his girl friend's garden. Ripe red tomatoes that burst to the tongue. I told him I shall either return soon to Greece, go to Mount Athos, where women are not allowed so much as to set foot on that peninsula of sacred ground. Tell that to Karen. Or I shall stay here for the rest of my life, repenting the world's acquisitions. It depends upon my oracular birds.

August 13

I was busy this morning, as usual, minding my own business and copying, even as a monk of old must have copied, words from one book into another. I was at ease yet concentrating, checking the text against the text. Speaking a few words aloud. Glancing away from my text to the ospreys on their high nest below me. Glancing again into the journal, completing its transformation into clear type on this old portable, tearing each used page from the journal.

I had only returned from the biffy when it happened. There, I had crumbled another three sheets of Karen's precious document. My stool was perfectly formed this morning, making a sickle-moon where it fell. I had, while there, on the three-holer bench, noticed a deer nosing at the wild flowers. I never bother to close the door. The doe came, on slender legs, to the yarrow. To the sage, to the ox-eye daisies, to the false lily of the valley. It touched, even, its quivering nose, to the enormous anthill, there by the wild grapes, just below the outhouse.

I had only checked my stool when I heard the sound. I heard what could only be the sound of an outboard motor, and at first I paid no attention. I returned diligently to my work. Fishermen, I thought, on their way to some imaginary spot where fish might actually be caught. A pair of campers dreaming some isolated beach where they might drink beer and paw each other and leave behind a few tin cans.

But, to my distress, the sound of the distant motor grew stronger and then stronger still, a high and insistent whine. A boat, apparently, was coming across the lake, not proceeding up or down. It could not be Billy; he'd said he would return in four days, and his word is iron.

Even then, I paid little attention and went on minding my own business, doing my transcribing. When I did glance up, finally, I noticed what I took to be a man seated in the stern of a smallish canoe with a large outboard motor available to his right hand.

I had gone back to the completed Portuguese section of my manuscript to make some final corrections. Perhaps for that reason I was not so much surprised as confused when I glanced up a minute later and realized there was not a man seated in the stern of the canoe but rather a man standing. It was surely the famous doctor, Manuel de Medeiros, his hand on the tiller; his being a dwarf had confused my judgment.

He struck quite a figure as a sailor, captain of his good ship, standing there and peering toward the forested shoreline, one last Magellan come to discover us. He had, for some reason, put on one of those admiral's caps for sale in tourist shops, over his thick blond hair. He was, unfortunately, made absurd by his size, for, even standing, he could hardly see over the upraised prow of the speeding canoe.

My thoughts, too, sped rapidly. The doctor was approaching the pilings, for whatever reasons I dread to think. He had slowed the motor somewhat so that he might more carefully study the shoreline. He looked for all the world like one of my baby ospreys, staring out at the airy nothing from the edge of the nest on top of the tallest piling; I could only laugh to myself.

And then it struck me that the sound of the motor must frighten the young ospreys into a premature attempt at flight, an omen I could ill afford. I went from laughter to distress. I knew I must, for all my instinct to remain anonymous, announce my boundaries.

By the best and finest and most demanding of all codes, by the code of the sea, I acted.

I went into the cabin and took down the .303 from its two nails over the door and slipped a cartridge into the magazine. I went back onto the veranda. I suspect I was concealed by the branches of the western red cedars that shelter the cabin.

I wanted both to indicate to de Medeiros where I was and to indicate to him that he should veer away from the pilings.

I raised the rifle. What I intended to do was to fire a shot across the bow of his boat, a sign and signal as old as gunpowder itself.

No man can live in a paradise. Nor woman either. The world will not allow it.

I fired the shot.

Unfortunately, I had not allowed for the remarkable speed of the canoe, even when it was slowed down; it is difficult to estimate the speed of a small boat moving across open water or the effect of its angle of passage; the most obvious landing place was just to the south of the pilings, closest to my cabin, yes, but closest also to the ospreys' nest.

It was an exquisite sunrise, though the light of the sun, rising behind me, had a further effect on my inability to judge time and space correctly; the slanting sun at my back distorted my sense of shadow and relationship.

Frankly, I am now of the opinion that de Medeiros was coming to my cabin to threaten my life. Or to try and bribe me. I was the only person on earth who might give evidence against him in the matter of Julie Magnuson's death. If I were to give any report at all, he would surely fall out of favor with Jack Deemer. But more than that, of course, he might well face a charge of murder.

There was, painted on the bow of the dark green canoe, a kind of mandala. It was an advertising of some sort for the manufacturer, but it was nevertheless not unlike a mandala, in its perfection of circles and inserted triangles; like an abstract hydrangea. I once went to Tehran for a collection of rugs for Jack Deemer, and only as I was flying back, the deal completed, the plane trying to land somewhere in a desert sandstorm, did I realize that each of the exquisite small rugs was a mandala, a design of the whole damned world.

I scored a bull's-eye without intending to. I had hoped to have the bullet strike the water to the port or far side and forward of the approaching canoe. Perhaps it fell short and ricocheted. Whatever the case, it struck the mandala dead center.

It hardly tore at all the canvas, in passing through and out on the far side of the canoe's bow. It caused not a tremor, so far as I could perceive, in the canoe's trajectory.

Ornithologists in general agree that young ospreys take their first flight early in the morning. Mine had been stretching their wings for an hour or more. But they had gone through exactly those same exercises every morning and each day of my presence.

As I say, I raised the rifle, took careful aim, allowing of course for all the variables, and pulled the trigger. De Medeiros had approached the shore, had swung in a half circle away. I had actually thought he was leaving. But then he began to make of his half circle a full; I saw he was going to come in this time to make a landing.

I pulled the trigger. Dr. de Medeiros lost his balance. It is suicide, as anyone knows, to stand up while hurtling straight

ahead with an outboard motor in a canoe, let alone to do the
same while making a turn, even if one is so small as to have
difficulty seeing over the raised bow. The good doctor lost
his balance even before the sound of the shot could have
reached him.

I cannot report with certainty what happened next, as
the startled ospreys, both of them, on the flat top of the
pilings, lifted their wings. It had struck me, earlier, that in
making my bargain with those omens of the sky I had
neglected to consider: what if one were to fly, one fail?

The morning light caught those raised wings and I
knew my fate hung in the balance. If the doctor came up
the traditional three times before going down altogether, I
cannot report that I counted for him, because I was watching
my two birds.

The two young ospreys, together and as one, raised
their wings at the shot.

The two birds did not so much climb into the waiting
air as step over a precipice, a ledge, a cliff, and into the
hollow air of an abyss. They must assume that something
there, invisible, would enable them to lift themselves up.
That there were tears in my eyes goes without saying. The
mother osprey, on the second piling, launched violently into
her own flight, gave a heart-rending cry.

Once, early in my career, I collected some things from
Hong Kong for Deemer. It was supposed to be a collection
of carved and ceramic horses, but in the booty I found a
book. The book was a collection of poems, translated into
English, and in the first poem, the first poem of all, was the
cry of the osprey. *Gwan-Gwan.* I remembered it, then, even
then, hearing the osprey; and I marveled at the accuracy of
the transliteration, from bird voice into human.

The two young birds were falling. *Gwan-Gwan.* They
must surely fall into the lake and drown or starve or be
caught by fish. The canoe, with its admiral gone, aimed
itself weakly toward shore.

And then, almost touching the water's throat, the two
birds, the two falling birds together and at once, realized

they might fly. Their wings caught their falling bodies. Their reaching wings found air. Against the fall they stroked their wings, the two young birds; skimming the blue water they found the invisible air, began to rise; awkwardly, they rose; they rose and faltered and rose; they found and lifted, above them, the blue sky; they tore, in their innocent talons, the sadness from my heart.